## Pink:
*Boldness*

Mix one love-shy publicist with a world-famous chef. Add a touch of boldness, a dash of spice, a hint of charm—and what do you get? A recipe for romance that simmers with passion...and boils down to love!

# NORA ROBERTS

### LANGUAGE OF LOVE

**Love has a language all its own, and for
centuries, flowers have symbolized
love's finest expression.
Discover the language of flowers
—and love—
in this romantic collection of 48 favorite
books by bestselling author Nora Roberts.**

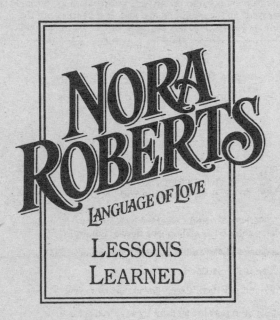

# NORA ROBERTS

## LANGUAGE OF LOVE

# LESSONS LEARNED

Silhouette® Books

Published by Silhouette Books New York

**America's Publisher of Contemporary Romance**

For Jill Gregory, a.k.a. The Baby,
one of my favorite roommates

SILHOUETTE BOOKS
300 East 42nd St., New York, N.Y. 10017

LESSONS LEARNED © 1986 by Nora Roberts.
First published as a Silhouette Special Edition.

Language of Love edition published February 1993.

ISBN: 0-373-51025-X

Printed in U.S.A.

# Chapter One

So he was gorgeous. And rich...and talented. And sexy; you shouldn't forget that he was outrageously sexy.

It hardly mattered to Juliet. She was a professional, and to a professional, a job was a job. In this case, great looks and personality were bound to help, but that was business. Strictly business.

No, personally it didn't matter a bit. After all, she'd met a few gorgeous men in her life. She'd met a few rich ones too, and so forth, though she had to admit she'd never met a man with all those elusive qualities rolled up in one. She'd certainly never had the opportunity to work with one. Now she did.

The fact was, Carlo Franconi's looks, charm, reputation and skill were going to make her job a pleasure. So she was told. Still, with her office door closed, Juliet scowled down at the eight-by-ten glossy black-and-white publicity photo. It looked to her as though he'd be more trouble than pleasure.

Carlo grinned cockily up at her, dark, almond-shaped eyes amused and appreciative. She wondered if the photographer had been a woman. His full thick hair was appealingly disheveled with a bit of curl along the nape of his neck and over his ears. Not too much—just enough to disarm. The strong facial bones, jauntily curved mouth, straight nose and expressive brows combined to create a face destined to sabotage any woman's common sense. Gift or cultivated talent, Juliet wasn't certain, but she'd have to use it to her advantage. Author tours could be murder.

A cook book. Juliet tried, and failed, not to sigh. Carlo
Franconi's *The Italian Way*, was, whether she liked it or not
her biggest assignment to date. Business was business.

She loved her job as publicist and was content for the
moment with Trinity Press, the publisher she currently
worked for, after a half-dozen job changes and upward
jumps since the start of her career. At twenty-eight, the
ambition she'd started with as a receptionist nearly ten year
before had eased very little. She'd worked, studied, hustled
and sweated for her own office and position. She had them
but she wasn't ready to relax.

In two years, by her calculations, she'd be ready to make
the next jump: her own public relations firm. Naturally
she'd have to start out small, but it was building the busi
ness that was exciting. The contacts and experience she
gained in her twenties would help her solidify her ambi
tions in her thirties. Juliet was content with that.

One of the first things she'd learned in public relation
was that an account was an account, whether it was a big
blockbuster best-seller already slated to be a big block
buster film or a slim volume of poetry that would barely
earn out its advance. Part of the challenge, and the fun, wa
finding the right promotional hook.

Now, she had a cookbook and a slick Italian chef. Fran
coni, she thought wryly, had a track record—with women
and in publishing. The first was a matter of hot interest to
the society and gossip sections of the international press. I
wasn't necessary to cook to be aware of Franconi's name
The second was the reason he was being pampered on the
road with a publicist.

His first two cookbooks had been solid best-sellers. For
good reason, Juliet admitted. It was true she couldn't fry a
egg without creating a gooey inedible glob, but she recog
nized quality and style. Franconi could make linguini sound
like a dish to be prepared while wearing black lace. H
turned a simple spaghetti dish into an erotic event.

Sex. Juliet tipped back in her chair and wiggled her stockinged toes. That's what he had. That's just what they'd use. Before the twenty-one-day author tour was finished, she'll have made Carlo Franconi the world's sexiest cook. Any red-blooded American woman would fantasize about him preparing an intimate dinner for two. Candlelight, pasta and romance.

One last study of his publicity shot and the charmingly crooked grin assured her he could handle it.

In the meantime, there was a bit more groundwork to cover. Creating a schedule was a pleasure, adhering to one a challenge. She thrived on both.

Juliet lifted the phone, noticed with resignation that she'd broken another nail, then buzzed her assistant. "Terry, get me Diane Maxwell. She's program coordinator on the Simpson Show' in L.A."

"Going for the big guns?"

Juliet gave a quick, unprofessional grin. "Yeah." She replaced the phone and started making hurried notes. No reason not to start at the top, she told herself. That way, if you fell on your face, at least the trip would be worth it.

As she waited, she looked around her office. Not the top, but a good ways from the bottom. At least she had a window. Juliet could still shudder thinking of some of the walled-in cubicles she'd worked in. Now, twenty stories below, New York rushed, bumped, pushed and shoved its way through another day. Juliet Trent had learned how to do the same thing after moving from the relatively easygoing suburb of Harrisburg, Pennsylvania.

She might've grown up in a polite little neighborhood where only a stranger drove over twenty-five miles per hour and everyone kept the grass clipped close to their side of the chain-link fences, but Juliet had acclimated easily. The truth was she liked the pace, the energy and the "I dare you" tone of New York. She'd never go back to the bee-humming, hedge-clipping quiet of suburbia where everyone knew who you were, what you did and how you did it. She preferred the anonymity and the individuality of crowds.

Perhaps her mother had molded herself into the perfect suburban wife, but not Juliet. She was an eighties woman, independent, self-sufficient and moving up. There was an apartment in the west Seventies that she'd furnished, slowly, meticulously and, most important, personally. Juliet had enough patience to move step by step as long as the result was perfect. She had a career she could be proud of and an office she was gradually altering to suit her own tastes. Leaving her mark wasn't something she took lightly. It had taken her four months to choose the right plants for her work space, from the four-foot split-leaf philodendron to the delicate white-blossomed African violet.

She'd had to make do with the beige carpet, but the six-foot Dali print on the wall opposite her window added life and energy. The narrow-beveled mirror gave an illusion of space and a touch of elegance. She had her eye on a big, gaudy Oriental urn that would be perfect for a spray of equally gaudy peacock feathers. If she waited a bit longer the price might come down from exorbitant to ridiculous. Then she'd buy it.

Juliet might put on a very practical front to everyone, including herself, but she couldn't resist a sale. As a result, her bank balance wasn't as hefty as her bedroom closet. She wasn't frivolous. No, she would have been appalled to hear the word applied to her. Her wardrobe was organized, well tended and suitable. Perhaps twenty pairs of shoes could be considered excessive, but Juliet rationalized that she was often on her feet ten hours a day and deserved the luxury. In any case, she'd earned them, from the sturdy sneakers, the practical black pumps to the strappy evening sandals. She'd earned them with innumerable long meetings, countless waits in airports and endless hours on the phone. She'd earned them on author tours, where the luck of the draw could have you dealing with the brilliant, the funny, the inept, the boring or the rude. Whatever she had to deal with, the results had to be the same. Media, media and more media.

She'd learned how to deal with the press, from the *New York Times* reporter to the stringer on the small-town weekly. She knew how to charm the staff of talk shows, from the accepted masters to the nervous imitators. Learning had been an adventure, and since she'd allowed herself very few in her personal life, professional success was all the sweeter.

When the intercom buzzed, she caught her tongue between her teeth. Now, she was going to apply everything she'd learned and land Franconi on the top-rated talk show in the States.

Once she did, she thought as she pressed the button, he'd better make the most of it. Or she'd slit his sexy throat with his own chef's knife.

"Ah, *mi amore. Squisito.*" Carlo's voice was a low purr designed to accelerate the blood pressure. The bedroom voice wasn't something he'd had to develop, but something he'd been born with. Carlo had always thought a man who didn't use God-given gifts was less than a fool. *"Bellisimo,"* he murmured and his eyes were dark and dreamy with anticipation.

It was hot, almost steamy, but he preferred the heat. Cold slowed down the blood. The sun coming through the window had taken on the subtle gold texture with tints of red that spoke of the end of the day and hinted at the pleasures of night. The room was rich with scent so he breathed it in. A man was missing a great deal of life if he didn't use and appreciate all of his senses. Carlo believed in missing nothing.

He watched his love of the moment with a connoisseur's eye. He'd caress, whisper to, flatter—it never mattered to him if it took moments or hours to get what he wanted. As long as he got what he wanted. To Carlo, the process, the anticipation, the moves themselves were equally as satisfy-

ing as the result. Like a dance, he'd always thought. Like a
song. An aria from *The Marriage of Figaro* played in the
background while he seduced.

Carlo believed in setting the scene because life was a play
not simply to be enjoyed, but to be relished.

*"Bellisimo,"* he whispered and bent nearer what he
adored. The clam sauce simmered erotically as he stirred it.
Slowly, savoring the moment, Carlo lifted the spoon to his
lips and with his eyes half-closed, tasted. The sound of
pleasure came from low in his throat. *"Squisito."*

He moved from the sauce to give the same loving attention to his *zabaglione.* He believed there wasn't a woman
alive who could resist the taste of that rich, creamy custard
with the zing of wine. As usual, it was a woman he was expecting.

The kitchen was as much a den of pleasure to him as the
bedroom. It wasn't an accident that he was one of the most
respected and admired chefs in the world, or that he was one
of the most engaging lovers. Carlo considered it a matter of
destiny. His kitchen was cleverly arranged, as meticulously
laid out for the seduction of sauces and spices as his bedroom was for the seduction of women. Yes, Carlo Franconi believed life was to be relished. Every drop of it.

When the knock on the front door reverberated through
the high-ceilinged rooms of his home, he murmured to his
pasta before he removed his apron. As he went to answer, he
rolled down the silk sleeves of his shirt but didn't stop for
adjustments in any of the antique mirrors that lined the
walls. He wasn't so much vain, as confident.

He opened the door to a tall, stately woman with honey-
toned skin and dark glossy eyes. Carlo's heart moved as it
did whenever he saw her. *"Mi amore."* Taking her hand, he
pressed his mouth to the palm, while his eyes smiled into
hers. *"Bella. Molto bella."*

She stood in the evening light for a moment, dark, lovely,
with a smile only for him. Only a fool wouldn't have known

he'd welcomed dozens of women in just this way. She wasn't a fool. But she loved him.

"You're a scoundrel, Carlo." The woman reached out to touch his hair. It was dark and thick and difficult to resist. "Is this the way you greet your mother?"

"This is the way—" he kissed her hand again "—I greet a beautiful woman." Then he wrapped both arms around her and kissed her cheeks. "This is the way I greet my mother. It's a fortunate man who can do both."

Gina Franconi laughed as she returned her son's hug. "To you, all women are beautiful."

"But only one is my mother." With his arm around her waist, he led her inside.

Gina approved, as always, the fact that his home was spotless, if a bit too exotic for her taste. She often wondered how the poor maid managed to keep the ornately carved archways dusted and polished and the hundreds of windowpanes unstreaked. Because she was a woman who'd spent fifteen years of her life cleaning other people's homes and forty cleaning her own, she thought of such things.

She studied one of his new acquisitions, a three-foot ivory owl with a small rodent captured in one claw. A good wife, Gina mused, would guide her son's tastes toward less eccentric paths.

"An aperitif, Mama?" Carlo walked over to a tall smoked-glass cabinet and drew out a slim black bottle. "You should try this," he told her as he chose two small glasses and poured. "A friend sent it to me."

Gina set aside her red snakeskin bag and accepted the glass. The first sip was hot, potent, smooth as a lover's kiss and just as intoxicating. She lifted a brow as she took the second sip. "Excellent."

"Yes, it is. Anna has excellent taste."

Anna, she thought, with more amusement than exasperation. She'd learned years before that it didn't do any good to be exasperated with a man, especially if you loved him. "Are all your friends women, Carlo?"

"No." He held his glass up, twirling it. "But this one was. She sent me this as a wedding present."

"A—"

"Her wedding," Carlo said with a grin. "She wanted a husband, and though I couldn't accommodate her, we parted friends." He held up the bottle as proof.

"Did you have it analyzed before you drank any?" Gina asked dryly.

He touched the rim of his glass to hers. "A clever man turns all former lovers into friends, Mama."

"You've always been clever." With a small movement of her shoulders she sipped again and sat down. "I hear you're seeing the French actress."

"As always, your hearing's excellent."

As if it interested her, Gina studied the hue of the liqueur in her glass. "She is, of course, beautiful."

"Of course."

"I don't think she'll give me grandchildren."

Carlo laughed and sat beside her. "You have six grandchildren and another coming, Mama. Don't be greedy."

"But none from my son. My only son," she reminded him with a tap of her finger on his shoulder. "Still, I haven't given you up yet."

"Perhaps if I could find a woman like you."

She shot him back arrogant look for arrogant look. "Impossible, *caro*."

His feeling exactly, Carlo thought as he guided her into talk about his four sisters and their families. When he looked at this sleek, lovely woman, it was difficult to think of her as the mother who'd raised him, almost single-handedly. She'd worked, and though she'd been known to storm and rage, she'd never complained. Her clothes had been carefully mended, her floors meticulously scrubbed while his father had spent endless months at sea.

When he concentrated, and he rarely did, Carlo could recall an impression of a dark, wiry man with a black mustache and an easy grin. The impression didn't bring on resentment or even regret. His father had been a seaman before his parents had married, and a seaman he'd remained. Carlo's belief in meeting your destiny was unwavering. But while his feelings for his father were ambivalent, his feelings for his mother were set and strong.

She'd supported each of her children's ambitions, and when Carlo had earned a scholarship to the Sorbonne in Paris and the opportunity to pursue his interest in haute cuisine, she'd let him go. Ultimately, she'd supplemented the meager income he could earn between studies with part of the insurance money she'd received when her husband had been lost in the sea he'd loved.

Six years before, Carlo had been able to pay her back in his own way. The dress shop he'd bought for her birthday had been a lifelong dream for both of them. For him, it was a way of seeing his mother happy at last. For Gina it was a way to begin again.

He'd grown up in a big, boisterous, emotional family. It gave him pleasure to look back and remember. A man who grows up in a family of women learns to understand them, appreciate them, admire them. Carlo knew about women's dreams, their vanities, their insecurities. He never took a lover he didn't have affection for as well as desire. If there was only desire, he knew there'd be no friendship at the end, only resentment. Even now, the comfortable affair he was having with the French actress was ending. She'd be starting a film in a few weeks, and he'd be going on tour in America. That, Carlo thought with some regret, would be that.

"Carlo, you go to America soon?"

"Hmm. Yes." He wondered if she'd read his mind, knowing women were capable of doing so. "Two weeks."

"You'll do me a favor?"

"Of course."

"Then notice for me what the professional American woman is wearing. I'm thinking of adding some things to the shop. The Americans are so clever and practical."

"Not too practical, I hope." He swirled his drink. "My publicist is a Ms. Trent." Tipping back his glass, he accepted the heat and the punch. "I'll promise you to study every aspect of her wardrobe."

She gave his quick grin a steady look. "You're so good to me, Carlo."

"But of course, mama. Now I'm going to feed you like a queen."

Carlo had no idea what Juliet Trent looked like, but put himself in the hands of fate. What he did know, from the letters he'd received from her, was that Juliet Trent was the type of American his mother had described. Practical and clever. Excellent qualities in a publicist.

Physically was another matter. But again, as his mother had said, Carlo could always find beauty in a woman. Perhaps he did prefer, in his personal life, a woman with a lovely shell, but he knew how to dig beneath to find inner beauty. It was something that made life interesting as well as aesthetically pleasing.

Still, as he stepped off the plane into the terminal in L.A., he had his hand on the elbow of a stunning redhead.

Juliet did know what he looked like, and she first saw him, shoulder to shoulder with a luxuriously built woman in pencil-thin heels. Though he carried a bulky leather case in one hand, and a flight bag over his shoulder, he escorted the redhead through the gate as though they were walking into a ballroom. Or a bedroom.

Juliet took a quick assessment of the well-tailored slacks, the unstructured jacket and open-collared shirt. The well-heeled traveler. There was a chunk of gold and diamond on his finger that should've looked ostentatious and vulgar. Somehow it looked as casual and breezy as the rest of him. She felt formal and sticky.

She'd been in L.A. since the evening before, giving herself time to see personally to all the tiny details. Carlo

Franconi would have nothing to do but be charming, answer questions and sign his cookbook.

As she watched him kiss the redhead's knuckles, Juliet thought he'd be signing plenty of them. After all, didn't women do the majority of cookbook buying? Carefully smoothing away a sarcastic smirk, Juliet rose. The redhead was sending one last wistful look over her shoulder as she walked away.

"Mr. Franconi?"

Carlo turned away from the woman who'd proven to be a pleasant traveling companion on the long flight from New York. His first look at Juliet brought a quick flutter of interest and a subtle tug of desire he often felt with a woman. It was a tug he could either control or let loose, as was appropriate. This time, he savored it.

She didn't have merely a lovely face, but an interesting one. Her skin was very pale, which should have made her seem fragile, but the wide, strong cheekbones undid the air of fragility and gave her face an intriguing diamond shape. Her eyes were large, heavily lashed and artfully accented with a smoky shadow that only made the cool green shade of the irises seem cooler. Her mouth was only lightly touched with a peach-colored gloss. It had a full, eye-drawing shape that needed no artifice. He gathered she was wise enough to know it.

Her hair was caught somewhere between brown and blond so that its shade was soft, natural and subtle. She wore it long enough in the back to be pinned up in a chignon when she wished, and short enough on the top and sides so that she could style it from fussy to practical as the occasion, and her whim, demanded. At the moment, it was loose and casual, but not windblown. She'd stopped in the ladies' room for a quick check just after the incoming flight had been announced.

"I'm Juliet Trent," she told him when she felt he'd stared long enough. "Welcome to California." As he took the hand she offered, she realized she should've expected him to kiss it rather than shake. Still, she stiffened, hardly more than an instant, but she saw by the lift of brow, he'd felt it.

"A beautiful woman makes a man welcome anywhere."

His voice was incredible—the cream that rose to the top and then flowed over something rich. She told herself it only pleased her because it would record well and took his statement literally. Thinking of the redhead, she gave him an easy, not entirely friendly smile. "Then you must have had a pleasant flight."

His native language might have been Italian, but Carlo understood nuances in any tongue. He grinned at her. "Very pleasant."

"And tiring," she said remembering her position. "Your luggage should be in by now." Again, she glanced at the large case he carried. "Can I take that for you?"

His brow lifted at the idea of a man dumping his burden on a woman. Equality, to Carlo, never crossed the border into manners. "No, this is something I always carry myself."

Indicating the way, she fell into step beside him. "It's a half-hour ride to the Beverly Wilshire, but after you've settled in, you can rest all afternoon. I'd like to go over tomorrow's schedule with you this evening."

He liked the way she walked. Though she wasn't tall, she moved in long, unhurried strides that made the red side-pleated skirt she wore shift over her hips. "Over dinner?"

She sent him a quick sidelong look. "If you like."

She'd be at his disposal, Juliet reminded herself, for the next three weeks. Without appearing to think about it, she skirted around a barrel-chested man hefting a bulging garment bag and a briefcase. Yes, he liked the way she walked, Carlo thought again. She was a woman who could take care of herself without a great deal of fuss.

"At seven? You have a talk show in the morning that starts at seven-thirty so we'd best make it an early evening."

Seven-thirty A.M. Carlo thought, only briefly, about jet ag and time changes. "So, you put me to work quickly."

"That's what I'm here for, Mr. Franconi." Juliet said it cheerfully as she stepped up to the slowly moving baggage belt. "You have your stubs?"

An organized woman, he thought as he reached into the inside pocket of his loose-fitting buff-colored jacket. In silence, he handed them to her, then hefted a pullman and a garment bag from the belt himself.

Gucci, she observed. So he had taste as well as money. Juliet handed the stubs to a skycap and waited while Carlo's luggage was loaded onto the pushcart. "I think you'll be pleased with what we have for you, Mr. Franconi." She walked through the automatic doors and signaled for her limo. "I know you've always worked with Jim Collins in the past on your tours in the States; he sends his best."

"Does Jim like his executive position?"

"Apparently."

Though Carlo expected her to climb into the limo first, he stepped back. With a bow to women professionals, Carlo ducked inside and took his seat. "Do you like yours, Ms. Trent?"

She took the seat across from him then sent him a straight-shooting, level look. Juliet could have no idea how much he admired it. "Yes, I do."

Carlo stretched out his legs—legs his mother had once said that had refused to stop growing long after it was necessary. He'd have preferred driving himself, particularly after the long, long flight from Rome where someone else had been at the controls. But if he couldn't, the plush laziness of the limo was the next best thing. Reaching over, he switched on the stereo so that Mozart poured out, quiet but vibrant. If he'd been driving, it would've been rock, loud and rambunctious.

"You've read my book, Ms. Trent?"

"Yes, of course. I couldn't set up publicity and promotion for an unknown product." She sat back. It was easy to

do her job when she could speak the simple truth. "I wa
impressed with the attention to detail and the clear direc
tions. It seemed a very friendly book, rather than simply
kitchen tool."

"Hmm." He noticed her stockings were very pale pin
and had a tiny line of dots up one side. It would interest h
mother that the practical American businesswoman coul
enjoy the frivolous. It interested him that Juliet Trent coul
"Have you tried any of the recipes?"

"No, I don't cook."

"You don't . . ." His lazy interest came to attention. "A
all?"

She had to smile. He looked so sincerely shocked. As h
watched the perfect mouth curve, he had to put the next tu
of desire in check. "When you're a failure at something, M
Franconi, you leave it to someone else."

"I could teach you." The idea intrigued him. He nev
offered his expertise lightly.

"To cook?" She laughed, relaxing enough to let her he
slip out of her shoe as she swung her foot. "I don't thin
so."

"I'm an excellent teacher," he said with a slow smile.

Again, she gave him the calm, gunslinger look. "I don
doubt it. I, on the other hand, am a poor student."

"Your age?" When her look narrowed, he smile
charmingly. "A rude question when a woman's reached
certain stage. You haven't."

"Twenty-eight," she said so coolly his smile became
grin.

"You look younger, but your eyes are older. I'd find it
pleasure to give you a few lessons, Ms. Trent."

She believed him. She, too, understood nuances. "A pi
our schedule won't permit it."

He shrugged easily and glanced out the window. But th
L.A. freeway didn't interest him. "You put Philadelphia
the schedule as I requested?"

"We'll have a full day there before we fly up to Boston. Then we'll finish up in New York."

"Good. I have a friend there. I haven't seen her in nearly year."

Juliet was certain he had—friends—everywhere.

"You've been to Los Angeles before?" he asked her.

"Yes. Several times on business."

"I've yet to come here for pleasure myself. What do you think of it?"

As he had, she glanced out the window without interest. "I prefer New York."

"Why?"

"More grit, less gloss."

He liked her answer, and her phrasing. Because of it, he studied her more closely. "Have you ever been to Rome?"

"No." He thought he heard just a trace of wistfulness in her voice. "I haven't been to Europe at all."

"When you do, come to Rome. It was built on grit."

Her mind drifted a bit as she thought of it, and her smile remained. "I think of fountains and marble and cathedrals."

"You'll find them—and more." She had a face exquisite enough to be carved in marble, he thought. A voice quiet and smooth enough for cathedrals. "Rome rose and fell and clawed its way back up again. An intelligent woman understands such things. A romantic woman understands the fountains."

She glanced out again as the limo pulled up in front of the hotel. "I'm afraid I'm not very romantic."

"A woman named Juliet hasn't a choice."

"My mother's selection," she pointed out. "Not mine."

"You don't look for Romeo?"

Juliet gathered her briefcase. "No, Mr. Franconi. I don't."

He stepped out ahead of her and offered his hand. When Juliet stood on the curb, he didn't move back to give her room, instead experimented with the sensation of bodies

brushing, lightly, even politely on a public street. Her gaz
came up to his, not wary but direct.

He felt it, the pull. Not the tug that was impersonal an
for any woman, but the pull that went straight to the gut an
was for one woman. So he'd have to taste her mouth. Afte
all, he was a man compelled to judge a great deal by taste
But he could also bide his time. Some creations took a lon
time and had complicated preparations to perfect. Like Ju
liet, he insisted on perfection.

"Some women," he murmured, "never need to look
only to evade and avoid and select."

"Some women," she said just as quietly, "choose not t
select at all." Deliberately, she turned her back on him t
pay off the driver. "I've already checked you in, Mr. Fran
coni," she said over her shoulder as she handed his key t
the waiting bellboy. "I'm just across the hall from you
suite."

Without looking at him, Juliet followed the bellboy int
the hotel and to the elevators. "If it suits you, I'll make res
ervations here in the hotel for dinner at seven. You can jus
tap on my door when you're ready." With a quick check o
her watch she calculated the time difference and figured sh
could make three calls to New York and one to Dallas be
fore office hours were over farther east. "If you need any
thing, you've only to order it and charge it to the room."

She stepped from the elevator, unzipping her purse an
pulling out her own room key as she walked. "I'm su
you'll find your suite suitable."

He watched her brisk, economic movements. "I'm sure
will."

"Seven o'clock then." She was already pushing her ke
into the lock as the bellboy opened the first door to the sui
across the hall. As she did, her mind was already on the cal
she'd make the moment she'd shed her jacket and shoes.

"Juliet."

She paused, her hair swinging back as she looked over he
shoulder at Carlo. He held her there, a moment longer, i

silence. "Don't change your scent," he murmured. "Sex without flowers, femininity without vulnerability. It suits you."

While she continued to stare over her shoulder, he disappeared inside the suite. The bellboy began his polite introductions to the accommodations of the suite. Something Carlo said caused him to break off and laugh.

Juliet turned her key with more strength than necessary, pushed open her door, then closed it again with the length of her body. For a minute, she just leaned there, waiting for her system to level.

Professional training had prevented her from stammering and fumbling and making a fool of herself. Professional training had helped her to keep her nerves just at the border where they could be controlled and concealed. Still, under the training, there was a woman. Control had cost her. Juliet was dead certain there wasn't a woman alive who would be totally unaffected by Carlo Franconi. It wasn't calm for her ego to admit she was simply part of a large, varied group.

He'd never know it, she told herself, but her pulse had been behaving badly since he'd first taken her hand. It was still behaving badly. Stupid, she told herself and threw her bag down on a chair. Then she thought it best if she followed it. Her legs weren't steady yet. Juliet let out a long, deep breath. She'd just have to wait until they were.

So he was gorgeous. And rich ... and talented. And outrageously sexy. She'd already known that, hadn't she? The trouble was, she wasn't sure how to handle him. Not nearly as sure as she had to be.

# Chapter Two

She was a woman who thrived on tight scheduling, minute details and small crises. These were the things that kept you alert, sharp and interested. If her job had been simple, there wouldn't have been much fun to it.

She was also a woman who liked long, lazy baths in mountains of bubbles and big, big beds. These were the things that kept you sane. Juliet felt she'd earned the second after she'd dealt with the first.

While Carlo amused himself in his own way, Juliet spent an hour and a half on the phone, then another hour revising and fine-tuning the next day's itinerary. A print interview had come through and had to be shuffled in. She shuffled. Another paper was sending a reporter and photographer to the book signing. Their names had to be noted and remembered. Juliet noted, circled and committed to memory. The way things were shaping up, they'd be lucky to manage a two-hour breather the next day. Nothing could've pleased her more.

By the time she'd closed her thick, leather-bound notebook, she was more than ready for the tub. The bed, unfortunately, would have to wait. Ten o'clock, she promised herself. By ten, she'd be in bed, snuggled in, curled up and unconscious.

She soaked, designating precisely forty-five minutes for her personal time. In the bath, she didn't plot or plan or estimate. She clicked off the busy, business end of her brain and enjoyed.

Relaxing—it took the first ten minutes to accomplish that completely. Dreaming—she could pretend the white, star

ard-size tub was luxurious, large and lush. Black marble
erhaps and big enough for two. It was a secret ambition of
uliet's to own one like it eventually. The symbol, she felt,
f ultimate success. She'd have bristled if anyone had called
er goal romantic. Practical, she'd insist. When you worked
ard, you needed a place to unwind. This was hers.

Her robe hung on the back of the door—jade green,
easingly brief and silk. Not a luxury as far as she was con-
erned, but a necessity. When you often had only short
natches to relax, you needed all the help you could get. She
onsidered the robe as much an aid in keeping pace as the
ottles of vitamins that lined the counter by the sink. When
he traveled, she always took them.

After she'd relaxed and dreamed a bit, she could appre-
iate soft, hot water against her skin, silky bubbles hissing,
team rising rich with scent.

He'd told her not to change her scent.

Juliet scowled as she felt the muscles in her shoulders
ense. Oh no. Deliberately she picked up the tiny cake of
otel soap and rubbed it up and down her arms. Oh no, she
ouldn't let Carlo Franconi intrude on her personal time.
'hat was rule number one.

He'd purposely tried to unravel her. He'd succeeded. Yes,
e had succeeded, Juliet admitted with a stubborn nod. But
hat was over now. She wouldn't let it happen again. Her job
as to promote his book, not his ego. To promote, she'd go
bove and beyond the call of duty with her time, her energy
nd her skill, but not with her emotions.

Franconi wasn't flying back to Rome in three weeks with
smug smile on his face unless it was professionally gener-
ted. That instant knife-sharp attraction would be dealt
ith. Priorities, Juliet mused, were the order of the day. He
ould add all the American conquests to his list he chose—
s long as she wasn't among them.

In any case, he didn't seriously interest her. It was simply
hat basic, primal urge. Certainly there wasn't any intellect
volved. She preferred a different kind of man—steady

rather than flashy, sincere rather than charming. That wa
the kind of man a woman of common sense looked for whe
the time was right. Juliet judged the time would be right i
about three years. By then, she'd have established th
structure for her own firm. She'd be financially indepenc
ent and creatively content. Yes, in three years she'd be read
to think about a serious relationship. That would fit he
schedule nicely.

Settled, she decided, and closed her eyes. It was a nic
comfortable word. But the hot water, bubbles and stear
didn't relax her any longer. A bit resentful, she released th
plug and stood up to let the water drain off her. The wic
mirror above the counter and sink was fogged, but on
lightly. Through the mist she could see Juliet Trent.

Odd, she thought, how pale and soft and vulnerable
naked woman could look. In her mind, she was stron
practical, even tough. But she could see, in the damp, mis
mirror, the fragility, even the wistfulness.

Erotic? Juliet frowned a bit as she told herself sl
shouldn't be disappointed that her body had been built c
slim, practical lines rather than round and lush ones. Sl
should be grateful that her long legs got her where she wa
going and her narrow hips helped keep her silhouette in
business suit trim and efficient. Erotic would never be a c
reer plus.

Without makeup, her face looked too young, too trus
ing. Without careful grooming, her hair looked too wil
too passionate.

Fragile, young, passionate. Juliet shook her head. N
qualities for a professional woman. It was fortunate th
clothes and cosmetics could play down or play up certa
aspects. Grabbing a towel, she wrapped it around hersel
then taking another she wiped the steam from the mirrc
No more mists, she thought. To succeed you had to s
clearly.

With a glance at the tubes and bottles on the counter sl
began to create the professional Ms. Trent.

Because she hated quiet hotel rooms, Juliet switched on the television as she started to dress. The old Bogart–Bacall movie pleased her and was more relaxing than a dozen bubble baths. She listened to the well-known dialogue while she drew on her smoke-colored stockings. She watched the shimmering restrained passion as she adjusted the straps of a sheer black teddy. While the plot twisted and turned, she zipped on the narrow black dress and knotted the long strand of pearls under her breasts.

Caught up, she sat on the edge of the bed, running a brush through her hair as she watched. She was smiling, absorbed, distracted, but it would've shocked her if anyone had said she was romantic.

When the knock sounded at her door, she glanced at her watch. 7:05. She'd lost fifteen minutes dawdling. To make up for it, Juliet had her shoes on, her earrings clipped and her bag and notebook at hand in twelve seconds flat. She went to the door ready with a greeting and an apology.

A rose. Just one, the color of a young girl's blush. When Carlo handed it to her, she didn't have anything to say at all. Carlo, however, had no problem.

*"Bella."* He had her hand to his lips before she'd thought to counter the move. "Some women look severe or cold in black. Others..." His survey was long and male, but his smile made it gallant rather than calculating. "In others it simply enhances their femininity. I'm disturbing you?"

"No, no, of course not. I was just—"

"Ah, I know this movie."

Without waiting for an invitation, he breezed passed her into the room. The standard, single hotel room didn't seem so impersonal any longer. How could it? He brought life, energy, passion into the air as if it were his mission.

"Yes, I've seen it many times." The two strong faces dominated the screen. Bogart's creased, heavy-eyed, weary—Bacall's smooth, steamy and challenging. *"Passione,"* he murmured and made the word seem like honey to be tasted. Incredibly, Juliet found herself swallowing. "A man and a woman can bring many things to each other, but without passion, everything else is tame. *Si?*"

Juliet recovered herself. Franconi wasn't a man to discuss passion with. The subject wouldn't remain academic for long. "Perhaps." She adjusted her evening bag and her notebook. But she didn't put the rose down. "We've a lot to discuss over dinner, Mr. Franconi. We'd best get started."

With his thumbs still hooked in the pockets of his taupe slacks, he turned his head. Juliet figured hundreds of women had trusted that smile. She wouldn't. With a careless flick, he turned off the television. "Yes, it's time we started."

What did he think of her? Carlo asked himself the question and let the answer come in snatches, twined through the evening.

Lovely. He didn't consider his affection for beautiful women a weakness. He was grateful that Juliet didn't find the need to play down or turn her natural beauty into severity, nor did she exploit it until it was artificial. She'd found a pleasing balance. He could admire that.

She was ambitious, but he admired that as well. Beautiful women without ambition lost his interest quickly.

She didn't trust him. That amused him. As he drank his second glass of Beaujolais, he decided her wariness was a compliment. In his estimation, a woman like Juliet would only be wary of a man if she were attracted in some way.

If he were honest, and he was, he'd admit that most women were attracted to him. It seemed only fair, as he was attracted to them. Short, tall, plump, thin, old or young, he found women a fascination, a delight, an amusement. He respected them, perhaps only as a man who had grown up surrounded by women could do. But respect didn't mean he couldn't enjoy.

He was going to enjoy Juliet.

"'Hello, L.A.' is on first tomorrow." Juliet ran down her notes while Carlo nibbled on pâté. "It's the top-rated morning talk show on the coast, not just in L.A. Liz Marks hosts. She's very personable—not too bubbly. Los Angeles doesn't want bubbly at 8:00 A.M.''

"Thank God."

"In any case, she has a copy of the book. It's important that you get the title in a couple of times if she doesn't. You have the full twenty minutes, so it shouldn't be a problem. You'll be autographing at Books, Incorporated on Wilshire Boulevard between one and three." Hastily, she made herself a note to contact the store in the morning for a last check. "You'll want to plug that, but I'll remind you just before airtime. Of course, you'll want to mention that you're beginning a twenty-one-day tour of the country here in California."

"Mmm-hmm. The pâté is quite passable. Would you like some?"

"No thanks. Just go ahead." She checked off her list and reached for her wine without looking at him. The restaurant was quiet and elegant, but it didn't matter. If they'd been in a loud crowded bar on the Strip, she'd still have gone on with her notes. "Right after the morning show, we go to a radio spot. Then we'll have brunch with a reporter from the *Times*. You've already had an article in the *Trib*. I've got a clipping for you. You'd want to mention your other two books, but concentrate on the new one. It wouldn't hurt to bring up some of the major cities we'll hit. Denver, Dallas, Chicago, New York. Then there's the autographing, a spot on the evening news and dinner with two book reps. The next day—"

"One day at a time," he said easily. "I'll be less likely to snarl at you."

"All right." She closed her notebook and sipped at her wine again. "After all, it's my job to see to the details, yours to sign books and be charming."

He touched his glass to hers. "Then neither of us should have a problem. Being charming is my life."

Was he laughing at himself, she wondered, or at her? "From what I've seen, you excel at it."

"A gift, *cara*." Those dark, deep-set eyes were amused and exciting. "Unlike a skill that's developed and trained."

So, he was laughing at both of them, she realized. It would be both difficult and wise not to like him for it.

When her steak was served, Juliet glanced at it. Carlo, however, studied his veal as though it were a fine old painting. No, Juliet realized after a moment, he studied it as though it were a young, beautiful woman.

"Appearances," he told her, "in food, as in people, are essential." He was smiling at her when he cut into the veal. "And, as in people, they can be deceiving."

Juliet watched him sample the first bite, slowly, his eyes half-closed. She felt an odd chill at the base of her spine. He'd sample a woman the same way, she was certain. Slowly.

"Pleasant," he said after a moment. "No more, no less."

She couldn't prevent the quick smirk as she cut into her steak. "Yours is better of course."

He moved his shoulders. A statement of arrogance. "Of course. Like comparing a pretty young girl with a beautiful woman." When she glanced up he was holding out his fork. Over it, his eyes studied her. "Taste," he invited and the simple word made her blood shiver. "Nothing should ever go untasted, Juliet."

She shrugged, letting him feed her the tiny bite of veal. It was spicy, just bordering on rich and hot on her tongue. "It's good."

"Good, *si*. Nothing Franconi prepares is ever merely good. Good, I'd pour into the garbage, feed to the dogs in the alley." She laughed, delighting him. "If something isn't special, then it's ordinary."

"True enough." Without realizing it, she slipped out of her shoes. "But then, I suppose I've always looked at food as a basic necessity."

"Necessity?" Carlo shook his head. Though he'd heard such sentiment before, he still considered it a sacrilege. "Oh, *madonna*, you have much to learn. When one knows how to eat, how to appreciate, it's second only to making love. Scents, textures, tastes. To eat only to fill your stomach? Barbaric."

"Sorry." Juliet took another bite of steak. It was tender and cooked well. But it was only a piece of meat. She'd never have considered it sensual or romantic, but simply filling. "Is that why you became a cook? Because you think food's sexy?"

He winced. "Chef, *cara mia.*"

She grinned, showing him for the first time a streak of humor and mischief. "What's the difference?"

"What's the difference between a plow horse and a thoroughbred? Plaster and porcelain?"

Enjoying herself, she touched her tongue to the rim of her glass. "Some might say dollar signs."

"No, no, no, my love. Money is only a result, not a cause. A cook makes hamburgers in a greasy kitchen that smells of onions behind a counter where people squeeze plastic bottles of ketchup. A chef creates..." He gestured, a circle of a hand. "An experience."

She lifted her glass and swept her lashes down, but she didn't hide the smile. "I see."

Though he could be offended by a look when he chose, and be ruthless with the offender, Carlo liked her style. "You're amused. But you haven't tasted Franconi." He waited until her eyes, both wry and wary, lifted to him. "Yet."

He had a talent for turning the simplest statement into something erotic, she observed. It would be a challenge to skirt around him without giving way. "But you haven't told me why you became a chef."

"I can't paint or sculpt. I haven't the patience or the talent to compose sonnets. There are other ways to create, to embrace art."

She saw, with surprise mixed with respect, that he was quite serious. "But paintings, sculpture and poetry remain centuries after they've been created. If you make a soufflé, it's here, then it's gone."

"Then the challenge is to make it again, and again. Art needn't be put behind glass or bronzed, Juliet, merely appreciated. I have a friend . . ." He thought of Summer Lyndon—no, Summer Cocharan now. "She makes pastries like an angel. When you eat one, you're a king."

"Then is cooking magic or art?"

"Both. Like love. And I think you, Juliet Trent, eat much too little."

She met his look as he'd hoped she would. "I don't believe in overindulgence, Mr. Franconi. It leads to carelessness."

"To indulgence then." He lifted his glass. The smile was back, charming and dangerous. "Carefully."

Anything and everything could go wrong. You had to expect it, anticipate it and avoid it. Juliet knew just how much could be botched in a twenty-minute, live interview at 7:30 A.M. on a Monday. You hoped for the best and made do with the not too bad. Even she didn't expect perfection on the first day of a tour.

It wasn't easy to explain why she was annoyed when she got it.

The morning spot went beautifully. There was no other way to describe it, Juliet decided as she watched Liz Marks talk and laugh with Carlo after the camera stopped taping. If a shrewd operator could be called a natural, Carlo was indeed a natural. During the interview, he'd subtly and completely dominated the show while charmingly blinding his host to it. Twice he'd made the ten-year veteran of morning talk shows giggle like a girl. Once, once, Juliet remembered with astonishment, she'd seen the woman blush.

Yeah. She shifted the strap of her heavy briefcase on her arm. Franconi was a natural. It was bound to make her job easier. She yawned and cursed him.

Juliet always slept well in hotel rooms. *Always*. Except for last night. She might've been able to convince someone else that too much coffee and first-day jitters had kept her awake. But she knew better. She could drink a pot of coffee at ten and fall asleep on command at eleven. Her system was very disciplined. Except for last night.

She'd nearly dreamed of him. If she hadn't shaken herself awake at 2:00 A.M., she would have dreamed of him. That was no way to begin a very important, very long author tour. She told herself now if she had to choose between some silly fantasies and honest fatigue, she'd take the fatigue.

Stifling another yawn, Juliet checked her watch. Liz had her arm tucked through Carlo's and looked as though she'd keep it there unless someone pried her loose. With a sigh, Juliet decided she'd have to be the crowbar.

"Ms. Marks, it was a wonderful show." As she crossed over, Juliet deliberately held out her hand. With obvious reluctance, Liz disengaged herself from Carlo and accepted it.

"Thank you, Miss..."

"Trent," Juliet supplied without a waver.

"Juliet is my publicist," Carlo told Liz, though the two women had been introduced less than an hour earlier. "She guards my schedule."

"Yes, and I'm afraid I'll have to rush Mr. Franconi along. He has a radio spot in a half-hour."

"If you must." Juliet was easily dismissed as Liz turned back to Carlo. "You have a delightful way of starting the morning. A pity you won't be in town longer."

"A pity," Carlo agreed and kissed Liz's fingers. Like an old movie, Juliet thought impatiently. All they needed were violins.

"Thank you again, Ms. Marks." Juliet used her most diplomatic smile as she took Carlo's arm and began to lead him out of the studio. After all, she'd very likely need Liz Marks again. "We're in a bit of a hurry," she muttered as they worked their way back to the reception area. The taping was over and she had other fish to fry. "This radio show's one of the top-rated in the city. Since it leans heavily on top forties and classic rock, its audience, at this time of day, falls mainly in the eighteen to thirty-five range. Excellent buying power. That gives us a nice mix with the audience from this morning's show which is generally in the twenty-five to fifty, primarily female category."

Listening with all apparent respect, Carlo reached the waiting limo first and opened the door himself. "You consider this important?"

"Of course." Because she was distracted by what she thought was a foolish question, Juliet climbed into the limo ahead of him. "We've a solid schedule in L.A." And she didn't see the point in mentioning there were some cities on the tour where they wouldn't be quite so busy. "A morning talk show with a good reputation, a popular radio show, two print interviews, two quick spots on the evening news and the 'Simpson Show.'" She said the last with a hint of relish. The "Simpson Show" offset what she was doing to the budget with limos.

"So you're pleased."

"Yes, of course." Digging into her briefcase, she took out her folder to recheck the name of her contact at the radio station.

"Then why do you look so annoyed?"

"I don't know what you're talking about."

"You get a line right . . . here," he said as he ran a fingertip between her eyebrows. At the touch, Juliet jerked back before she could stop herself. Carlo only cocked his head, watching her. "You may smile and speak in a quiet, polite voice, but that line gives you away."

"I was very pleased with the taping," she said again.

"But?"

All right, she thought, he was asking for it. "Perhaps it annoys me to see a woman making a fool of herself." Juliet stuffed the folder back into her briefcase. "Liz Marks is married, you know."

"Wedding rings are things I try to be immediately aware of," he said with a shrug. "Your instructions were to be charming, weren't they?"

"Perhaps *charm* has a different meaning in Italy."

"As I said, you must come to Rome."

"I suppose you enjoy having women drooling all over you."

He smiled at her, easy, attractive, innocent. "But of course."

A gurgle of laughter bubbled in her throat but she swallowed it. She wouldn't be charmed. "You'll have to deal with some men on this tour as well."

"I promise not to kiss Simpson's fingers."

This time the laughter escaped. For a moment, she relaxed with it, let it come. Carlo saw, too briefly, the youth and energy beneath the discipline. He'd like to have kept her like that longer—laughing, at ease with him, and with herself. It would be a challenge, he mused, to find the right sequence of buttons to push to bring laughter to her eyes more often. He liked challenges—particularly when there was a woman connected to them.

"Juliet." Her name flowed off his tongue in a way only the European male had mastered. "You mustn't worry. Your tidily married Liz only enjoyed a mild flirtation with a man she'll more than likely never see again. Harmless. Perhaps because of it, she'll find more romance with her husband tonight."

Juliet eyed him a moment in her straight-on, no-nonsense manner. "You think quite of lot of yourself, don't you?"

He grinned, not sure if he was relieved or if he regretted the fact that he'd never met anyone like her before. "No more than is warranted, *cara*. Anyone who has character

leaves a mark on another. Would you like to leave the world
without making a ripple?"

No. No, that was one thing she was determined not to do.
She sat back determined to hold her own. "I suppose some
of us insist on leaving more ripples than others."

He nodded. "I don't like to do anything in a small way."

"Be careful, Mr. Franconi, or you'll begin to believe your
own image."

The limo had stopped, but before Juliet could scoot toward the door, Carlo had her hand. When she looked at him
this time, she didn't see the affable, amorous Italian chef,
but a man of power. A man, she realized, who was well
aware of how far it could take him.

She didn't move, but wondered how many other women
had seen the steel beneath the silk.

"I don't need imagery, Juliet." His voice was soft,
charming, beautiful. She heard the razor-blade cut beneath
it. "Franconi is Franconi. Take me for what you see, or go
to the devil."

Smoothly, he climbed from the limo ahead of her, turned
and took her hand, drawing her out with him. It was a move
that was polite, respectful, even ordinary. It was a move,
Juliet realized, that expressed their positions. Man to
woman. The moment she stood on the curb, she removed
her hand.

With two shows and a business brunch under their belts,
Juliet left Carlo in the bookstore, already swamped with
women crowded in line for a glimpse at and a few words
with Carlo Franconi. They'd handled the reporter and
photographer already, and a man like Franconi wouldn't
need her help with a crowd of women. Armed with change
and her credit card, she went to find a pay phone.

For the first forty-five minutes, she spoke with her assistant in New York, filling her pad with times, dates and
names while L.A. traffic whisked by outside the phone.

booth. As a bead of sweat trickled down her back, she wondered if she'd chosen the hottest corner in the city.

Denver still didn't look as promising as she'd hoped, but Dallas... Juliet caught her bottom lip between her teeth as she wrote. Dallas was going to be fabulous. She might need to double her daily dose of vitamins to get through that twenty-four-hour stretch, but it would be fabulous.

After breaking her connection with New York, Juliet dialed her first contact in San Francisco. Ten minutes later, she was clenching her teeth. No, her contact at the department store couldn't help coming down with a virus. She was sorry, genuinely sorry he was ill. But did he have to get sick without leaving someone behind with a couple of working brain cells?

The young girl with the squeaky voice knew about the cooking demonstration. Yes, she knew all about it and wasn't it going to be fun? Extension cords? Oh my, she really didn't know a thing about that. Maybe she could ask someone in maintenance. A table—chairs? Well golly, she supposed she could get something, if it was really necessary.

Juliet was reaching in her bag for her purse-size container of aspirin before it was over. The way it looked now, she'd have to get to the department store at least two hours before the demonstration to make sure everything was taken care of. That meant juggling the schedule.

After completing her calls, Juliet left the corner phone booth, aspirin in hand, and headed back to the bookstore, hoping they could give her a glass of water and a quiet corner.

No one noticed her. If she'd just crawled in from the desert on her belly, no one would have noticed her. The small, rather elegant bookstore was choked with laughter. No bookseller stood behind the counter. There was a magnet in the left-hand corner of the room. Its name was Franconi.

It wasn't just women this time, Juliet noticed with interest. There were men sprinkled in the crowd. Some of them might have been dragged along by their wives, but they were having a time of it now. It looked like a cocktail party, minus the cigarette smoke and empty glasses.

She couldn't even see him, Juliet realized as she worked her way toward the back of the store. He was surrounded, enveloped. Jingling the aspirin in her hand, she was glad she could find a little corner by herself. Perhaps he got all the glory, she mused. But she wouldn't trade places with him.

Glancing at her watch, she noted he had another hour and wondered whether he could dwindle the crowd down in the amount of time. She wished vaguely for a stool, dropped the aspirin in the pocket of her skirt and began to browse.

"Fabulous, isn't he?" Juliet heard someone murmur on the other side of a book rack.

"God, yes. I'm so glad you talked me into coming."

"What're friends for?"

"I thought I'd be bored to death. I feel like a kid at a rock concert. He's got such . . ."

"Style," the other voice supplied. "If a man like that ever walked into my life, he wouldn't walk out again."

Curious, Juliet walked around the stacks. She wasn't sure what she expected—young housewives, college students. What she saw were two attractive women in their thirties, both dressed in sleek professional suits.

"I've got to get back to the office." One woman checked a trim little Rolex watch. "I've got a meeting at three."

"I've got to get back to the courthouse."

Both women tucked their autographed books into leather briefcases.

"How come none of the men I date can kiss my hand without making it seem like a staged move in a one-act play?"

"Style. It all has to do with style."

With this observation, or complaint, the two women disappeared into the crowd.

At three-fifteen, he was still signing, but the crowd had thinned enough that Juliet could see him. Style, she was forced to agree, he had. No one who came up to his table, book in hand was given a quick signature, practiced smile and brush-off. He talked to them. Enjoyed them, Juliet corrected, whether it was a grandmother who smelled of lavender or a young woman with a toddler on her hip. How did he know the right thing to say to each one of them, she wondered, that made them leave the table with a laugh or a smile or a sigh?

First day of the tour, she reminded herself. She wondered if he could manage to keep himself up to this level for three weeks. Time would tell, she decided and calculated she could give him another fifteen minutes before she began to ease him out the door.

Even with the half-hour extension, it wasn't easy. Juliet began to see the pattern she was certain would set the pace of the tour. Carlo would charm and delight, and she would play the less attractive role of drill sergeant. That's what she was paid for, Juliet reminded herself as she began to smile, chat and urge people toward the door. By four there were only a handful of stragglers. With apologies and an iron grip, Juliet disengaged Carlo.

"That went very well," she began, nudging him onto the street. "One of the booksellers told me they'd nearly sold out. Makes you wonder how much pasta's going to be cooked in L.A. tonight. Consider this just one more triumph today."

"*Grazie.*"

"*Prego.* However, we won't always have the leeway to run an hour over," she told him as the door of the limo shut behind her. "It would help if you try to keep an eye on the time and pick up the pace say half an hour before finishing time. You've got an hour and fifteen minutes before airtime—"

"Fine." Pushing a button, Carlo instructed the driver to cruise.

"But—"

"Even I need to unwind," he told her, then opened up a small built-in cabinet to reveal the bar. "Cognac," he decided and poured two glasses without asking. "You've had two hours to window-shop and browse." Leaning back, he stretched out his legs.

Juliet thought of the hour and a half she'd spent on the phone, then the time involved in easing customers along. She'd been on her feet for two and a half hours straight, but she said nothing. The cognac went down smooth and warm.

"The spot on the news should run four, four and a half minutes. It doesn't seem like much time, but you'd be surprised how much you can cram in. Be sure to mention the book title, and the autographing and demonstration at the college tomorrow afternoon. The sensual aspect of food, cooking and eating's a great angle. If you'll—"

"Would you care to do the interview for me?" he asked so politely she glanced up.

So, he could be cranky, she mused. "You handle interviews beautifully, Mr. Franconi, but—"

"Carlo." Before she could open her notebook, he had his hand on her wrist. "It's Carlo, and put the damn notes away for ten minutes. Tell me, my very organized Juliet Trent, why are we here together?"

She started to move her hand but his grip was firmer than she'd thought. For the second time, she got the full impression of power, strength and determination. "To publicize your book."

"Today went well, *si*?"

"Yes, so far—"

"Today went well," he said again and began to annoy her with the frequencies of his interrupting. "I'll go on this local news show, talk for a few minutes, then have this necessary business dinner when I would much rather have a bottle of wine and a steak in my room. With you. Alone. Then I could see you without your proper little business suit and your proper little business manner."

She wouldn't permit herself to shudder. She wouldn't permit herself to react in any way. "Business is what we're here for. It's all I'm interested in."

"That may be." His agreement was much too easy. In direct contrast, he moved his hand to the back of her neck, gently, but not so gently she could move aside. "But we have an hour before business begins again. Don't lecture me on timetables."

The limo smelled of leather, she realized all at once. Of leather and wealth and Carlo. As casually as possible, she sipped from her glass. "Timetables, as you pointed out yourself this morning, are part of my job."

"You have an hour off," he told her, lifting a brow before she could speak. "So relax. Your feet hurt, so take your shoes off and drink your cognac." He set down his own drink, then moved her briefcase to the floor so there was nothing between them. "Relax," he said again but wasn't displeased that she'd stiffened. "I don't intend to make love with you in the back of a car. This time." He smiled as temper flared in her eyes because he'd seen doubt and excitement as well. "One day, one day soon, I'll find the proper moment for that, the proper place, the proper mood."

He leaned closer, so that he could just feel her breath flutter on his lips. She'd swipe at him now, he knew, if he took the next step. He might enjoy the battle. The color that ran along her cheekbones hadn't come from a tube or pot, but from passion. The look in her eyes was very close to a dare. She expected him to move an inch closer, to press her back against the seat with his mouth firm on hers. She was waiting for him, poised, ready.

He smiled while his lips did no more than hover until he knew the tension in her had built to match the tension in him. He let his gaze shift down to her mouth so that he could imagine the taste, the texture, the sweetness. Her chin stayed lifted even as he brushed a thumb over it.

He didn't care to do the expected. In a long, easy move, he leaned back, crossed his feet at the ankles and closed his eyes.

"Take off your shoes," he said again. "My schedule and yours should merge very well."

Then, to her astonishment, he was asleep. Not feigning it, she realized, but sound asleep, as if he'd just flicked a switch.

With a click, she set her half-full glass down and folded her arms. Angry, she thought. Damn right she was angry because he hadn't kissed her. Not because she wanted him to, she told herself as she stared out the tinted window. But because he'd denied her the opportunity to show her claws.

She was beginning to think she'd love drawing some Italian blood.

# Chapter Three

Their bags were packed and in the limo. As a precaution, Juliet had given Carlo's room a quick, last minute going over to make sure he hadn't left anything behind. She still remembered being on the road with a mystery writer who'd forgotten his toothbrush eight times on an eight-city tour. A quick look was simpler than a late night search for a drugstore.

Check-out at the hotel had gone quickly and without any last minute hitches. To her relief, the charges on Carlo's room bill had been light and reasonable. Her road budget might just hold. With a minimum of confusion, they'd left the Wilshire. Juliet could only hope check-in at the airport, then at the hotel in San Francisco would go as well.

She didn't want to think about the "Simpson Show."

A list of demographics wasn't necessary here. She knew Carlo had spent enough time in the States off and on to know how important his brief demonstration on the proper way to prepare *biscuit tortoni* and his ten minutes on the air would be. It was the top-rated nighttime show in the country and had been for fifteen years. Bob Simpson was an American institution. A few minutes on his show could boost the sale of books even in the most remote areas. Or it could kill it.

And boy oh boy, she thought, with a fresh gurgle of excitement, did it look impressive to have the "Simpson Show" listed on her itinerary. She offered a last minute prayer that Carlo wouldn't blow it.

* * *

She checked the little freezer backstage to be certain the dessert Carlo had prepared that afternoon was in place and ready. The concoction had to freeze for four hours, so they'd play the before-and-after game for the viewers. He'd make it up on the air, then *voilà*, they'd produce the completed frozen dessert within minutes.

Though Carlo had already gone over the procedure, the tools and ingredients with the production manager and the director, Juliet went over them all again. The whipped cream was chilling and so far none of the crew had pilfered any macaroons. The brand of dry sherry Carlo had insisted on was stored and ready. No one had broken the seal for a quick sample.

Juliet nearly believed she could whip up the fancy frozen dessert herself if necessary and only thanked God she wouldn't have to give a live culinary demonstration in front of millions of television viewers.

*He* didn't seem to be feeling any pressure, she thought as they settled in the greenroom. No, he'd already given the little half-dressed blonde on the sofa a big smile and offered her a cup of coffee from the available machine.

Coffee? Even for Hollywood, it took a wild imagination to consider the contents of the coffeepot. Juliet had taken one sip of what tasted like lukewarm mud and set the cup aside.

The little blonde was apparently a new love interest on one of the popular nighttime soaps, and she was jittery with nerves. Carlo sat down on the sofa beside her and began chatting away as though they were old friends. By the time the greenroom door opened again, she was giggling.

The greenroom itself was beige—pale, unattractive beige and cramped. The air conditioning worked, but miserably. Still Juliet knew how many of the famous and near-famous had sat in that dull little room chewing their nails. Or taking quick sips from a flask.

Carlo had exchanged the dubious coffee for plain water and was sprawled on the sofa with one arm tossed over the back. He looked as easy as a man entertaining in his own home. Juliet wondered why she hadn't tossed any antacids in her bag.

She made a pretense of rechecking the schedule while Carlo charmed the rising star and the "Simpson Show" murmured away on the twenty-five inch color console across the room.

Then the monkey walked in. Juliet glanced up and saw the long-armed, tuxedoed chimpanzee waddle in with his hand caught in that of a tall thin man with harassed eyes and a nervous grin. Feeling a bit nervous herself, Juliet looked over at Carlo. He nodded to both newcomers then went back to the blonde without missing a beat. Even as Juliet told herself to relax, the chimp grinned, threw back his head and let out a long, loud announcement.

The blonde giggled, but looked as though she'd cut and run if the chimp came one step closer—tux or no tux.

"Behave, Butch." The thin man cleared his throat as he swept his gaze around the room. "Butch just finished a picture last week," he explained to the room in general. "He's feeling a little restless."

With a jiggle of the sequins that covered her, the blonde walked to the door when her name was announced. With some satisfaction, Carlo noted that she wasn't nearly as edgy as she'd been when he'd sat down. She turned and gave him a toothy smile. "Wish me luck, darling."

"The best."

To Juliet's disgust, the blonde blew him a kiss as she sailed out.

The thin man seemed to relax visibly. "That's a relief. Blondes make Butch overexcited."

"I see." Juliet thought of her own hair that could be considered blond or brown depending on the whim. Hopefully Butch would consider it brown and unstimulating.

"But where's the lemonade?" The man's nerves came
back in full force. "They know Butch wants lemonade be
fore he goes on the air. Calms him down."

Juliet bit the tip of her tongue to hold back a snicker
Carlo and Butch were eyeing each other with a kind of tol
erant understanding. "He seems calm enough," Carlo ven
tured.

"Bundle of nerves," the man disagreed. "I'll never be
able to get him on camera."

"I'm sure it's just an oversight." Because she was used to
soothing panic, Juliet smiled. "Maybe you should ask one
of the pages."

"I'll do that." The man patted Butch on the head and
went back through the door.

"But—" Juliet half rose, then sat again. The chimp stood
in the middle of the room, resting his knuckles on the floor
"I'm not sure he should've left Cheetah."

"Butch," Carlo corrected. "I think he's harmless
enough." He sent the chimp a quick grin. "He certainly ha
an excellent tailor."

Juliet looked over to see the chimp grinning and wink
ing. "Is he twitching," she asked Carlo, "or is he flirtin
with me?"

"Flirting, if he's a male of any taste," he mused. "An
as I said his tailoring is quite good. What do you say, Butch
You find my Juliet attractive?"

Butch threw back his head and let out a series of sound
Juliet felt could be taken either way.

"See? He appreciates a beautiful woman."

Appreciating the ridiculous, Juliet laughed. Whether h
was attracted to the sound or simply felt it was time he mad
his move, Butch bowlegged his way over to her. Still grin
ning, he put his hand on Juliet's bare knee. This time, sh
was certain he winked.

"I never make so obvious a move on first acquain
tance," Carlo observed.

"Some women prefer the direct approach." Deciding he was harmless, Juliet smiled down at Butch. "He reminds me of someone." She sent Carlo a mild look. "It must be that ingratiating grin." Before she'd finished speaking, Butch climbed into her lap and wrapped one of his long arms around her. "He's kind of sweet." With another laugh, she looked down into the chimp's face. "I think he has your eyes, Carlo."

"Ah, Juliet, I think you should—"

"Though his might be more intelligent."

"Oh, I think he's smart, all right." Carlo coughed into his hand as he watched the chimp's busy fingers. "Juliet, if you'd—"

"Of course he's smart, he's in movies." Enjoying herself, Juliet watched the chimp grin up at her. "Have I seen any of your films, Butch?"

"I wouldn't be surprised if they're blue."

She tickled Butch under the chin. "Really, Carlo, how crude."

"Just a guess." He let his gaze run over her. "Tell me Juliet, do you feel a draft?"

"No. I'd say it's entirely too warm in here. This poor thing is all wrapped up in a tux." She clucked at Butch and he clacked his teeth at her.

"Juliet, do you believe people can reveal their personalities by the clothes they wear? Send signals, if you understand what I mean."

"Hmm?" Distracted, she shrugged and helped Butch straighten his tie. "I suppose so."

"I find it interesting that you wear pink silk under such a prim blouse."

"I beg your pardon?"

"An observation, *mi amore*," He let his gaze wander down again. "Just an observation."

Sitting very still, Juliet moved only her head. In a moment, her mouth was as open as her blouse. The monkey with the cute face and excellent tailor had nimbly undone every one of the buttons.

Carlo gave Butch a look of admiration. "I must ask him how he perfected that technique."

"Why you son of a—"

"Not me." Carlo put a hand to his heart. "I'm an inno-cent bystander."

Juliet rose abruptly, dumping the chimp onto the floor. As she ducked into the adjoining rest room, she heard the laughter of two males—one a chimp, the other a rat.

Juliet took the ride to the airport where they would leave for San Diego in excruciatingly polite silence.

"Come now, *cara*, the show went well. Not only was the title mentioned three times, but there was that nice close-up of the book. My *tortoni* was a triumph, and they liked my anecdote on cooking the long, sensual Italian meal."

"You're a real prince with anecdotes," she murmured.

"*Amore*, it was the monkey who tried to undress you, not I." He gave a long, self-satisfied sigh. He couldn't remem-ber when he'd enjoyed a . . . demonstration quite so much. "If I had, we'd have missed the show altogether."

"You just had to tell that story on the air, didn't you?" She sent him a cool, killing look. "Do you know how many millions of people watch that show?"

"It was a good story." In the dim light of the limo, she saw the gleam in his eyes. "Most millions of people like good stories."

"Everyone I work with will have seen that show." She found her jaw was clenched and deliberately relaxed it. "Not only did you just—just *sit* there and let that happy fingered little creature half strip me, but then you broadcast it on national television."

"*Madonna*, you'll remember I did try to warn you."

"I remember nothing of the kind."

"But you were so enchanted with Butch," he continued "I confess, it was difficult not to be enchanted myself." He let his gaze roam down to her tidily buttoned blouse. "You've lovely skin, Juliet; perhaps I was momentarily distracted. I throw myself, a simple, weak man, on your mercy."

"Oh, shut up." She folded her arms and stared straight ahead, not speaking again until the driver pulled to the curb at their airline.

Juliet pulled her carry-on bag out of the trunk. She knew the chance was always there that the bags could be lost—sent to San Jose while she went to San Diego—so she always carried her absolute essentials with her. She handed over both her ticket and Carlo's so the check-in could get underway while she paid off the driver. It made her think of her budget. She'd managed to justify limo service in L.A., but it would be cabs and rented cars from here on. Goodbye glamour, she thought as she pocketed her receipt. Hello reality.

"No, this I'll carry."

She turned to see Carlo indicate his leather-bound box of about two feet in length, eight inches in width. "You're better off checking something that bulky."

"I never check my tools." He slung a flight bag over his shoulder and picked up the box by its handle.

"Suit yourself," she said with a shrug and moved through the automatic doors with him. Fatigue was creeping in, she realized, and she hadn't had to prepare any intricate desserts. If he were human, he'd be every bit as weary as she. He might annoy her in a dozen ways, but he didn't gripe. Juliet bit back a sigh. "We've a half-hour before they'll begin boarding. Would you like a drink?"

He gave her an easy smile. "A truce?"

She returned it despite herself. "No, a drink."

"Okay."

They found a dark, crowded lounge and worked their way through to a table. She watched Carlo maneuver his box, with some difficulty, around people, over chairs and ultimately under their table. "What's in there?"

"Tools," he said again. "Knives, properly weighted, stainless steel spatulas of the correct size and balance. My own cooking oil and vinegar. Other essentials."

"You're going to lug oil and vinegar through airport terminals from coast to coast?" With a shake of her head, she glanced up at a waitress. "Vodka and grapefruit juice."

"Brandy. Yes," he said, giving his attention back to Juliet after he'd dazzled the waitress with a quick smile. "Because there's no brand on the American market to compare with my own." He picked up a peanut from the bowl on the table. "There's no brand on any market to compare with my own."

"You could still check it," she pointed out. "After all, you check your shirts and ties."

"I don't trust my tools to the hands of baggage carriers." He popped the peanut into his mouth. "A tie is a simple thing to replace, even a thing to become bored with. But an excellent whisk is entirely different. Once I teach you to cook, you'll understand."

"You've got as much chance teaching me to cook as you do flying to San Diego without the plane. Now, you know you'll be giving a demonstration of preparing linguini and clam sauce on 'A.M. San Diego.' The show airs at eight, so we'll have to be at the studio at six to get things started."

As far as he could see, the only civilized cooking to be done at that hour would be a champagne breakfast for two. "Why do Americans insist on rising at dawn to watch television?"

"I'll take a poll and find out," she said absently. "In the meantime, you'll make up one dish that we'll set aside, exactly as we did tonight. On the air you'll be going through each stage of preparation, but of course we don't have enough time to finish; that's why we need the first dish. Now, for the good news." She sent a quick smile to the waitress as their drinks were served. "There's been a bit of a mix-up at the studio, so we'll have to bring the ingredients along ourselves. I need you to give me a list of what you'll eed. Once I see you settled into the hotel, I'll run out and pick them up. There's bound to be an all-night market.''

In his head, he went over the ingredients for his *linguini on vongole biance*. True, the American market would have some of the necessities, but he considered himself fortunate that he had a few of his own in the case at his feet. The clam sauce was his specialty, not to be taken lightly.

"Is shopping for groceries at midnight part of a publicist's job?''

She smiled at him. Carlo thought it was not only lovely, but perhaps the first time she'd smiled at him and meant it. "On the road, anything that needs to be done is the publicist's job. So, if you'll run through the ingredients, I'll write them down.''

"Not necessary." He swirled and sipped his brandy. "I'll go with you.''

"You need your sleep." She was already rummaging for a pencil. "Even with a quick nap on the plane you're only going to get about five hours.''

"So are you," he pointed out. When she started to speak again, he lifted his brow in that strange silent way he had of interrupting. "Perhaps I don't trust an amateur to pick out my clams.''

Juliet watched him as she drank. Or perhaps he was a gentleman, she mused. Despite his reputation with women, and a healthy dose of vanity, he was one of that rare breed of men who knew how to be considerate of women without patronizing them. She decided to forgive him for Butch after all.

"Drink up, Franconi." And she toasted him, perhaps in friendship. "We've a plane to catch.''

"*Salute.*" He lifted his glass to her.

They didn't argue again until they were on the plane.

Grumbling only a little, Juliet helped him stow his fancy box of tools under the seat. "It's a short flight." She checked her watch and calculated the shopping would indeed go beyond midnight. She'd have to take some of the vile tasting brewer's yeast in the morning. "I'll see you when we land."

He took her wrist when she would have gone past him. "Where are you going?"

"To my seat."

"You don't sit here?" He pointed to the seat beside him.

"No, I'm in coach." Impatient, she had to shift to let another oncoming passenger by.

"Why?"

"Carlo, I'm blocking the aisle."

"Why are you in coach?"

She let out a sigh of a parent instructing a stubborn child. "Because the publisher is more than happy to spring for first-class ticket for a best-selling author and celebrity. There's a different style for publicists. It's called coach." Someone bumped a briefcase against her hip. Damn if she wouldn't have a bruise. "Now if you'd let me go, I could stop being battered and go sit down."

"First class is almost empty," he pointed out. "It's simple matter to upgrade your ticket."

She managed to pull her arm away. "Don't buck the system, Franconi."

"I always buck the system," he told her as she walked down the aisle to her seat. Yes, he did like the way she moved.

"Mr. Franconi." A flight attendant beamed at him. "May I get you a drink after take-off?"

"What's your white wine?"

When she told him he settled into his seat. A bit pedestrian, he thought, but not entirely revolting. "You noticed the young woman I was speaking with. The honey-colored hair and the stubborn chin."

Her smile remained bright and helpful though she thought it was a shame that he had his mind on another woman. "Of course, Mr. Franconi."

"She'll have a glass of wine, with my compliments."

Juliet would have considered herself fortunate to have an isle seat if the man beside her hadn't already been sprawled out and snoring. Travel was so glamorous, she thought wryly as she slipped her toes out of her shoes. Wasn't she lucky to have another flight to look forward to the very next night?

Don't complain, Juliet, she warned herself. When you have your own agency, you can send someone else on the down-and-dirty tours.

The man beside her snored through take-off. On the other side of the aisle a woman held a cigarette in one hand and a lighter in the other in anticipation of the no smoking sign blinking off. Juliet took out her pad and began to work.

"Miss?"

Stifling a yawn, Juliet glanced up at the flight attendant. "I'm sorry, I didn't order a drink."

"With Mr. Franconi's compliments."

Juliet accepted the wine as she looked up toward first class. He was sneaky, she told herself. Trying to get under her defenses by being nice. She let her notebook close as she sighed and sat back.

It was working.

She barely finished the wine before touchdown, but it had relaxed her. Relaxed her enough, she realized, that all she wanted to do was find a soft bed and a dark room. In an hour—or two, she promised herself and gathered up her flight bag and briefcase.

She found Carlo was waiting for her in first class with a very young, very attractive flight attendant. Neither of them seemed the least bit travel weary.

"Ah, Juliet, Deborah knows of a marvelous twenty-four hour market where we can find everything we need."

Juliet looked at the willowy brunette and managed a smile. "How convenient."

He took the flight attendant's hand and, inevitably Juliet thought, kissed it. *"Arrivederci."*

"Don't waste time, do you?" Juliet commented the moment they deplaned.

"Every moment lived is a moment to be enjoyed."

"What a quaint little sentiment." She shifted her bag and aimed for baggage claim. "You should have it tattooed."

"Where?"

She didn't bother to look at his grin. "Where it would be most attractive, naturally."

They had to wait longer than she liked for their luggage, and by then the relaxing effects of the wine had worn off. There was business to be seen to. Because he enjoyed watching her in action, Carlo let her see to it.

She secured a cab, tipped the skycap and gave the driver the name of the hotel. Scooting in beside Carlo, she caught his grin. "Something funny?"

"You're so efficient, Juliet."

"Is that a compliment or an insult?"

"I never insult women." He said it so simply, she was absolutely certain it was true. Unlike Juliet, he was completely relaxed and not particularly sleepy. "If this was Rome, we'd go to a dark little café, drink heavy red wine and listen to American music."

She closed her window because the air was damp and chilly. "The tour interfering with your night life?"

"So far I find myself enjoying the stimulating company."

"Tomorrow you're going to find yourself worked to a frazzle."

Carlo thought of his background and smiled. At nine he'd spent the hours between school and supper washing dishes and mopping up kitchens. At fifteen he'd waited tables and spent his free time learning of spices and sauces. In Paris he'd combined long, hard study with work as an assistant chef. Even now, his restaurant and clients had him keeping twelve-hour days. Not all of his background was in the neatly typed bio Juliet had in her briefcase.

"I don't mind work, as long as it interests me. I think you're the same."

"I have to work," she corrected. "But it's easier when you enjoy it."

"You're more successful when you enjoy it. It shows with you. Ambition, Juliet, without a certain joy, is cold, and when achieved leaves a flat taste."

"But I am ambitious."

"Oh yes." He turned to look at her, starting off flutters she'd thought herself too wise to experience. "But you're not cold."

For a moment, she thought she'd be better off if he were wrong. "Here's the hotel." She turned from him, relieved to deal with details. "We need you to wait," she instructed the driver. "We'll be going out again as soon as we check in. The hotel has a lovely view of the bay I'm told." She walked into the lobby with Carlo as the bellboy dealt with their luggage. "It's a shame we won't have time to enjoy it. Franconi and Trent," she told the desk clerk.

The lobby was quiet and empty. Oh, the lucky people who were sleeping in their beds, she thought and pushed at a strand of hair that had come loose.

"We'll be checking out first thing tomorrow, and we won't be able to come back, so be sure you don't leave anything behind in your room."

"But of course you'll check anyway."

She sent him a sidelong look as she signed the form. "Just part of the service." She pocketed her key. "The luggage can be taken straight up." Discreetly, she handed the bellboy a folded bill. "Mr. Franconi and I have an errand."

"Yes, ma'am."

"I like that about you." To Juliet's surprise, Carlo linked arms with her as they walked back outside.

"What?"

"Your generosity. Many people would've slipped out without tipping the bellboy."

She shrugged. "Maybe it's easier to be generous when it' not your money."

"Juliet." He opened the door to the waiting cab and ges tured her in. "You're intelligent enough. Couldn't you— how is it—stiff the bellboy then write the tip down on you expense account?"

"Five dollars isn't worth being dishonest."

"Nothing's worth being dishonest." He gave the drive the name of the market and settled back. "Instinct tells m if you tried to tell a lie—a true lie—your tongue would fa out."

"Mr. Franconi." She planted the tongue in question i her cheek. "You forget, I'm in public relations. If I didn lie, I'd be out of a job."

"A true lie," he corrected.

"Isn't that a contradiction in terms?"

"Perhaps you're too young to know the variety of truth and lies. Ah, you see? This is why I'm so fond of you country." Carlo leaned out the window as they approache the big, lighted all-night market. "In America, you wan cookies at midnight, you can buy cookies at midnight. Suc practicality."

"Glad to oblige. Wait here," she instructed the drive then climbed out opposite Carlo. "I hope you know wha you need. I'd hate to get into the studio at dawn and find had to run out and buy whole peppercorns or something."

"Franconi knows linguini." He swung an arm around h shoulder and drew her close as they walked inside. "You first lesson, my love."

He led her first to the seafood section where he clucke and muttered and rejected and chose until he had the prope number of clams for two dishes. She'd seen women give much time and attention to choosing an engagement ring

Juliet obliged him by pushing the cart as he walked alor beside her, looking at everything. And touching. Can boxes, bottles—she waited as he picked up, examined ar ran his long artist's fingers over the labels as he read ever ngredient. Somewhat amused, she watched his diamond wink in the fluorescent light.

"Amazing what they put in this prepackaged garbage," he commented as he dropped a box back on the shelf.

"Careful, Franconi, you're talking about my staple diet."

"You should be sick."

"Prepackaged food's freed the American woman from the kitchen."

"And destroyed a generation of taste buds." He chose his spices carefully and without haste. He opened three brands of oregano and sniffed before he settled on one. "I tell you, Juliet, I admire your American convenience, its practicality, but I would rather shop in Rome where I can walk along the stalls and choose vegetables just out of the ground, fish fresh from the sea. Everything isn't in a can, like the music."

He didn't miss an aisle, but Juliet forgot her fatigue in fascination. She'd never seen anyone shop like Carlo Franconi. It was like strolling through a museum with an art student. He breezed by the flour, scowling at each sack. She was afraid for a moment, he'd rip one open and test the contents. "This is a good brand?"

Juliet figured she bought a two-pound bag of flour about once a year. "Well, my mother always used this, but—"

"Good. Always trust a mother."

"She's a dreadful cook."

Carlo set the flour firmly in the basket. "She's a mother."

"An odd sentiment from a man no mother can trust."

"For mothers, I have the greatest respect. I have one myself. Now, we need garlic, mushrooms, peppers. Fresh."

Carlo walked along the stalls of vegetables, touching, squeezing and sniffing. Cautious, Juliet looked around for clerks, grateful they'd come at midnight rather than midday. "Carlo, you really aren't supposed to handle everything quite so much."

"If I don't handle, how do I know what's good and what's just pretty?" He sent her a quick grin over his

shoulder. "I told you, food was much like a woman. The
put mushrooms in this box with wrap over it." Disgusted
he tore the wrapping off before Juliet could stop him.

"Carlo! You can't open it."

"I want only what I want. You can see, some are to
small, too skimpy." Patiently, he began to pick out th
mushrooms that didn't suit him.

"Then we'll throw out what you don't want when we ge
back to the hotel." Keeping an eye out for the night man
ager, she began to put the discarded mushrooms back in th
box. "Buy two boxes if you need them."

"It's a waste. You'd waste your money?"

"The publisher's money," she said quickly, as she put th
broken box into the basket. "He's glad to waste i
Thrilled."

He paused for a moment, then shook his head. "No, n
I can't do it." But when he started to reach into the baske
Juliet moved and blocked his way.

"Carlo, if you break open another package, we're goin
to be arrested."

"Better to go to jail than to buy mushrooms that will d
me no good in the morning."

She grinned at him and stood firm. "No, it's not."

He ran a fingertip over her lips before she could read
"For you then, but against my better judgment."

"*Grazie.* Do you have everything now?"

His gaze followed the path his finger had traced just a
slowly. "No."

"Well, what next?"

He stepped closer and because she hadn't expected it, sl
found herself trapped between him and the grocery car
"Tonight is for first lessons," he murmured then ran h
hands along either side of her face.

She should laugh. Juliet told herself it was ludicrous th
he'd make a pass at her under the bright lights of the veg
table section of an all-night market. Carlo Franconi, a ma

who'd made seduction as much an art as his cooking wouldn't choose such a foolish setting.

But she saw what was in his eyes, and she didn't laugh.

Some women, he thought as he felt her skin soft and warm under his hands, were made to be taught slowly. Very slowly. Some women were born knowing; others were born wondering.

With Juliet, he would take time and care because he understood. Or thought he did.

She didn't resist, but her lips had parted in surprise. He touched his to hers gently, not in question, but with patience. Her eyes had already given him the answer.

He didn't hurry. It didn't matter to him where they were, that the lights were bright and the music manufactured. It only mattered that he explore the tastes that waited for him. So he tasted again, without pressure. And again.

She found she was bracing herself against the cart with her fingers wrapped around the metal. Why didn't she walk away? Why didn't she just brush him aside and stalk out of the store? He wasn't holding her there. On her face his hands were light, clever but not insistent. She could move. She could go. She should.

She didn't.

His thumbs trailed under her chin, tracing there. He felt the pulse, rapid and jerky, and kept his hold easy. He meant to keep it so, but even he hadn't guessed her taste would be so unique.

Neither of them knew who took the next step. Perhaps they took it together. His mouth wasn't so light on hers any longer, nor was hers so passive. They met, triumphantly, and clung.

Her fingers weren't wrapped around the cart now, but gripping his shoulders, holding him closer. Their bodies fit. Perfectly. It should have warned her. Giving without thought was something she never did, until now. In giving, she took, but she never thought to balance the ledger.

His mouth was warm, full. His hands never left her face, but they were firm now. She couldn't have walked away so easily. She wouldn't have walked away at all.

He'd thought he had known everything there was to expect from a woman—fire, ice, temptation. But a lesson was being taught to both. Had he ever felt this warmth before? This kind of sweetness? No, because if he had, he'd remember. No tastes, no sensations ever experienced were forgotten.

He knew what it was to desire a woman—many women—but he hadn't known what it was to crave. For a moment, he filled himself with the sensation. He wouldn't forget.

But he knew that a cautious man takes a step back and a second breath before he steps off a cliff. With a murmur in his own language, he did.

Shaken, Juliet gripped the cart again for balance. Cursing herself for an idiot, she waited for her breath to even out.

"Very nice," Carlo said quietly and ran a finger along her cheek. "Very nice, Juliet."

An eighties woman, she reminded herself as her heart thudded. Strong, independent, sophisticated. "I'm so glad you approve."

He took her hand before she could slam the cart down the aisle. Her skin was still warm, he noted, her pulse still unsteady. If they'd been alone... Perhaps it was best this way. For now. "It isn't a matter of approval, *cara mia*, but of appreciation."

"From now on, just appreciate me for my work, okay?" A jerk, and she freed herself of him and shoved the cart away. Without regard for the care he'd taken in selecting them, Juliet began to drop the contents of the cart on the conveyor belt at check-out.

"You didn't object," he reminded her. He'd needed to find his balance as well, he realized. Now he leaned against the cart and gave her a cocky grin.

"I didn't want a scene."

He took the peppers from the basket himself before she could wound them. "Ah, you're learning about lies."

When her head came up, he was surprised her eyes didn't bore right through him. "You wouldn't know truth if you fell into it."

"Darling, mind the mushrooms," he warned her as she swung the package onto the belt. "We don't want them bruised. I've a special affection for them now."

She swore at him, loudly enough that the checker's eyes widened. Carlo continued to grin and thought about lesson two.

He thought they should have it soon. Very soon.

# Chapter Four

There were times when you knew everything could go wrong, should go wrong, and probably would go wrong, but somehow it didn't. Then there were the other times.

Perhaps Juliet was grouchy because she'd spent another restless night when she couldn't afford to lose any sleep. That little annoyance she could lay smack at Carlo's door, even though it didn't bring any satisfaction. But even if she'd been rested and cheerful, the ordeal at Gallegher's Department Store would have had her steaming. With a good eight hours' sleep, she might have kept things from boiling over.

First, Carlo insisted on coming with her two hours before he was needed. Or wanted. Juliet didn't care to spend the first two hours of what was bound to be a long, hectic day with a smug, self-assured, egocentric chef who looked as though he'd just come back from two sun-washed weeks on the Riviera.

Obviously, *he* didn't need any sleep, she mused as they took the quick, damp cab ride from hotel to mall.

Whatever the tourist bureau had to say about sunny California, it was raining—big, steady drops of it that immediately made the few minutes she'd taken to fuss with her hair worthless.

Prepared to enjoy the ride, Carlo looked out the window. He liked the way the rain plopped in puddles. It didn't matter to him that he'd heard it start that morning, just past four. "It's a nice sound," he decided. "It makes things more quiet, more...subtle, don't you think?"

Breaking away from her own gloomy view of the rain, Juliet turned to him. "What?"

"The rain." Carlo noted she looked a bit hollow-eyed. Good. She hadn't been unaffected. "Rain changes the look of things."

Normally, she would have agreed. Juliet never minded dashing for the subway in a storm or strolling along Fifth Avenue in a drizzle. Today, she considered it her right to look on the dark side. "This one might lower the attendance in your little demonstration by ten percent."

"So?" He gave an easy shrug as the driver swung into the parking lot of the mall.

What she didn't need at that moment was careless acceptance. "Carlo, the purpose of all this is exposure."

He patted her hand. "You're only thinking of numbers. You should think instead of my *pasta con pesto*. In a few hours, everyone else will."

"I don't think about food the way you do," she muttered. It still amazed her that he'd lovingly prepared the first linguini at 6:00 A.M., then the second two hours later for the camera. Both dishes had been an exquisite example of Italian cooking at its finest. He'd looked more like a film star on holiday than a working chef, which was precisely the image Juliet had wanted to project. His spot on the morning show had been perfect. That only made Juliet more pessimistic about the rest of the day. "It's hard to think about food at all on this kind of a schedule."

"That's because you didn't eat anything this morning."

"Linguini for breakfast doesn't suit me."

"My linguini is always suitable."

Juliet gave a mild snort as she stepped from the cab into the rain. Though she made a dash for the doors, Carlo was there ahead of her, opening one. "Thanks." Inside, she ran a hand through her hair and wondered how soon she could come by another cup of coffee. "You don't need to do anything for another two hours." And he'd definitely be in the way while things were being set up on the third floor.

"So, I'll wander." With his hands in his pockets, he looked around. As luck would have it, they'd entered straight into the lingerie department. "I find your American malls fascinating."

"I'm sure." Her voice was dry as he fingered the border of lace on a slinky camisole. "You can come upstairs with me first, if you like."

"No, no." A saleswoman with a face that demanded a second look adjusted two negligees and beamed at him. "I think I'll just roam around and see what your shops have to offer." He beamed back. "So far, I'm charmed."

She watched the exchange and tried not to clench her teeth. "All right, then, if you'll just be sure to—"

"Be in Special Events on the third floor at eleven-forty-five," he finished. In his friendly, casual way, he kissed her forehead. She wondered why he could touch her like a cousin and make her think of a lover. "Believe me, Juliet, nothing you say to me is forgotten." He took her hand, running his thumb over her knuckles. That was definitely not the touch of a cousin. "I'll buy you a present."

"It isn't necessary."

"A pleasure. Things that are necessary are rarely a pleasure."

Juliet disengaged her hand while trying not to dwell on the pleasure he could offer. "Please, don't be later than eleven-forty-five, Carlo."

"Timing, *mi amore*, is something I excel in."

I'll bet, she thought as she started toward the escalator. She'd have bet a week's pay he was already flirting with the lingerie clerk.

It only took ten minutes in Special Events for Juliet to forget Carlo's penchant for romancing anything feminine.

The little assistant with the squeaky voice was still in charge as her boss continued his battle with the flu. She was young, cheerleader pretty and just as pert. She was also completely over her head.

"Elise," Juliet began because it was still early on enough for her to have some optimism. "Mr. Franconi's going to need a working area in the kitchen department. Is everything set?"

"Oh yes." Elise gave Juliet a toothy, amiable grin. "I'm getting a nice folding table from Sporting Goods."

Diplomacy, Juliet reminded herself, was one of the primary rules of PR. "I'm afraid we'll need something a bit sturdier. Perhaps one of the islands where Mr. Franconi could prepare the dish and still face the audience. Your supervisor and I had discussed it."

"Oh, is that what he meant?" Elise looked blank for a moment, then brightened. Juliet began to think dark thoughts about mellow California. "Well, why not?"

"Why not," Juliet agreed. "We've kept the dish Mr. Franconi is to prepare as simple as possible. You do have all the ingredients listed?"

"Oh, yes. It sounds just delicious. I'm a vegetarian, you know."

Of course she was, Juliet thought. Yogurt was probably the high point of her day. "Elise, I'm sorry if it seems I'm rushing you along, but I really need to work out the setup as soon as possible."

"Oh sure." All cooperation, Elise flashed her straight-toothed smile. "What do you want to know?"

Juliet offered up a prayer. "How sick is Mr. Francis?" she asked, thinking of the level-headed, businesslike man she had dealt with before.

"Just miserable." Elise swung back her straight California-blond hair. "He'll be out the rest of the week."

No help there. Accepting the inevitable, Juliet gave Elise her straight, no-nonsense look. "All right, what have you got so far?"

"Well, we've taken a new blender and some really lovely bowls from Housewares."

Juliet nearly relaxed. "That's fine. And the range?"

Elise smiled. "Range?"

"The range Mr. Franconi needs to cook the spaghetti for this dish. It's on the list."

"Oh. We'd need elecricity for that, wouldn't we?"

"Yes." Juliet folded her hands to keep them from clenching. "We would. For the blender, too."

"I guess I'd better check with maintenance."

"I guess you'd better." Diplomacy, tact, Juliet reminded herself as her fingers itched for Elise's neck. "Maybe I'll just go over to the kitchen layouts and see which one would suit Mr. Franconi best."

"Terrific. He might want to do his interview right there."

Juliet had taken two steps before she stopped and turned back. "Interview?"

"With the food editor of the *Sun*. She'll be here at eleven-thirty."

Calm, controlled, Juliet pulled out her itinerary of the San Diego stop. She skimmed it, though she knew every word by heart. "I don't seem to have anything listed here."

"It came up at the last minute. I called your hotel at nine but you'd already checked out."

"I see." Should she have expected Elise to phone the television studio and leave a message? Juliet looked into the personality-plus smile. No, she supposed not. Resigned, she checked her watch. The setup could be dealt with in time if she started immediately. Carlo would just have to be paged. "How do I call mall management?"

"Oh, you can call from my office. Can I do anything?"

Juliet thought of and rejected several things, none of which were kind. "I'd like some coffee, two sugars."

She rolled up her sleeves and went to work.

By eleven, Juliet had the range, the island and the ingredients Carlo had specified neatly arranged. It had taken only one call, and some finesse, to acquire two vivid flower arrangements from a shop in the mall.

She was on her third coffee and considering a fourth when Carlo wandered over. "Thank God." She drained the last from the styrofoam cup. "I thought I was going to have to send out a search party."

"Search party?" Idly he began looking around the kitchen set. "I came when I heard the page."

"You've been paged five times in the last hour."

"Yes?" He smiled as he looked back at her. Her hair was beginning to stray out of her neat bun. He might have stepped off the cover of *Gentlemen's Quarterly*. "I only just heard. But then, I spent some time in the most fantastic record store. Such speakers. Quadraphonic."

"That's nice." Juliet dragged a hand through her already frazzled hair.

"There's a problem?"

"Her name's Elise. I've come very close to murdering her half a dozen times. If she smiles at me again, I just might." Juliet gestured with her hand to brush it off. This was no time for fantasies, no matter how satisfying. "It seems things were a bit disorganized here."

"But you've seen to that." He bent over to examine the range as a driver might a car before Le Mans. "Excellent."

"You can be glad you've got electricity rather than your imagination," she muttered. "You have an interview at eleven-thirty with a food editor, Marjorie Ballister, from the *Sun*."

He only moved his shoulders and examined the blender. "All right."

"If I'd known it was coming up, I'd have bought a paper so we could have seen her column and gauged her style. As it is—"

"*Non importante*. You worry too much, Juliet."

She could have kissed him. Strictly in gratitude, but she could have kissed him. Considering that unwise, she smiled instead. "I appreciate your attitude, Carlo. After the last hour of dealing with the inept, the insane and the unbearable, it's a relief to have someone take things in stride."

"Franconi always takes things in stride." Juliet started to sink into a chair for a five-minute break.

"*Dio!* What joke is this?" She was standing again an lonking down at the little can he held in his hand. "Wh would sabotage my pasta?"

"Sabotage?" Had he found a bomb in the can? "Wha are you talking about?"

"This!" He shook the can at her. "What do you cal this?"

"It's basil," she began, a bit unsteady when she lifted he gaze and caught the dark, furious look in his eyes. "It's o your list."

"Basil!" He went off in a stream of Italian. "You dar call this basil?"

Soothe, Juliet reminded herself. It was part of the job "Carlo, it says basil right on the can."

"On the can." He said something short and rude as h dropped it into her hand. "Where in your clever notes doe it say Franconi uses basil from a can?"

"It just says basil," she said between clenched teeth. "B a-s-i-l."

"Fresh. On your famous list you'll see fresh. *Accidenti* Only a philistine uses basil from a can for *pasta con pesto* Do I look like a philistine?"

She wouldn't tell him what he looked like. Later, sh might privately admit that temper was spectacular on him Dark and unreasonable, but spectacular. "Carlo, I realiz things aren't quite as perfect here as both of us would like but—"

"I don't need perfect," he tossed at her. "I can cook in sewer if I have to, but not without the proper ingredients."

She swallowed—though it went down hard—pride, tem per and opinion. She only had fifteen minutes left until th interview. "I'm sorry, Carlo. If we could just compromis on this—"

"Compromise?" When the word came out like an ob scenity, she knew she'd lost the battle. "Would you ask Pi casso to compromise on a painting?"

Juliet stuck the can into her pocket. "How much fresh basil do you need?"

"Three ounces."

"You'll have it. Anything else?"

"A mortar and pestle, marble."

Juliet checked her watch. She had forty-five minutes to handle it. "Okay. If you'll do the interview right here, I'll take care of this and we'll be ready for the demonstration at noon." She sent up a quick prayer that there was a gourmet shop within ten miles. "Remember to get in the book title and the next stop on the tour. We'll be hitting another Gallegher's in Portland, so it's a good tie-in. Here." Digging into her bag she brought out an eight-by-ten glossy. "Take the extra publicity shot for her in case I don't get back. Elise didn't mention a photographer."

"You'd like to chop and dice that bouncy little woman," Carlo observed, noting that Juliet was swearing very unprofessionally under her breath.

"You bet I would." She dug in again. "Take a copy of the book. The reporter can keep it if necessary."

"I can handle the reporter," he told her calmly enough. "You handle the basil."

It seemed luck was with her when Juliet only had to make three calls before she found a shop that carried what she needed. The frenzied trip in the rain didn't improve her disposition, nor did the price of a marble pestle. Another glance at her watch reminded her she didn't have time for temperament. Carrying what she considered Carlo's eccentricities, she ran back to the waiting cab.

At exactly ten minutes to twelve, dripping wet, Juliet rode up to the third floor of Gallegher's. The first thing she saw was Carlo, leaning back in a cozy wicker dinette chair laughing with a plump, pretty middle-aged woman with a pad and pencil. He looked dashing, amiable and most of all, dry. She wondered how it would feel to grind the pestle into his ear.

"Ah, Juliet." All good humor, Carlo rose as she walked up to the table. "You must meet Marjorie. She tells me she's eaten my pasta in my restaurant in Rome."

"Loved every sinful bite. How do you do? You must be the Juliet Trent Carlo bragged about."

Bragged about? No, she wouldn't be pleased. But Juliet set her bag on the table and offered her hand. "It's nice to meet you. I hope you can stay for the demonstration."

"Wouldn't miss it." She twinkled at Carlo. "Or a sample of Franconi's pasta."

Juliet felt a little wave of relief. Something would be salvaged out of the disaster. Unless she was way off the mark, Carlo was about to be given a glowing write-up.

Carlo was already taking the little sack of basil out of the bag. "Perfect," he said after one sniff. "Yes, yes, this is excellent." He tested the pestle weight and size. "You'll see over at our little stage a crowd is gathering," he said easily to Juliet. "So we moved here to talk, knowing you'd see us as soon as you stepped off the escalator."

"Very good." They'd both handled things well, she decided. It was best to take satisfaction from that. A quick glance showed her that Elise was busy chatting away with a small group of people. Not a worry in the world, Juliet thought nastily. Well, she'd already resigned herself to that. Five minutes in the rest room for some quick repairs, she calculated, and she could keep everything on schedule.

"You have everything you need now, Carlo?"

He caught the edge of annoyance, and her hand, smiling brilliantly. "*Grazie, cara mia*. You're wonderful."

Perhaps she'd rather have snarled, but she returned the smile. "Just doing my job. You have a few more minutes before we should begin. If you'll excuse me, I'll just take care of some things and be right back."

Juliet kept up a brisk, dignified walk until she was out of sight, then made a mad dash for the rest room, pulling out her brush as she went in.

"What did I tell you?" Carlo held the bag of basil in his palm to judge the weight. "She's fantastic."

"And quite lovely," Marjorie agreed. "Even when she's damp and annoyed."

With a laugh, Carlo leaned forward to grasp both of Marjorie's hands. He was a man who touched, always. "A woman of perception. I knew I liked you."

She gave a quick dry chuckle, and for a moment felt twenty years younger. And twenty pounds lighter. It was a talent of his that he was generous with. "One last question, Carlo, before your fantastic Ms. Trent rushes you off. Are you still likely to fly off to Cairo or Cannes to prepare one of your dishes for an appreciative client and a stunning fee?"

"There was a time this was routine." He was silent a moment, thinking of the early years of his success. There'd been mad, glamorous trips to this country and to that, preparing fettuccine for a prince or cannelloni for a tycoon. It had been a heady, spectacular time.

Then he'd opened his restaurant and had learned that the solid continuity of his own place was so much more fulfilling than the flash of the single dish.

"From time to time I would still make such trips. Two months ago there was Count Lequine's birthday. He's an old client, an old friend, and he's fond of my spaghetti. But my restaurant is more rewarding to me." He gave her a quizzical look as a thought occurred to him. "Perhaps I'm setting down?"

"A pity you didn't decide to settle in the States." She closed her pad. "I guarantee if you opened a Franconi's right here in San Diego, you'd have clientele flying in from all over the country."

He took the idea, weighed it in much the same way he had the basil, and put it in a corner of his mind. "An interesting thought."

"And a fascinating interview. Thank you." It pleased her that he rose as she did and took her hand. She was a tough outspoken feminist who appreciated genuine manners and genuine charm. "I'm looking forward to a taste of you pasta. I'll just ease over and try to get a good seat. Her comes your Ms. Trent."

Marjorie had never considered herself particularly ro mantic, but she'd always believed where there was smoke there was fire. She watched the way Carlo turned his head saw the change in his eyes and the slight tilt of his mouth There was fire all right, she mused. You only had to b within five feet to feel the heat.

Between the hand dryer and her brush, Juliet had man aged to do something with her hair. A touch here, a da' there, and her makeup was back in shape. Carrying he raincoat over her arm, she looked competent and collected She was ready to admit she'd had one too many cups o coffee.

"Your interview went well?"

"Yes." He noticed, and approved, that she'd taken th time to dab on her scent. "Perfectly."

"Good. You can fill me in later. We'd better get started.'

"In a moment." He reached in his pocket. "I told you I' buy you a present."

There was a flutter of surprised pleasure she tried to ig nore. Just wired from the coffee, she told herself. "Carlo, told you not to. We don't have time—"

"There's always time." He opened the little box himsel and drew out a small gold heart with an arrow of diamond running through it. She'd been expecting something alon the line of a box of chocolates.

"Oh, I—" Words were her business, but she'd lost them "Carlo, really, you can't—"

"Never say can't to Franconi," he murmured and bega to fasten the pin to her lapel. He did so smoothly, with n fumbling. After all, he was a man accustomed to such fem inine habits. "It's very delicate, I thought, very elegant. S it suits you." Narrowing his eyes, he stood back then nod ded. "Yes, I was sure it would."

It wasn't possible to remember her crazed search for fresh basil when he was smiling at her in just that way. It was barely possible to remember how furious she was over the lackadaisical setup for the demonstration. Instinctively, she put up her hand and ran a finger over the pin. "It's lovely." Her lips curved, easily, sweetly, as he thought they didn't do often enough. "Thank you."

He couldn't count or even remember the number of presents he'd given, or the different styles of gratitude he'd received. Somehow, he was already sure this would be one he wouldn't forget.

"*Prègo.*"

"Ah, Ms. Trent?"

Juliet glanced over to see Elise watching her. Present or no present, it tightened her jaw. "Yes, Elise. You haven't met Mr. Franconi yet."

"Elise directed me from the office to you when I answered the page," Carlo said easily, more than appreciating Juliet's aggravation.

"Yes." She flashed her touchdown smile. "I thought your cookbook looked just super, Mr. Franconi. Everyone's dying to watch you cook something." She opened a little pad of paper with daisies on the cover. "I thought you could spell what it is so I could tell them when I announce you."

"Elise, I have everything." Juliet managed charm and diplomacy to cover a firm nudge out the door. "Why don't I just announce Mr. Franconi?"

"Great." She beamed. Juliet could think of no other word for it. "That'll be a lot easier."

"We'll get started now, Carlo, if you just step over there behind those counters, I'll go give the announcements." Without waiting for an assent, she gathered up the basil, mortar and pestle and walked over to the area that she'd prepared. In the most natural of moves, she set everything down and turned to the audience. Three hundred, she judged. Maybe even over. Not bad for a rainy day in a department store.

"Good afternoon." Her voice was pleasant and well pitched. There'd be no need for a microphone in the relatively small space. Thank God, because Elise had botched that minor detail as well. "I want to thank you all for coming here today, and to thank Gallegher's for providing such a lovely setting for the demonstration."

From a few feet away, Carlo leaned on a counter and watched her. She was, as he'd told the reporter, fantastic. No one would guess she'd been up and on her feet since dawn.

"We all like to eat." This drew the murmured laughter she'd expected. "But I've been told by an expert that eating is more than a basic necessity, it's an experience. Not all of us like to cook, but the same expert told me that cooking is both art and magic. This afternoon, the expert, Carlo Franconi, will share with you the art, the magic and the experience with his own *pasta con pesto*."

Juliet started the applause herself, but it was picked up instantly. As Carlo stepped out, she melted back. Center stage was his the moment he stepped on it.

"It's a fortunate man," he began, "who has the opportunity to cook for so many beautiful women. Some of you have husbands?" At the question there was a smatter of chuckles and the lifting of hands. "Ah well." He gave a very European shrug. "Then I must be content to cook."

She knew Carlo had chosen that particular dish because it took little time in preparation. After the first five minutes, Juliet was certain not one member of the audience would have budged if he'd chosen something that took hours. She wasn't yet convinced cooking was magic, but she was certain he was.

His hands were as skilled and certain as a surgeon's, his tongue as glib as a politician's. She watched him measure, grate, chop and blend and found herself just as entertained as she might have been with a well produced one-act play.

One woman was bold enough to ask a question. It opened the door and dozens of others followed. Juliet needn't have worried that the noise and conversations would disturb him. Obviously he thrived on the interaction. He wasn't, she decided, simply doing his job or fulfilling an obligation. He was enjoying himself.

Calling one woman up with him, Carlo joked about all truly great chefs requiring both inspiration and assistance. He told her to stir the spaghetti, made a fuss out of showing her the proper way to stir by putting his hand over hers and undoubtedly sold another ten books then and there.

Juliet had to grin. He'd done it for fun, not for sales. He was fun, Juliet realized, even if he did take his basil too seriously. He was sweet. Unconsciously, she began to toy with the gold and diamonds on her lapel. Uncommonly considerate and uncommonly demanding. Simply uncommon.

As she watched him laugh with his audience, something began to melt inside of her. She sighed with it, dreaming. There were certain men that prompted a woman, even a practical woman, to dream.

One of the women seated closer to her leaned toward a companion. "Good God, he's the sexiest man I've ever seen. He could keep a dozen lovers patiently waiting."

Juliet caught herself and dropped her hand. Yes, he could keep a dozen lovers patiently waiting. She was sure he did. Deliberately she tucked her hands in the pockets of her skirt. She'd be better off remembering she was encouraging this public image, even exploiting it. She'd be better off remembering that Carlo himself had told her he needed no imagery.

If she started believing half the things he said to her, she might just find herself patiently waiting. The thought of that was enough to stop the melting. Waiting didn't fit into her schedule.

When every last bite of pasta had been consumed, and every last fan had been spoken with, Carlo allowed himself to think of the pleasures of sitting down with a cool glass of wine.

Juliet already had his jacket.

"Well done, Carlo." As she spoke, she began to help him
into it. "You can leave California with the satisfaction of
knowing you were a smashing success."

He took her raincoat from her when she would've
shrugged into it herself. "The airport."

She smiled at his tone, understanding. "We'll pick up our
bags in the holding room at the hotel on the way. Look at it
this way. You can sit back and sleep all the way to Portland
if you like."

Because the thought had a certain appeal, he cooper-
ated. They rode down to the first floor and went out the west
entrance where Juliet had told the cab to wait. She let out a
quick sigh of relief when it was actually there.

"We get into Portland early?"

"Seven." Rain splattered against the cab's windshield.
Juliet told herself to relax. Planes took off safely in the rain
every day. "You have a spot on 'People of Interest,' but not
until nine-thirty. That means we can have breakfast at a
civilized hour and go over the scheduling."

Quickly, efficiently, she checked off her San Diego list and
noted everything had been accomplished. She had time for
a quick, preliminary glance at her Portland schedule before
the cab pulled up to the hotel.

"Just wait here," she ordered both the driver and Carlo.
She was up and out of the cab and, because they were running it close, managed to have the bags installed in the trunk
within seven minutes. Carlo knew because it amused him to
time her.

"You, too, can sleep all the way to Portland."

She settled in beside him again. "No, I've got some work
to do. The nice thing about planes is that I can pretend I'm
in my office and forget I'm thousands of feet off the
ground."

"I didn't realize flying bothered you."

"Only when I'm in the air." Juliet sat back and closed her
eyes, thinking to relax for a moment. The next thing she
knew, she was being kissed awake.

Disoriented, she sighed and wrapped her arms around Carlo's neck. It was soothing, so sweet. And then the heat began to rise.

*"Cara."* She'd surprised him, but that had brought its own kind of pleasure. "Such a pity to wake you."

"Hmm?" When she opened her eyes, his face was close, her mouth still warm, her heart still thudding. She jerked back and fumbled with the door handle. "That was uncalled for."

"True enough." Leisurely, Carlo stepped out into the rain. "But it was illuminating. I've already paid the driver, Juliet," he continued when she started to dig into her purse. "The baggage is checked. We board from gate five." Taking her arm, and his big leather case, he led her into the terminal.

"You didn't have to take care of all that." She'd have pulled her arm away if she'd had the energy. Or so she told herself. "The reason I'm here is to—"

"Promote my book," he finished easily. "If it makes you feel better, I've been known to do the same when I traveled with your predecessor."

The very fact that it did, made her feel foolish as well. "I appreciate it, Carlo. It's not that I mind you lending a hand, it's that I'm not used to it. You'd be surprised how many authors are either helpless or careless on the road."

"You'd be surprised how many chefs are temperamental and rude."

She thought of the basil and grinned. "No!"

"Oh yes." And though he'd read her thoughts perfectly, his tone remained grave. "Always flying off the handle, swearing, throwing things. It leads to a bad reputation for all of us. Here, they're boarding. If only they have a decent Bordeaux."

Juliet stifled a yawn as she followed him through. "I'll need my boarding pass, Carlo."

"I have it." He flashed them both for the flight atten
dant and nudged Juliet ahead. "Do you want the window
or the aisle?"

"I need my pass to see which I've got."

"We have 2A and B. Take your pick."

Someone pushed past her and bumped her solidly. I
brought a sinking sensation of déjà vu. "Carlo, I'm i
coach, so—"

"No, your tickets are changed. Take the window."

Before she could object, he'd maneuvered her over and
slipped in beside her. "What do you mean my ticket's bee
changed? Carlo, I have to get in the back before I cause a
scene."

"Your seat's here." After handing Juliet her boarding
pass he stretched out his legs. "*Dio*, what a relief."

Frowning, Juliet studied her stub—2A. "I don't know
how they could've made a mistake like this. I'd better see to
it right away."

"There's no mistake. You should fasten your belt," he
advised, then did so himself. "I changed your tickets for the
remaining flights on the tour."

Juliet reached to undo the clasp he'd just secured. "You—
but you can't."

"I told you, don't say can't to Franconi." Satisfied with
her belt, he dealt with his own. "You work as hard as I do—
why should you travel in tourist?"

"Because I'm paid to work. Carlo, let me out so I can fix
this before we take off."

"No." For the first time, his voice was blunt and final. "
prefer your company to that of a stranger or an empty seat."
When he turned his head, his eyes were like his voice. "
want you here. Leave it."

Juliet opened her mouth and closed it again. Profession
ally, she was on shaky ground either direction she went. She
was supposed to see to his needs and wants within reason
Personally, she'd counted on the distance, at least during

flight time, to keep her balanced. With Carlo, even a little distance could help.

He was being kind, she knew. Considerate. But he was also being stubborn. There was always a diplomatic way to handle such things.

She gave him a patient smile. "Carlo—"

He stopped her by simply closing his mouth over hers, quietly, completely and irresistibly. He held her there a moment, one hand on her cheek, the other over the fingers which had frozen in her lap. Juliet felt the floor tilt and her head go light.

We're taking off, she thought dimly, but knew the plane hadn't left the ground.

His tongue touched hers briefly, teasingly; then it was only his lips again. After brushing a hand through her hair, he leaned back. "Now, go back to sleep awhile," he advised. "This isn't the place I'd choose to seduce you."

Sometimes, Juliet decided, silence was the best diplomacy. Without another word, she closed her eyes and slept.

# Chapter Five

Colorado. The Rockies, Pike's Peak, Indian ruins, aspens and fast-running streams. It sounded beautiful, exciting. But a hotel room was a hotel room after all.

They'd been busy in Washington State. For most of their three-day stay, Juliet had had to work and think on her feet. But the media had been outstanding. Their schedule had been so full her boss back in New York had probably done handstands. Her report on their run on the coast would be a publicist's dream. Then there was Denver.

What coverage she'd managed to hustle there would barely justify the plane fare. One talk show at the ungodly hour of 7:00 A.M. and one miserly article in the food section of a local paper. No network or local news coverage of the autographing, no print reporter who'd confirm an appearance. Lousy.

It was 6:00 A.M. when Juliet dragged herself out of the shower and began to search through her unpacked garment bag for a suit and a fresh blouse. The cleaners was definitely a priority the minute they moved on to Dallas.

At least Carlo wasn't cooking this morning. She didn't think she could bear to look at food in any form for at least two hours.

With any luck she could come back to the hotel after the show, catch another hour's sleep and then have breakfast in her room while she made her morning calls. The autographing wasn't until noon, and their flight out wasn't until early the next morning.

That was something to hold on to, Juliet told herself as she looked for the right shade of stockings. For the first time in a week, they had an evening free with no one to entertain, no one to be entertained by. A nice, quiet meal somewhere close by and a full night's sleep. With that at the end of the tunnel, she could get through the morning.

With a grimace, she gulped down her daily dose of brewer's yeast.

It wasn't until she was fully dressed that she woke up enough to remember she hadn't dealt with her makeup. With a shrug Juliet slipped out of her little green jacket and headed for the bathroom. She stared at the front door with a combination of suspicion and bad temper when she heard the knock. Peeking through the peephole, she focused on Carlo. He grinned at her, then crossed his eyes. She only swore a little as she pulled open the door.

"You're early," she began, then caught the stirring aroma of coffee. Looking down, she saw that he carried a tray with a small pot, cups and spoons. "Coffee," she murmured, almost like a prayer.

"Yes." He nodded as he stepped into the room. "I thought you'd be ready, though room service isn't." He walked over to a table, saw that her room could fit into one section of his suite and set down the tray. "So, we deliver."

"Bless you." It was so sincere he grinned again as she crossed the room. "How did you manage it? Room service doesn't open for half an hour."

"There's a small kitchen in my suite. A bit primitive, but adequate to brew coffee."

She took the first sip, black and hot, and she closed her eyes. "It's wonderful. Really wonderful."

"Of course. I fixed it."

She opened her eyes again. No, she decided, she wouldn't spoil gratitude with sarcasm. After all, they'd very nearly gotten along for three days running. With the help of her shower, the yeast and the coffee, she was feeling almost human again.

"Relax," she suggested. "I'll finish getting ready." Expecting him to sit, Juliet took her cup and went into the bathroom to deal with her face and hair. She was dotting on foundation when Carlo leaned on the doorjamb.

"*Mi amore*, doesn't this arrangement strike you as impractical?"

She tried not to feel self-conscious as she smoothed on the thin, translucent base. "Which arrangement is that?"

"You have this—broom closet," he decided as he gestured toward her room. Yes, it was small enough that the subtle, feminine scent from her shower reached all the corners. "While I have a big suite with two baths, a bed big enough for three friends and one of those sofas that unfold."

"You're the star," she murmured as she brushed color over the slant of her cheeks.

"It would save the publisher money if we shared the suite."

She shifted her eyes in the mirror until they met his. She'd have sworn, absolutely sworn, he meant no more than that. That is, if she hadn't known him. "He can afford it," she said lightly. "It just thrills the accounting department at tax time."

Carlo moved his shoulders then sipped from his cup again. He'd known what her answer would be. Of course, he'd enjoy sharing his rooms with her for the obvious reason, but neither did it sit well with him that her accommodations were so far inferior to his.

"You need a touch more blusher on your left cheek," he said idly, not noticing her surprised look. What he'd noticed was the green silk robe that reflected in the mirror from the back of the door. Just how would she look in that? Carlo wondered. How would she look out of it?

After a narrowed-eyed study, Juliet discovered he'd been right. She picked up her brush again and evened the color. "You're a very observant man."

"Hmm?" He was looking at her again, but mentally, he'd changed her neat, high-collared blouse and slim skirt for the provocative little robe.

"Most men wouldn't notice unbalanced blusher." She picked up a grease pencil to shadow her eyes.

"I notice everything when it comes to a woman." There was still a light fog near the top of the mirror from the steam of her shower. Seeing it gave Carlo other, rather pleasant mental images. "What you're doing now gives you a much different look."

Relaxed again, she laughed. "That's the idea."

"But no." He stepped in closer so he could watch over her shoulder. The small, casual intimacy was as natural for him as it was uncomfortable for her. "Without the pots of paint, your face is younger, more vulnerable, but no less attractive than it is with them. Different..." Easily, he picked up her brush and ran it through her hair. "It's not more, not less, simply different. I like both of your looks."

It wasn't easy to keep her hand steady. Juliet set down the eye-shadow and tried the coffee instead. Better to be cynical than be moved, she reminded herself and gave him a cool smile. "You seem right at home in the bathroom with a woman fixing her face."

He liked the way her hair flowed as he brushed it. "I've done it so often."

Her smile became cooler. "I'm sure."

He caught the tone, but continued to brush as he met her eyes in the glass. "Take it as you like, *cara*, but remember, I grew up in a house with five women. Your powders and bottles hold no secrets to me."

She'd forgotten that, perhaps because she'd chosen to forget anything about him that didn't connect directly with the book. Yet now it made her wonder. Just what sort of insight did a man get into women when he'd been surrounded by them since childhood? Frowning a bit, she picked up her mascara.

"Were you a close family?"

"We are a close family," he corrected. "My mother's a widow who runs a successful dress shop in Rome." It was typical of him not to mention that he'd bought it for her.

"My four sisters all live within thirty kilometers. Perhaps no longer share the bathroom with them, but little else changes."

She thought about it. It sounded cozy and easy and rather sweet. Juliet didn't believe she could relate at all. "You mother must be proud of you."

"She'd be prouder if I added to her growing horde o grandchildren."

She smiled at that. It sounded more familiar. "I know what you mean."

"You should leave your hair just like this," he told her a he set down the brush. "You have a family?"

"My parents live in Pennsylvania."

He struggled with geography a moment. "Ah, then you' visit them when we go to Philadelphia."

"No." The word was flat as she recapped the tube o mascara. "There won't be time for that."

"I see." And he thought he was beginning to. "You hav brothers, sisters?"

"A sister." Because he was right about her hair, Juliet le it be and slipped out for her jacket. "She married a docto and produced two children, one of each gender, before sh was twenty-five."

Oh yes, he was beginning to see well enough. Though th words had been easy, the muscles in her shoulders had bee tight. "She makes an excellent doctor's wife?"

"Carrie makes a perfect doctor's wife."

"Not all of us are meant for the same things."

"I wasn't." She picked up her briefcase and her purse "We'd better get going. They said it would take about fif teen minutes to drive to the studio."

Strange, he thought, how people always believed thei tender spots could go undetected. For now, he'd leave he with the illusion that hers had.

Because the directions were good and the traffic was light Juliet drove the late model Chevy she'd rented with confi dence. Carlo obliged by navigating because he enjoyed the poised, skilled way she handled the wheel.

"You haven't lectured me on today's schedule," he pointed out. "Turn right here at this light."

Juliet glanced in the mirror, switched lanes then made the turn. She wasn't yet sure what his reaction would be to the fact that there barely was one. "I've decided to give you a break," she said brightly, knowing how some authors snarled and ranted when they had a dip in exposure. "You have this morning spot, then the autographing at World of Books downtown."

He waited, expecting the list to go on. When he turned to her, his brow was lifted. "And?"

"That's all." She heard the apology in her voice as she stopped at a red light. "It happens sometimes, Carlo. Things just don't come through. I knew it was going to be light here, but as it happens they've just started shooting a major film using Denver locations. Every reporter, every news team, every camera crew is covering it this afternoon. The bottom line is we got bumped."

"Bumped? Do you mean there is no radio show, no lunch with a reporter, no dinner engagement?"

"No, I'm sorry. It's just—"

*"Fantastico!"* Grabbing her face with both hands he kissed her hard. "I'll find out the name of this movie and go to its premiere."

The little knot of tension and guilt vanished. "Don't take it so hard, Carlo."

He felt as though he'd just been paroled. "Juliet, did you think I'd be upset? *Dio*, for a week it's been nothing but go here, rush there."

She spotted the TV tower and turned left. "You've been wonderful," she told him. The best time to admit it, she decided, was when they only had two minutes to spare. "Not everyone I've toured with has been as considerate."

She surprised him. He preferred it when a woman could do so. He twined a lock of the hair he'd brushed around his finger. "So, you've forgiven me for the basil?"

She smiled and had to stop herself from reaching up to touch the heart on her lapel. "I'd forgotten all about it."

He kissed her cheek in a move so casual and friendly she didn't object. "I believe you have. You've a kind heart, Juliet. Such things are beauty in themselves."

He could soften her so effortlessly. She felt it, fought it and, for the moment, surrendered to it. In an impulsive, uncharacteristic move, she brushed the hair on his forehead. "Let's go in. You've got to wake up Denver."

Professionally, Juliet should've been cranky at the lack of obligations and exposure in Denver. It was going to leave a few very obvious blanks on her overall report. Personally, she was thrilled.

According to schedule, she was back in her room by eight. By 8:03, she'd stripped out of her suit and had crawled, naked and happy, into her still rumpled bed. For exactly an hour she slept deeply, and without any dreams she could remember. By ten-thirty, she'd gone through her list of phone calls and an enormous breakfast. After freshening her makeup, she dressed in her suit then went downstairs to meet Carlo in the lobby.

It shouldn't have surprised her that he was huddled in one of the cozy lounging areas with three women. It shouldn't have irked her. Pretending it did neither, Juliet strolled over. It was then she noticed that all three women were built stupendously. That shouldn't have surprised her either.

"Ah, Juliet." He smiled, all grace, all charm. She didn't stop to wonder why she'd like to deck him. "Always prompt. Ladies." He turned to bow to all three of them. "It's been a pleasure."

"Bye-bye, Carlo." One of them sent him a look that could have melted lead. "Remember, if you're ever in Tucson..."

"How could I forget?" Hooking his arm with Juliet's, he strolled outside. "Juliet," he murmured, "where is Tucson?"

"Don't you ever quit?" she demanded.

"Quit what?"

"Collecting women."

He lifted a brow as he pulled open the door on the driver's side. "Juliet, one collects matchbooks, not women."

"It would seem there are some who consider them on the same level."

He blocked her way before she could slip inside. "Any who do are too stupid to matter." He walked around the side of the car and opened his own door before she spoke again.

"Who were they anyhow?"

Soberly, Carlo adjusted the brim of the buff-colored fedora he wore. "Female body-builders. It seems they're having a convention."

A muffled laugh escaped before she could prevent it. "Figures."

"Indeed yes, but such muscular ones." His expression was still grave as he lowered himself into the car. Juliet remained quiet a moment, then gave up and laughed out loud. Damn, she'd never had as much fun on tour with anyone. She might as well accept it. "Tucson's in Arizona," she told him with another laugh. "And it's not on the itinerary."

They would have been on time for the autographing if they hadn't run into the detour. Traffic was clogged, rerouted and bad tempered as roads were blocked off for the film being shot. Juliet spent twenty minutes weaving, negotiating and cursing until she found she'd done no more than make a nice big circle.

"We've been here before," Carlo said idly and received a glowering look.

"Oh, really?" Her sweet tone had an undertone of arsenic.

He merely shifted his legs into a less cramped position. "It's an interesting city," he commented. "I think perhaps if you turn right at the next corner, then left two corners beyond, we'll find ourselves on the right track.''

Juliet meticulously smoothed her carefully written directions when she'd have preferred to crumple them into a ball. "The book clerk specifically said—"

"I'm sure she's a lovely woman, but things seem a bit confused today." It didn't particularly bother him. The blast of a horn made her jolt. Amused, Carlo merely looked over. "As someone from New York City, you should be used to such things."

Juliet set her teeth. "I never drive in the city."

"I do. Trust me, *innamorata*."

Not on your life, Juliet thought, but turned right. It took nearly ten minutes in the crawling traffic to manage the next two blocks, but when she turned left she found herself, as Carlo had said, on the right track. She waited, resigned, for him to gloat.

"Rome moves faster" was all he said.

How could she anticipate him? she wondered. He didn't rage when you expected, didn't gloat when it was natural. With a sigh, she gave up. "Anything moves faster." She found herself in the right block, but parking space was at a premium. Weighing the ins and outs, Juliet swung over beside a car at the curb. "Look, Carlo, I'm going to have to drop you off. We're already running behind. I'll find a place to park and be back as soon as I can."

"You're the boss," he said, still cheerful after forty-five minutes of teeth-grinding traffic.

"If I'm not there in an hour, send up a flare."

"My money's on you."

Still cautious, she waited until she saw him swing into the bookstore before she fought her way into traffic again.

Twenty frustrating minutes later, Juliet walked into the dignified little bookstore herself. It was, she noted with a sinking stomach, too quiet and too empty. A clerk with a thin-striped tie and shined shoes greeted her.

"Good morning. May I help you?"

"I'm Juliet Trent, Mr. Franconi's publicist."

"Ah yes, right this way." He glided across the carpet to a set of wide steps. "Mr. Franconi's on the second level. It's unfortunate that the traffic and confusion have discouraged people from coming out. Of course, we rarely do these things." He gave her a smile and brushed a piece of lint from the sleeve of his dark blue jacket. "The last time was . . . let me see, in the fall. J. Jonathan Cooper was on tour. I'm sure you've heard of him. He wrote *Metaphysical Force and You*."

Juliet bit back a sigh. When you hit dry ground, you just had to wait for the tide.

She spotted Carlo in a lovely little alcove on a curvy love seat. Beside him was a woman of about forty with a neat suit and pretty legs. Such things didn't warrant even a raised brow. But to Juliet's surprise, Carlo wasn't busy charming her. Instead, he was listening intently to a young boy who sat across from him.

"I've worked in the kitchens there for the last three summers. I'm not allowed to actually prepare anything, but I can watch. At home, I cook whenever I can, but with school and the job, it's mostly on weekends."

"Why?"

The boy stopped in midstream and looked blank. "Why?"

"Why do you cook?" Carlo asked. He acknowledged Juliet with a nod, then gave his attention back to the boy.

"Because. . ." The boy looked at his mother, then back at Carlo. "Well, it's important. I like to take things and put them together. You have to concentrate, you know, and be careful. But you can make something really terrific. It looks good and it smells good. It's . . . I don't know." His voice lowered in embarrassment. "Satisfying, I guess."

"Yes." Pleased, Carlo smiled at him. "That's a good answer."

"I have both your other books," the boy blurted out. "I've tried all your recipes. I even made your *pasta al tre formaggi* for this dinner party at my aunt's."

"And?"

"They liked it." The boy grinned. "I mean they really liked it."

"You want to study."

"Oh yeah." But the boy dropped his gaze to where his hands rubbed nervously over his knees. "Thing is we can't really afford college right now, so I'm hoping to get some restaurant work."

"In Denver?"

"Any place where I could start cooking instead of wiping up."

"We've taken up enough of Mr. Franconi's time." The boy's mother rose, noting there was now a handful of people milling around on the second level with Carlo's books in hand. "I want to thank you." She offered her hand to Carlo as he rose with her. "It meant a great deal to Steven to talk with you."

"My pleasure." Though he was gracious as always, he turned back to the boy. "Perhaps you'd give me your address. I know of some restaurant owners here in the States. Perhaps one of them needs an apprentice chef."

Stunned, Steven could do nothing but stare. "You're very kind." His mother took out a small pad and wrote on it. Her hand was steady, but when she handed the paper to Carlo and looked at him, he saw the emotion. He thought of his own mother. He took the paper, then her hand.

"You have a fortunate son, Mrs. Hardesty."

Thoughtful, Juliet watched them walk away, noting that Steven looked over his shoulder with the same, blank, baffled expression.

So he has a heart, Juliet decided, touched. A heart that wasn't altogether reserved for *amore*. But she saw Carlo slip the paper into his pocket and wondered if that would be the end of it.

The autographing wasn't a smashing success. Six books by Juliet's count. That had been bad enough, but then there'd been The Incident.

Looking at the all but empty store, Juliet had considered hitting the streets with a sign on her back, then the homey little woman had come along bearing all three of Carlo's books. Good for the ego, Juliet thought. That was before the woman had said something that caused Carlo's eyes to chill and his voice to freeze. All Juliet heard was the name LaBare.

"I beg your pardon, Madame?" Carlo said in a tone Juliet had never heard from him. It could've sliced through steel.

"I said I keep all your books on a shelf in my kitchen, right next to André LaBare's. I love to cook."

"LaBare?" Carlo put his hand over his stack of books as a protective parent might over a threatened child. "You would dare put my work next to that—that peasant's?"

Thinking fast, Juliet stepped up and broke into the conversation. If ever she'd seen a man ready to murder, it was Carlo. "Oh, I see you have all of Mr. Franconi's books. You must love to cook."

"Well, yes I—"

"Wait until you try some of his new recipes. I had the *pasta con pesto* myself. It's wonderful." Juliet started to take the woman's books from under Carlo's hand and met with resistance and a stubborn look. She gave him one of her own and jerked the books away. "Your family's going to be just thrilled when you serve it," Juliet went on, keeping her voice pleasant as she led the woman out of the line of fire. "And the fettuccine..."

"LaBare is a swine." Carlo's voice was very clear and reached the stairs. The woman glanced back nervously.

"Men." Juliet made her voice a conspiratorial whisper. "Such egos."

"Yes." Gathering up her books, the woman hurried down the stairs and out of the store. Juliet waited until she was out of earshot before she pounced on Carlo.

"How could you?"

"How could I?" He rose, and though he skimmed just under six feet, he looked enormous. "She would *dare* speak that name to me? She would *dare* associate the work of an artist with the work of a jackass? LaBare—"

"At the moment, I don't give a damn who or what this LaBare is." Juliet put a hand on his shoulder and shoved him back onto the love seat. "What I do care about is you scaring off the few customers we have. Now behave yourself."

He sat where he was only because he admired the way she'd ordered him to. Fascinating woman, Carlo decided, finding it wiser to think of her than LaBare. It was wiser to think of flood and famine than of LaBare.

The afternoon had dragged on and on, except for the young boy, Carlo thought and touched the paper in his pocket. He'd call Summer in Philadelphia about young Steven Hardesty.

But other than Steven and the woman who upped his blood pressure by speaking of LaBare, Carlo had found himself perilously close to boredom. Something he considered worse than illness.

He needed some activity, a challenge—even a small one. He glanced over at Juliet as she spoke with a clerk. That was no small challenge. The one thing he'd yet to be in Juliet's company was bored. She kept him interested. Sexually? Yes, that went without saying. Intellectually. That was a plus, a big one.

He understood women. It wasn't a matter of pride, but to Carlo's thinking, a matter of circumstance. He enjoyed women. As lovers, of course, but he also enjoyed them as companions, as friends, as associates. It was a rare thing when a man could find a woman to be all of those things. That's what he wanted from Juliet. He hadn't resolved i

et, only felt it. Convincing her to be his friend would be as
challenging, and as rewarding, as it would be to convince her
to be his lover.

No, he realized as he studied her profile. With this
woman, a lover would come easier than a friend. He had
two weeks left to accomplish both. With a smile, he decided to start the campaign in earnest.

Half an hour later, they were walking the three blocks to
the parking garage Juliet had found.

"This time I drive," he told Juliet as they stepped inside
the echoing gray building. When she started to object, he
held out his hand for the keys. "Come, my love, I've just
survived two hours of boredom. Why should you have all
the fun?"

"Since you put it that way." She dropped the keys in his
hand, relieved that whatever had set him off before was
forgotten.

"So now we have a free evening."

"That's right." With a sigh she leaned back in her seat
and waited for him to start the engine.

"We'll have dinner at seven. Tonight, I make the arrangements."

A hamburger in her room, an old movie and bed. Juliet
let the wish come and go. Her job was to pamper and entertain as much as possible. "Whatever you like."

Carlo pulled out of the parking space with a squeal of
tires that had Juliet bolting up. "I'll hold you to that, *cara*."

He zoomed out of the garage and turned right with hardly
a pause. "Carlo—"

"We should have champagne to celebrate the end of our
first week. You like champagne?"

"Yes, I—Carlo, the light's changing."

He breezed through the amber light, skimmed by the
bumper of a battered compact and kept going. "Italian
food. You have no objection?"

"No." She gripped the door handle until her knuckles
turned white. "That truck!"

"Yes, I see it." He swerved around it, zipped throug
another light and cut a sharp right. "You have plans for th
afternoon?"

Juliet pressed a hand to her throat, thinking she might b
able to push out her voice. "I was thinking of making u;
of the hotel spa. If I live."

"Good. Me, I think I'll go shopping."

Juliet's teeth snapped together as he changed lanes i
bumper-to-bumper traffic. "How do I notify next of kin?

With a laugh, Carlo swung in front of their hotel. "Don
worry, Juliet. Have your whirlpool and your sauna. Knoc
on my door at seven."

She looked back toward the street. Pamper and ente
tain, she remembered. Did that include risking your life
Her supervisor would think so. "Maybe I should go wi1
you."

"No, I insist." He leaned over, cupping her neck befo:
she'd recovered enough to evade. "Enjoy," he murmure
lightly against her lips. "And think of me as your skin grov
warm and your muscles grow lax."

In self-defense, Juliet hurried out of the car. Before sl
could tell him to drive carefully, he was barreling back o
into the street. She offered a prayer for Italian maniacs the
went inside.

By seven, she felt reborn. She'd sweated out fatigue in tl
sauna, shocked herself awake in the pool and splurged on
massage. Life, she thought as she splashed on her scent, ha
its good points after all. Tomorrow's flight to Dallas wou
be soon enough to draft her Denver report. Such as it wa
Tonight, all she had to worry about was eating. Aft
pressing a hand to her stomach, Juliet admitted she w
more than ready for that.

With a quick check, she approved the simple ivory dre
with the high collar and tiny pearly buttons. Unless Car
had picked a hot dog stand it would suit. Grabbing her ev
ning bag, she slipped across the hall to knock on Carlo
door. She only hoped he'd chosen some place close by. Tl

ast thing she wanted to do was fight Denver's downtown
raffic again.

The first thing she noticed when Carlo opened his door
vere the rolled up sleeves of his shirt. It was cotton, over-
ized and chic, but her eyes were drawn to the surprising
cord of muscles in his forearms. The man did more than lift
poons and spatulas. The next thing she noticed was the
erotic scents of spices and sauce.

"Lovely." Carlo took both hands and drew her inside.
She pleased him, the smooth, creamy skin, the light, subtle
cent, but more, the confused hesitation in her eyes as she
glanced over to where the aroma of food was strongest.

"An interesting cologne," she managed after a moment.
'But don't you think you've gotten a bit carried away?"

"*Innamorata*, you don't wear Franconi's spaghetti sauce,
ou absorb it." He kissed the back of her hand. "Antici-
bate it." Then the other. "Savor it." This time her palm.

A smart woman wasn't aroused by a man who used such
lamboyant tactics. Juliet told herself that as the chills raced
p her arms and down again. "Spaghetti sauce?" Slipping
er hands from his, she linked them behind her back.

"I found a wonderful shop. The spices pleased me very
much. The burgundy was excellent. Italian, of course."

"Of course." Cautious, she stepped farther into the suite.
'You spent the day cooking?"

"Yes. Though you should remind me to speak to the ho-
el owner about the quality of this stove. All in all, it went
quite well."

She told herself it wasn't wise to encourage him when she
ad no intention of eating alone with him in his suite. Per-
aps if she'd been made out of rock she could have resisted
vandering toward the little kitchenette. Her mouth wa-
ered. "Oh God."

Delighted, Carlo slipped an arm around her waist and led
er to the stove. The little kitchen itself was in shambles.
She'd never seen so many pots and bowls and spoons

jammed into a sink before. Counters were splattered an
streaked. But the smells. It was heaven, pure and simple.

"The senses, Juliet. There's not one of us who isn't rule
by them. First, you smell, and you begin to imagine." H
fingers moved lightly over her waist. "Imagine. You ca
almost taste it on your tongue from that alone."

"Hmm." Knowing she was making a mistake, sh
watched him take the lid off the pot on the stove. The tan
made her close her eyes and just breathe. "Oh, Carlo."

"Then we look, and the imagination goes one step fur
ther." His fingers squeezed lightly at her waist until sh
opened her eyes and looked into the pot. Thick, red, sim
mering, the sauce was chunky with meat, peppers and spice
Her stomach growled.

"Beautiful, yes?"

"Yes." She wasn't aware that her tongue slid out over he
lips in anticipation. He was.

"And we hear." Beside the sauce a pot of water began t
boil. In an expert move, he measured pasta by sight and sli
it in. "Some things are destined to be mated." With a slo
ted spoon, he stirred gently. "Without each other, they ar
incomplete. But when merged..." he adjusted the flame, "
treasure. Pasta and the sauce. A man and a woman. Com
you'll have some burgundy. The champagne's for later."

It was time to take a stand, even though she took it by th
stove. "Carlo, I had no idea this was what you intended.
think—"

"I like surprises." He handed her a glass half filled wit
dark, red wine. "And I wanted to cook for you."

She wished he hadn't put it quite that way. She wished h
voice wasn't so warm, so deep, like his eyes. Like the fee
ings he could urge out of her. "I appreciate that Carlo, it
just that—"

"You had your sauna?"

"Yes, I did. Now—"

"It relaxed you. It shows."

She sighed, sipping at the wine without thinking. "Yes.

"This relaxes me. We eat together tonight." He tapped his glass to hers. "Men and women have done so for centuries. It has become civilized."

Her chin tilted. "You're making fun of me."

"Yes." Ducking into the refrigerator, he pulled out a small tray. "First you'll try my antipasto. Your palate should be prepared."

Juliet chose a little chunk of zucchini. "I'd think you'd prefer being served in a restaurant."

"Now and then. There are times I prefer privacy." He set down the tray. As he did, she took a small step back. Interested, he lifted a brow. "Juliet, do I make you nervous?"

She swallowed zucchini. "Don't be absurd."

"Am I?" On impulse, he set his wine down as well and took another step toward her. Juliet found her back pressed into the refrigerator.

"Carlo—"

"No, shh. We experiment." Gently, watching her, he brushed his lips over one cheek, then the other. He heard her breath catch then shudder out. Nerves—these he accepted. When a man and woman were attracted and close, there had to be nerves. Without them, passion was bland, like a sauce without spice.

But fear? Wasn't that what he saw in her eyes? Just a trace of it, only briefly. Nerves he'd use, play on, exploit. Fear was something different. It disturbed him, blocked him and, at the same time, moved him.

"I won't hurt you, Juliet."

Her eyes were direct again, level, though her hand was balled into a fist. "Won't you?"

He took her hand, slowly working it open. "No." In that moment, he promised both of them. "I won't. Now we'll eat."

Juliet held off the shudder until he'd turned around to stir and drain his pasta. Perhaps he wouldn't hurt her, she thought and recklessly tossed back her wine. But she might hurt herself.

He didn't fuss. He merely perfected. It occurred to Juliet, as she watched him put the last touches on the meal that he was no different here in the little hotel kitchen than he'd been before the camera. Juliet added her help in the only way she'd have dared. She set the table.

Yes, it was a mistake, she told herself as she arranged plates. But no one but a fool would walk away from anything that smelled like that sauce. She wasn't a fool. She could handle herself. The moment of weak fear she'd felt in the kitchen was past. She'd enjoy a take-your-shoes-off meal, drink two glasses of really excellent burgundy, then go across the hall and catch eight hours' sleep. The merry-go round would continue the next day.

She selected a marinated mushroom as Carlo brought in the platter of spaghetti. "Better," he said when she smiled at him. "You're ready to enjoy yourself."

With a shrug, Juliet sat. "If one of the top chefs in the world wants to cook me dinner, why should I complain?"

"*The* top," he corrected and gestured for her to serve herself. She did, barely conquering greed.

"Does it really relax you to stand in a kitchen?"

"It depends. Sometimes it relaxes, sometimes it excites. Always it pleases. No, don't cut." With a shake of his head he reached over. "Americans. You roll it onto the fork."

"It falls off when I do."

"Like this." With his hands on her wrists, he guided her. Her pulse was steady, he noted, but not slow. "Now." Still holding her hand, he lifted the fork toward her mouth. "Taste."

As she did, he had the satisfaction of watching her face. Spices exploded on her tongue. Heat seeped through, mellowing to warmth. She savored it, even as she thought of the next bite. "Oh, this is no little sin."

Nothing could have delighted him more. With a laugh, he sat back and started on his own plate. "Small sins are only small pleasures. When Franconi cooks for you, food is no a basic necessity."

She was already rolling the next forkful. "You win that one. Why aren't you fat?"

*"Prègo?"*

"If I could cook like this..." She tasted again and sighed. "I'd look like one of your meatballs."

With a chuckle, he watched her dig in. It pleased him to see someone he cared for enjoying what he'd created. After years of cooking, he'd never tired of it. "So, your mother didn't teach you to cook?"

"She tried." Juliet accepted a piece of the crusty bread he offered but set it aside as she rolled more spaghetti. First things first. "I never seemed to be very good at the things she wanted me to be good at. My sister plays the piano beautifully; I can barely remember the scales."

"So, what did you want to do instead of taking piano lessons?"

"Play third base." It came out so easily, it stunned her. Juliet had thought she'd buried that along with a dozen other childhood frustrations. "It just wasn't done," she said with a shrug. "My mother was determined to raise two well rounded ladies who would become two well rounded, successful wives. Win some, lose some."

"You think she's not proud of you?"

The question hit a target she hadn't known was exposed. Juliet reached for her wine. "It's not a matter of pride, but of disappointment, I suppose. I disappointed her; I confused my father. They still wonder what they did wrong."

"What they did wrong was not to accept what you are."

"Maybe," she murmured. "Or maybe I was determined to be something they couldn't accept. I've never worked it out."

"Are you unhappy with your life?"

Surprised, she glanced up. Unhappy? Sometimes frustrated, harassed and pressured. But unhappy? "No. No, I'm not."

"Then perhaps that's your answer."

Juliet took a moment to study him. He was more than gorgeous, more than sexy, more than all those qualities she'd once cynically attributed to him. "Carlo." For the first time she reached out to touch him, just his hand, but he thought it a giant step. "You're a very nice man."

"But of course I am." His fingers curled over hers because he couldn't resist. "I could give you references."

With a laugh, Juliet backed off. "I'm sure you could." With concentration, dedication and just plain greed, she cleared off her plate.

"Time for dessert."

"Carlo!" Moaning, Juliet pressed a hand to her stomach. "Please, don't be cruel."

"You'll like it." He was up and in the kitchen before she found the strength to refuse again. "It's an old, old, Italian tradition. Back to the empire. American cheesecake is sometimes excellent, but this . . ." He brought out a small, lovely cake with cherries dripping lavishly over it.

"Carlo, I'll die."

"Just a taste with the champagne." He popped the cork with an expert twist and poured two fresh glasses. "Go, sit on the sofa, be comfortable."

As she did, Juliet realized why the Romans traditionally slept after a meal. She could've curled up in a happy little ball and been unconscious in moments. But the champagne was lively, insistent.

"Here." He brought over one plate with a small slice. "We'll share."

"One bite," she told him, prepared to stand firm. Then she tasted. Creamy, smooth, not quite sweet, more nutty. Exquisite. With a sigh of surrender, Juliet took another. "Carlo, you're a magician."

"Artist," he corrected.

"Whatever you want." Using all the willpower she had left, Juliet exchanged the cake for champagne. "I really can't eat another bite."

"Yes, I remember. You don't believe in overindulgence." But he filled her glass again.

"Maybe not." She sipped, enjoying that rich, luxurious aura only champagne could give. "But now I've gotten a different perspective on indulgence." Slipping out of her shoes, she laughed over the rim of her glass. "I'm converted."

"You're lovely." The lights were low, the music soft, the scents lingering and rich. He thought of resisting. The fear that had been in her eyes demanded he think of it. But just now, she was relaxed, smiling. The desire he'd felt tug the moment he'd seen her had never completely gone away.

Senses were aroused, heightened, by a meal. That was something he understood perfectly. He also understood that a man and a woman should never ignore whatever pleasure they could give to each other.

So he didn't resist, but took her face in his hands. There he could watch her eyes, feel her skin, nearly taste her. This time he saw desire, not fear but wariness. Perhaps she was ready for lesson two.

She could have refused. The need to do so went through her mind. But his hands were so strong, so gentle on her skin. She'd never been touched like that before. She knew how he'd kiss her and the sense of anticipation mixed with nerves. She knew, and wanted.

Wasn't she a woman who knew her own mind? She took her hands to his wrists, but didn't push away. Her fingers curled around and held as she touched her mouth to his. For a moment they stayed just so, allowing themselves to savor that first taste, that first sensation. Then slowly, mutually, they asked for more.

She seemed so small when he held her that a man could forget how strong and competent she was. He found himself wanting to treasure. Desire might burn, but when she was so pliant, so vulnerable, he found himself compelled to show only gentleness.

Had any man ever shown her such care? Juliet's head began to swim as his hands moved into her hair. Was there another man so patient? His heart was pounding against hers. She could feel it, like something wild and desperate. But his mouth was so soft, his hands so gentle. As though they'd been lovers for years, she thought dimly. And had all the time left in the world to continue to love.

No hurry, no rush, no frenzy. Just pleasure. Her heart opened reluctantly, but it opened. He began to pour through. When the phone shrilled, he swore and she sighed. They'd both been prepared to take all the chances.

"Only a moment," he murmured.

Still dreaming, she touched his cheek. "All right."

As he went to answer, she leaned back, determined not to think.

"*Cara!*" The enthusiasm in his voice, and the endearment had her opening her eyes again. With a warm laugh, Carlo went into a stream of Italian. Juliet had no choice but to think.

Affection. Yes, it was in his voice. She didn't have to understand the words. She looked around to see him smiling as he spoke to the woman on the other end. Resigned, Juliet picked up her champagne. It wasn't easy for her to admit she'd been a fool. Or for her to admit she'd been hurt.

She knew who he was. What he was. She knew how many women he'd seduced. Perhaps she was a woman who knew her own mind, and perhaps she wanted him. But she would never be eased into a long line of *others*. Setting down the champagne, she rose.

"*Si, si.* I love you."

Juliet turned away at the phrase I love you. How well it slid off his tongue, in any language. How little it meant, in any language.

"Interruptions. I'm sorry."

Juliet turned back and gave him her uncompromising look. "Don't be. The dinner was marvelous, Carlo, thank you. You should be ready to check out by eight."

"A moment," he murmured. Crossing over, he took her by the arms. "What's this? You're angry."

"Of course not." She tried to back away and failed. It was easy to forget just how strong he was. "Why should I be?"

"Reasons aren't always necessary for a woman."

Though he'd said it in a simple tone that offered no insult, her eyes narrowed. "The expert. Well, let me tell you something about *this* woman, Franconi. She doesn't think much of a man who makes love to her one minute then pushes another lover in her face the next."

He held up his hand as he struggled to follow her drift. "I'm not following you. Maybe my English is failing."

"Your English is perfect," she spit at him. "From what I just heard, so's your Italian."

"My..." His grin broke out. "The phone."

"Yes. The phone. Now, if you'll excuse me."

He let her get as far as the door. "Juliet, I admit I'm hopelessly enamored of the woman I was speaking to. She's beautiful, intelligent, interesting and I've never met anyone quite like her."

Furious, Juliet whirled around. "How marvelous."

"I think so. It was my mother."

She walked back to snatch up the purse she'd nearly forgotten. "I'd think a man of your experience and imagination could do better."

"So I could." He held her again, not so gently, not so patiently. "If it was necessary. I don't make a habit to explain myself, and when I do, I don't lie."

She took a deep breath because she was abruptly certain she was hearing the truth. Either way, she'd been a fool. "I'm sorry. It's none of my business in any case."

"No, it's not." He took her chin in his hand and held it. "I saw fear in your eyes before. It concerned me. Now I think it wasn't me you were afraid of, but yourself."

"That's none of your business."

"No, it's not," he said again. "You appeal to me, Juliet, in many ways, and I intend to take you to bed. But we'll wait until you aren't afraid."

She wanted to rage at him. She wanted to weep. He saw both things clearly. "We have an early flight in the morning, Carlo."

He let her go, but stood where he was for a long time after he'd heard her door shut across the hall.

# Chapter Six

Dallas was different. Dallas was Dallas without apology. Texas rich, Texas big and Texas arrogant. If it was the city that epitomized the state, then it did so with flair. Futuristic architecture and mind-twisting freeways abounded in a strange kind of harmony with the more sedate buildings downtown. The air was hot and carried the scents of oil, expensive perfumes and prairie dust. Dallas was Dallas, but it had never forgotten its roots.

Dallas held the excitement of a boomtown that was determined not to stop booming. It was full of downhome American energy that wasn't about to lag. As far as Juliet was concerned they could have been in downtown Timbuktu.

He acted as though nothing had happened—no intimate dinner, no arousal, no surrender, no cross words. Juliet wondered if he did it to drive her crazy.

Carlo was amiable, cooperative and charming. She knew better now. Under the amiability was a shaft of steel that wouldn't bend an inch. She'd seen it. One could say she'd felt it. It would have been a lie to say she didn't admire it.

Cooperative, sure. In his favor, Juliet had to admit that he'd never been on tour with anyone as willing to work without complaint. And touring was hard work, no matter how glamorous it looked on paper. Once you were into your second full week, it became difficult to smile unless you were cued. Carlo never broke his rhythm.

But he expected perfection—spelled his way—and wouldn't budge an inch until he got it.

Charming. No one could enchant a group of people wit
more style than Franconi. That alone made her job easie
No one would deny his charm unless they'd seen how col
his eyes could become. She had.

He had flaws like any other man, Juliet thought. R
membering that might help her keep an emotional di
tance. It always helped her to list the pros and cons of
situation, even if the situation was a man. The trouble wa
though flawed, he was damn near irresistible.

And he knew it. That was something else she had to r
mind herself of.

His ego was no small matter. That was something she'
be wise to balance against his unrestricted generosity. Va
ity about himself and his work went over the border int
arrogance. It didn't hurt her sense of perspective to weig
that against his innate consideration for others.

But then, there was the way he smiled, the way he said h
name. Even the practical, professional Juliet Trent had
difficult time finding a flaw to balance those little details.

The two days in Dallas were busy enough to keep h
driving along on six hours' sleep, plenty of vitamins an
oceans of coffee. They were making up for Denver all righ
She had the leg cramps to prove it.

Four minutes on the national news, an interview with or
of the top magazines in the country, three write-ups in th
Dallas press and two autograph sessions that sold clean ou
There was more, but those headed up her report. When sh
went back to New York, she'd go back in triumph.

She didn't want to think of the dinners with departmer
store executives that started at 10:00 P.M. and lasted until sh
was falling asleep in her bananas flambé. She couldn't bea
to count the lunches of poached salmon or shrimp sala
She'd had to refill her pocket aspirin bottles and stock up o
antacids. But it was worth it. She should have been thrille

She was miserable.

She was driving him mad. Polite, Carlo thought as the
prepared to sit through another luncheon interview. Yes, sl

vas polite. Her mother had taught her perfect manners even if she hadn't taught her to cook.

Competent? As far as he was concerned, he'd never known anyone, male or female, who was as scrupulously competent as Juliet Trent. He'd always admired that particular quality in a companion, insisted on it in an associate. Of course, Juliet was both. Precise, prompt, cool in a crisis and unflaggingly energetic. Admirable qualities all.

For the first time in his life he gave serious thought to strangling a woman.

Indifferent. That's what he couldn't abide. She acted as though there was nothing more between them than the next interview, the next television spot, the next plane. She acted as though there'd been no flare of need, of passion, of understanding between them. One would think she didn't want him with the same intensity that he wanted her.

He knew better. Didn't he?

He could remember her ripe, unhesitating response to him. Mouth to mouth, body to body. There'd been no indifference in the way her arms had held him. No, there'd been strength, pliancy, need, demand, but no indifference. Yet now...

They'd spent nearly two days exclusively in each other's company, but he'd seen nothing in her eyes, heard nothing in her voice that indicated more than a polite business association. They ate together, drove together, worked together. They did everything but sleep together.

He'd had his fill of polite. But he hadn't had his fill of Juliet.

He thought of her. It didn't bruise Carlo's pride to admit he thought of her a great deal. He often thought of women, and why not? When a man didn't think of a woman, he was better off dead.

He wanted her. It didn't worry him to admit that he wanted her more every time he thought of her. He'd wanted many women. He'd never believed in self-denial. When a man didn't want a woman, he *was* dead.

But... Carlo found it odd that "buts" so often followe[d]
any thoughts he had on Juliet. But he found himself dwell[-]
ing on her more often than he'd have once considere[d]
healthy. Though he didn't mind wanting a woman until h[e]
ached, he found Juliet could make him ache more than he'[d]
have once considered comfortable.

He might have been able to rationalize the threat to hi[s]
health and comfort. But... she was so damn indifferent.

If he did nothing else in the short time they had left i[n]
Dallas, he was going to change that.

Lunch was white linen, heavy silver flatware and thi[n]
crystal. The room was done in tones of dusty rose and pas[-]
tel greens. The murmur of conversation was just as quiet.

Carlo thought it a pity they couldn't have met the re[-]
porter at one of the little Tex-Mex restaurants over Mexi[-]
can beer with chili and nachos. Briefly, he promised himsel[f]
he'd rectify that in Houston.

He barely noticed the reporter was young and running o[n]
nerves as they took their seats. He'd decided, no matte[r]
what it took, he'd break through Juliet's inflexible shield o[f]
politeness before they stood up again. Even if he had to pla[y]
dirty.

"I'm so happy you included Dallas on your tour, M[r]
Franconi," the reporter began, already reaching for he[r]
water glass to clear her throat. "Mr. Van Ness sends hi[s]
apologies. He was looking forward to meeting you."

Carlo smiled at her, but his mind was on Juliet. "Yes?"

"Mr. Van Ness is the food editor for the *Tribune*." Julie[t]
spread her napkin over her lap as she gave Carlo informa[-]
tion she'd related less than fifteen minutes before. She sen[t]
him the friendliest of smiles and hoped he felt the barbs i[n]
it. "Ms. Tribly is filling in for him."

"Of course." Carlo smoothed over the gap of attention[.]
"Charmingly, I'm sure."

As a woman she wasn't immune to that top-cream voice[.]
As a reporter, she was well aware of the importance of he[r]
assignment. "It's all pretty confused." Ms. Tribly wipe[d]

damp hands on her napkin. "Mr. Van Ness is having a baby. That is, what I mean is, his wife went into labor just a couple of hours ago."

"So, we should drink to them." Carlo signaled a waiter. "Margaritas?" He phrased the question as a statement, earned a cool nod from Juliet and a grateful smile from the reporter.

Determined to pull off her first really big assignment, Ms. Tribly balanced a pad discreetly on her lap. "Have you been enjoying your tour through America, Mr. Franconi?"

"I always enjoy America." Lightly he ran a finger over the back of Juliet's hand before she could move it out of reach. "Especially in the company of a beautiful woman." She started to slide her hand away then felt it pinned under his. For a man who could whip up the most delicate of soufflés, his hands were as strong as a boxer's.

Wills sparked, clashed and fumed. Carlo's voice remained mild, soft and romantic. "I must tell you, Ms. Tribly, Juliet is an extraordinary woman. I couldn't manage without her."

"Mr. Franconi's very kind." Though Juliet's voice was as mild and quiet as his, the nudge she gave him under the table wasn't. "I handle the details; Mr. Franconi's the artist."

"We make an admirable team, wouldn't you say, Ms. Tribly?"

"Yes." Not quite sure how to handle that particular line, she veered off to safer ground. "Mr. Franconi, besides writing cookbooks, you own and run a successful restaurant in Rome and occasionally travel to prepare a special dish. A few months ago, you flew to a yacht in the Aegean to cook minestrone for Dimitri Azares, the shipping magnate."

"His birthday," Carlo recalled. "His daughter arranged a surprise." Again, his gaze skimmed over the woman whose hand he held. "Juliet will tell you, I'm fond of surprises."

"Yes, well." Ms. Tribly reached for her water glass again. "Your schedule's so full and exciting. I wonder if you still enjoy the basics as far as cooking."

"Most people think of cooking as anything from a chore to a hobby. But as I've told Juliet—" His fingers twined possessively with hers "—food is a basic need. Like making love, it should appeal to all the senses. It should excite, arouse, satisfy." He slipped his thumb around to skim over her palm. "You remember, Juliet?"

She'd tried to forget, had told herself she could. Now with that light, insistent brush of thumb, he was bringing it all back. "Mr. Franconi is a strong believer in the sensuality of food. His unusual flair for bringing this out has made him one of the top chefs in the world."

*"Grazie, mi amore,"* he murmured and brought her stiff hand to his lips.

She pressed her shoe down on the soft leather of his loafers and hoped she ground bones. "I think you, and your readers, will find that Mr. Franconi's book, *The Italian Way*, is a really stunning example of his technique, his style and his opinions, written in such a way that the average person following one of his recipes step by step can create something very special."

When their drinks were served, Juliet gave another tug on her hand thinking she might catch him off guard. She should have known better.

"To the new baby." He smiled over at Juliet. "It's always a pleasure to drink to life in all its stages."

Ms. Tribly sipped lightly at her margarita in a glass the size of a small birdbath. "Mr. Franconi, have you actually cooked and tasted every recipe that's in your book?"

"Of course." Carlo enjoyed the quick tang of his drink. There was a time for the sweet, and a time for the tart. His laugh came low and smooth as he looked at Juliet. "When something's mine, there's nothing I don't learn about it. A meal, Ms. Tribly, is like a love affair."

She broke the tip of her pencil and hurriedly dug out another. "A love affair?"

"Yes. It begins slowly, almost experimentally. Just a taste, to whet the appetite, to stir the anticipation. Then the flavor changes, perhaps something light, something cool to keep the senses stirred, but not overwhelmed. Then there's the spice, the meat, the variety. The senses are aroused; the mind is focused on the pleasure. It should be lingered over. But finally, there's dessert, the time of indulgence." When he smiled at Juliet, there was no mistaking his meaning. "It should be enjoyed slowly, savored, until the palate is satisfied and the body sated."

Ms. Tribly swallowed. "I'm going to buy a copy of your book for myself."

With a laugh, Carlo picked up his menu. "Suddenly, I have a huge appetite."

Juliet ordered a small fruit salad and picked at it for thirty minutes.

"I've really got to get back." After polishing off her meal and an apricot tart, Ms. Tribly gathered up her pad. "I can't tell you how much I've enjoyed this, Mr. Franconi. I'm never going to sit down to pot roast with the same attitude again."

Amused, Carlo rose. "It was a pleasure."

"I'll be glad to send a clipping of the article to your office, Ms. Trent."

"I'd appreciate that." Juliet offered her hand, surprised when the reporter held it an extra moment.

"You're a lucky woman. Enjoy the rest of your tour, Mr. Franconi."

"*Arrivederci.*" He was still smiling when he sat down to finish his coffee.

"You put on a hell of a show, Franconi."

He'd been expecting the storm. Anticipating it. "Yes, I think I did my—what was it you called it? Ah yes, my spiel very well."

"It was more like a three-act play." With calm, deliberate movements, she signed the check. "But the next time, don't cast me unless you ask first."

"Cast you?"

His innocence was calculated to infuriate. He never missed his mark. "You gave that woman the very clear impression that we were lovers."

"Juliet, I merely gave her the very correct impression that I respect and admire you. What she takes from that isn't my responsibility."

Juliet rose, placed her napkin very carefully on the table and picked up her briefcase. "Swine."

Carlo watched her walk out of the restaurant. No endearment could have pleased him more. When a woman called a man a swine, she wasn't indifferent. He was whistling when he walked out to join her. It pleased him even more to see her fumbling with the keys of the rented car parked at the curb. When a woman was indifferent, she didn't swear at inanimate objects.

"Would you like me to drive to the airport?"

"No." Swearing again, she jabbed the key into the lock. She'd control her temper. She would control it. Like hell. Slamming both hands down on the roof of the car, she stared at him. "Just what was the point of that little charade?"

*Squisito,* he thought briefly. Her eyes were a dangerous blade-sharp green. He'd discovered he preferred a woman with temper. "Charade?"

"All that hand-holding, those intimate looks you were giving me?"

"It's not a charade that I enjoy holding your hand, and that I find it impossible not to look at you."

She refused to argue with the car between them. In a few quick steps she was around the hood and toe to toe with him. "It was completely unprofessional."

"Yes. It was completely personal."

It was going to be difficult to argue at all if he turned everything she said to his own advantage.

"Don't ever do it again."

*"Madonna."* His voice was very mild, his move very calculated. Juliet found herself boxed in between him and the car. "Orders I'll take from you when they have to do with schedules and plane flights. When it comes to more personal things, I do as I choose."

It wasn't something she'd expected; that's why she lost her advantage. Juliet would tell herself that again and again—later. He had her by both shoulders and his eyes never left hers as he gave her a quick jerk. It wasn't the smooth, calculated seduction she'd have anticipated from him. It was rough, impulsive and enervating.

His mouth was on hers, all demand. His hands held her still, all power. She had no time to stiffen, to struggle or to think. He took her with him quickly, through a journey of heat and light. She didn't resist. Later, when she would tell herself she had, it would be a lie.

There were people on the sidewalk, cars in the street. Juliet and Carlo were unaware of everything. The heat of a Dallas afternoon soaked into the concrete beneath them. It blasted the air until it hummed. They were concerned with a fire of their own.

Her hands were at his waist, holding on, letting go. A car streaked by, country rock blasting through open windows. She never heard it. Though she'd refused wine at lunch, she tasted it on his tongue and was intoxicated.

Later, much later, he'd take time to think about what was happening. It wasn't the same. Part of him already knew and feared because it wasn't the same. Touching her was different than touching other women. Tasting her—lightly, deeply, teasingly—just tasting her was different than tasting other women. The feelings were new, though he'd have sworn he'd experienced all the feelings that any man was capable of.

He knew about sensations. He incorporated them in his work and in his life. But they'd never had this depth before. A man who found more and didn't reach for it was a fool.

He knew about intimacy. He expected, demanded it in everything he did. But it had never had this strength before.

New experiences were not to be refused, but explored and exploited. If he felt a small, nagging fear, he could ignore it. For now.

Later. They clung to each other and told themselves they'd think later. Time was unimportant after all. Now held all the meaning necessary.

He took his mouth from hers, but his hands held her still. It shocked him to realize they weren't quite steady. Women had made him ache. Women had made him burn. But no woman had ever made him tremble. "We need a place," he murmured. "Quiet, private. It's time to stop pretending this isn't real."

She wanted to nod, to simply put herself completely in his hands. Wasn't that the first step in losing control over your own life? "No, Carlo." Her voice wasn't as strong as she would have liked but she didn't back away. "We've got to stop mixing personal feelings with business. We've got just under two weeks to go on the road."

"I don't give a damn if it's two days or two years. I want to spend it making love with you."

She brought herself back enough to remember they were standing on a public street in the middle of afternoon traffic. "Carlo, this isn't the time to discuss it."

"Now is always the time. Juliet—" He cupped her face in his hand. "It's not me you're fighting."

He didn't have to finish the thought. She was all too aware that the war was within herself. What she wanted, what was wise. What she needed, what was safe. The tug-of-war threatened to split her apart, and the two halves, pu

# PLAY "LUCKY HEARTS" AND GET . . .

★ Exciting Silhouette Intimate Moments® novels—**FREE**
★ "Key to Your Heart" pendant necklace—FREE
★ Surprise mystery gift that will delight you—FREE

## THEN CONTINUE YOUR LUCKY STREAK WITH A SWEETHEART OF A DEAL

When you return the postcard on the opposite page, we'll send you the books and gifts you qualify for, absolutely free! Then, you'll get 6 new Silhouette Intimate Moments® novels every month, delivered right to your door months before they're available in stores. If you decide to keep them, you'll pay only $2.71* each plus 25¢ delivery and applicable sales tax, if any*. That's the complete price and—compared to cover prices of $3.39 each in stores—quite a bargain!

## Free Newsletter!

You'll get our subscribers-only newsletter—an insider's look at our most popular authors and their upcoming novels.

## Special Extras—Free!

When you join the Silhouette Reader Service™, you'll also get additional free gifts from time to time as a token of our appreciation for being a home subscriber.

back together, would never equal the whole she understood.

"Carlo, we have a plane to catch."

He said something soft and pungent in Italian. "You'll talk to me."

"No." She lifted her hands to grip his forearms. "Not about this."

"Then we'll stay right here until you change your mind."

They could both be stubborn, and with stubborness, they could both get nowhere. "We have a schedule."

"We have a great deal more than that."

"No, we don't." His brow lifted. "All right then, we can't. We have a plane to catch."

"We'll catch your plane, Juliet. But we'll talk in Houston."

"Carlo, don't push me into a corner."

"Who pushes?" he murmured. "Me or you?"

She didn't have an easy answer. "What I'll do is arrange for someone else to come out and finish the tour with you."

He only shook his head. "No, you won't. You're too ambitious. Leaving a tour in the middle wouldn't look good for you."

She set her teeth. He knew her too well already. "I'll get sick."

This time he smiled. "You're too proud. Running away isn't possible for you."

"It's not a matter of running." But of survival, she thought and quickly changed the phrase. "It's a matter of priorities."

He kissed her again, lightly. "Whose?"

"Carlo, we have business."

"Yes, of different sorts. One has nothing to do with the other."

"To me they do. Unlike you, I don't go to bed with everyone I'm attracted to."

Unoffended, he grinned. "You flatter me, *cara*."

She could have sighed. How like him to make her want to laugh while she was still furious. "Purely unintentional."

"I like you when you bare your teeth."

"Then you're going to enjoy the next couple of weeks." She pushed his hands away. "It's a long ride to the airport, Carlo. Let's get going."

Amiable as ever, he pulled his door open. "You're the boss."

A foolish woman might've thought she'd won a victory.

# Chapter Seven

Juliet was an expert on budgeting time. It was her business every bit as much as promotion. So, if she could budget time, she could just as easily overbudget it when the circumstances warranted. If she did her job well enough, hustled fast enough, she could create a schedule so tight that there could be no time for talk that didn't directly deal with business. She counted on Houston to cooperate.

Juliet had worked with Big Bill Bowers before. He was a brash, warm-hearted braggart who handled special events for Books, Etc., one of the biggest chains in the country. Big Bill had Texas sewed up and wasn't ashamed to say so. He was partial to long, exaggerated stories, ornate boots and cold beer.

Juliet liked him because he was sharp and tough and invariably made her job easier. On this trip, she blessed him because he was also long-winded and gregarious. He wouldn't give her or Carlo many private moments.

From the minute they arrived at Houston International, the six-foot-five, two hundred and sixty pound Texan made it his business to entertain. There was a crowd of people waiting at the end of the breezeway, some already packed together and chatting, but there was no overlooking Big Bill. You only had to look for a Brahma bull in a Stetson.

"Well now, there's little Juliet. Pretty as ever."

Juliet found herself caught in a good-natured, rib-cracking bear hug. "Bill." She tested her lungs gingerly as she drew away. "It's always good to be back in Houston. You look great."

"Just clean living, honey." He let out a boom of a laugh that turned heads. Juliet found her mood lifting automatically.

"Carlo Franconi, Bill Bowers. Be nice to him," she added with a grin. "He's not only big, he's the man who'll promote your books for the largest chain in the state."

"Then I'll be very nice." Carlo offered his hand and met an enormous, meaty paw.

"Glad you could make it." The same meaty hand gave Carlo a friendly pat on the back that could have felled a good-sized sapling. Juliet gave Carlo points for not taking a nosedive.

"It's good to be here" was all he said.

"Never been to Italy myself, but I'm partial to Eye-talian cooking. The wife makes a hell of a pot of spaghetti. Let me take that for you." Before Carlo could object, Bill had hefted his big leather case. Juliet couldn't prevent the smirk when Carlo glanced down at the case as though it were a small child boarding a school bus for the first time.

"Car's outside. We'll just pick up your bags and get going. Airports and hospitals, can't stand 'em." Bill started toward the terminal in his big, yard-long strides. "Hotel's all ready for you; I checked this morning."

Juliet managed to keep up though she still wore three-inch heels. "I knew I could depend on you, Bill. How's Betty?"

"Mean as ever," he said proudly of his wife. "With the kids up and gone, she's only got me to order around."

"But you're still crazy about her."

"A man gets used to mean after a while." He grinned, showing one prominent gold tooth. "No need to go by the hotel straight off. We'll show Carlo here what Houston's all about." As he walked he swung Carlo's case at his side.

"I'd like that." Diplomatically, Carlo moved closer to his side. "I could take that case..."

"No need for that. What you got in here, boy? Weighs like a steer."

"Tools," Juliet put in with an innocent smile. "Carlo's very temperamental."

"Man can't be too temperamental about his tools," Bill said with a nod. He tipped his hat at a young woman with a short skirt and lots of leg. "I've still got the same hammer my old man gave me when I was eight."

"I'm just as sentimental about my spatulas," Carlo murmured. But he hadn't, Juliet noted, missed the legs either.

"You got a right." A look passed between the two men that was essential male and pleased. Juliet decided it had more to do with long smooth thighs than tools. "Now, I figured you two must've had your fill of fancy restaurants and creamed chicken by now. Having a little barbecue over at my place. You can take off your shoes, let down your hair and eat real food."

Juliet had been to one of Bill's *little* barbecues before. It meant grilling a whole steer along with several chickens and the better part of a pig, then washing it all down with a couple hundred gallons of beer. It also meant she wouldn't see her hotel room for a good five hours. "Sounds great. Carlo, you haven't lived until you've tasted one of Bill's steaks grilled over mesquite."

Carlo slipped a hand over her elbow. "Then we should live first." The tone made her turn her head and meet the look. "Before we attend to business."

"That's the ticket." Bill stopped in front of the conveyor belt. "Just point 'em out and we'll haul 'em in."

They lived, mingling at Bill's little barbecue with another hundred guests. Music came from a seven-piece band that never seemed to tire. Laughter and splashing rose up from a pool separated from the patio by a spread of red flowering bushes that smelled of spice and heat. Above all was the scent of grilled meat, sauce and smoke. Juliet ate twice as much as she would normally have considered because her host filled her plate then kept an eagle eye on her.

It should have pleased her that Carlo was surrounded by a dozen or so Texas ladies in bathing suits and sundresses who had suddenly developed an avid interest in cooking. But, she thought nastily, most of them wouldn't know a stove from a can opener.

It should have pleased her that she had several men dancing attendance on her. She was barely able to keep the names and faces separate as she watched Carlo laugh with a six-foot brunette in two minuscule ribbons of cloth.

The music was loud, the air heavy and warm. Giving into necessity, Juliet had dug a pair of pleated shorts and a crop top out of her bag and changed. It occurred to her that it was the first time since the start of the tour that she'd been able to sit out in the sun, soak up rays and not have a pad and pencil in her hand.

Though the blonde beside her with the gleaming biceps was in danger of becoming both a bore and a nuisance, she willed herself to enjoy the moment.

It was the first time Carlo had seen her in anything other than her very proper suits. He'd already concluded, by the way she walked, that her legs were longer than one might think from her height. He hadn't been wrong. They seemed to start at her waist and continued down, smooth, slim and New York pale. The statuesque brunette beside him might not have existed for all the attention he paid her.

It wasn't like him to focus on a woman yards away when there was one right beside him. Carlo knew it, but not what to do about it. The woman beside him smelled of heat and musk—heavy and seductive. It made him think that Juliet's scent was lighter, but held just as much punch.

She had no trouble relaxing with other men. Carlo tipped back a beer as he watched her fold those long legs under her and laugh with the two men sitting on either side of her. She didn't stiffen when the young, muscle-bound hunk on her left put his hand on her shoulder and leaned closer.

It wasn't like him to be jealous. As emotional as he was, Carlo had never experienced that particular sensation. He'd

so felt that a woman had just as much right to flirt and
xperiment as he did. He found that particular rule didn't
pply to Juliet. If she let that slick-skinned, weight-lifting
*uffone* put his hand on her again . . .

He didn't have time to finish the thought. Juliet laughed
gain, set aside her plate and rose. Carlo couldn't hear
hatever she'd said to the man beside her, but she strolled
to the sprawling ranch house. Moments later, the bur-
ished, bare-chested man rose and followed her.

*"Maledetto!"*

"What?" The brunette stopped in the middle of what
e'd thought was an intimate conversation.

Carlo barely spared her a glance. *"Scusi."* Muttering, he
rode off in the direction Juliet had taken. There was mur-
er in his eye.

Fed up with fending off the attentions of Big Bill's hot-
ot young neighbor, Juliet slipped into the house through
e kitchen. Her mood might have been foul, but she con-
atulated herself on keeping her head. She hadn't taken a
unk out of the free-handed, self-appointed Adonis. She
dn't snarled out loud even once in Carlo's direction.

Attending to business always helped steady her temper.
'ith a check of her watch, Juliet decided she could get one
llect call through to her assistant at home. She'd no more
an picked up the receiver from the kitchen wall phone
an she was lifted off her feet.

"Ain't much to you. But it sure is a pleasure to look at
hat there is."

She barely suppressed the urge to come back with her el-
ow. "Tim." She managed to keep her voice pleasant while
e thought how unfortunate it was that most of his muscle
as from the neck up. "You're going to have to put me
wn so I can make my call."

"It's a party, sweetheart." Shifting her around with a flex
' muscle, he set her on the counter. "No need to go calling
ybody when you've got me around."

"You know what I think?" Juliet gauged that she coul
give him a quick kick below the belt, but tapped his shou
der instead. After all, he was Bill's neighbor. "I think yo
should get back out to the party before all the ladies mi
you."

"Got a better idea." He leaned forward, boxing her i
with a hand on each side. His teeth gleamed in the style c
the best toothpaste ads. "Why don't you and I go have
little party of our own? I imagine you New York ladies kno
how to have fun."

If she hadn't considered him such a jerk, she'd have bee
insulted for women in general and New York in particula
Patiently, Juliet considered the source. "We New York la
dies," she said calmly, "know how to say no. Now back of
Tim."

"Come on, Juliet." He hooked a finger in the neck of he
top. "I've got a nice big water bed down the street."

She put a hand on his wrist. Neighbor or not, she wa
going to belt him. "Why don't you go take a dive."

He only grinned as his hand slid up her leg. "Just wha
had in mind."

"Excuse me." Carlo's voice was soft as a snake from tl
doorway. "If you don't find something else to do with yo
hands quickly, you might lose the use of them."

"Carlo." Her voice was sharp, but not with relief. Sl
wasn't in the mood for a knight-in-armor rescue.

"The lady and I're having a private conversation." Ti
flexed his pectorals. "Take off."

With his thumbs hooked in his pockets, Carlo stroll
over. Juliet noted he looked as furious as he had over tl
canned basil. In that mood, there was no telling what he
do. She swore, let out a breath and tried to avoid a scen
"Why don't we all go outside?"

"Excellent." Carlo held out a hand to help her dow
Before she could reach for it, Tim blocked her way.

"You go outside, buddy. Juliet and I haven't finish
talking."

Carlo inclined his head then shifted his gaze to Juliet.
Have you finished talking?''

"Yes." She'd have slid off the counter, but that would
ave put her on top of Tim's shoulders. Frustrated, she sat
here she was.

"Apparently Juliet is finished." Carlo's smile was all
niability, but his eyes were flat and cold. "You seem to be
ocking her way."

"I told you to take off." Big and annoyed, he grabbed
arlo by the lapels.

"Cut it out, both of you." With a vivid picture of Carlo
eeding from the nose and mouth, Juliet grabbed a cookie
r shaped like a ten-gallon hat. Before she could use it, Tim
unted and bent over from the waist. As he gasped,
utching his stomach, Juliet only stared.

"You can put that down now," Carlo said mildly. "It's
ne we left." When she didn't move, he took the jar him-
lf, set it aside then lifted her from the counter. "You'll
:cuse us," he said pleasantly to the groaning Tim, then led
iliet outside.

"What did you do?"

"What was necessary."

Juliet looked back toward the kitchen door. If she hadn't
en it for herself... "You hit him."

"Not very hard." Carlo nodded to a group of sunbath-
s. "All his muscle is in his chest and his brain."

"But—" She looked down at Carlo's hands. They were
an-fingered and elegant with the flash of a diamond on the
nky. Not hands one associated with self-defense. "He was
vfully big."

Carlo lifted a brow as he took his sunglasses back out of
s pocket. "Big isn't always an advantage. The neighbor-
ood where I grew up was an education. Are you ready to
ive?"

No, his voice wasn't pleasant, she realized. It was cold. Ice
ld. Instinctively hers mirrored it. "I suppose I should
ank you."

"Unless of course you enjoyed being pawed. Perhaps Ti was just acting on the signals you were sending out."

Juliet stopped in her tracks. "What signals?"

"The ones women send out when they want to be pu sued."

Thinking she could bring her temper to order, she ga herself a moment. It didn't work. "He might have be bigger than you," she said between her teeth. "But I thi you're just as much of an ass. You're very much alike."

The lenses of his glasses were smoky, but she saw his ey narrow. "You compare what's between us with what ha pened in there?"

"I'm saying some men don't take no for an answer gr ciously. You might have a smoother style, Carlo, but you' after the same thing, whether it's a roll in the hay or a cru on a water bed."

He dropped his hand from her arm, then very delibe ately tucked both in his pockets. "If I've mistaken yo feelings, Juliet, I apologize. I'm not a man who finds necessary or pleasurable to pressure a woman. Do you wi to leave or stay?"

She felt a great deal of pressure—in her throat, behind h eyes. She couldn't afford the luxury of giving into it. "I like to get to the hotel. I still have some work to do t night."

"Fine." He left her there to find their host.

Three hours later, Juliet admitted working was impos ble. She'd tried all the tricks she knew to relax. A half-ho in a hot tub, quiet music on the radio while she watched t sun set from her hotel window. When relaxing failed, s went over the Houston schedule twice. They'd be runni from 7:00 A.M. to 5:00 P.M., almost nonstop. Their flight Chicago took off at 6:00.

There'd be no time to discuss, think or worry about a thing that had happened within the last twenty-four hou That's what she wanted. Yet when she tried to work on t two-day Chicago stand, she couldn't. All she could do was think about the man a few steps across the hall.

She hadn't realized he could be so cold. He was always so full of warmth, of life. True, he was often infuriating, but he infuriated with verve. Now, he'd left her in a vacuum.

No. Tossing her notebook aside, Juliet dropped her chin in her hand. No, she'd put herself there. Maybe she could have stood it if she'd been right. She'd been dead wrong. She hadn't sent any signals to the idiot Tim, and Carlo's opinion on that still made her steam, but... But she hadn't even thanked him for helping her when, whether she liked to admit it or not, she'd needed help. It didn't sit well with her to be in debt.

With a shrug, she rose from the table and began to pace the room. It might be better all around if they finished off the tour with him cold and distant. There'd certainly be less personal problems that way because there'd be nothing personal between them. There'd be no edge to their relationship because they wouldn't have a relationship. Logically, this little incident was probably the best thing that could have happened. It hardly mattered if she'd been right or wrong as long as the result was workable.

She took a glimpse around the small, tidy, impersonal room where she'd spend little more than eight hours, most of it asleep.

No, she couldn't stand it.

Giving in, Juliet stuck her room key in the pocket of her robe.

Women had made him furious before. Carlo counted on it to keep life from becoming too tame. Women had frustrated him before. Without frustrations, how could you fully appreciate success?

But hurt. That was something no woman had ever done to him before. He'd never considered the possibility. Frustration, fury, passion, laughter, shouting. No man who'd known so many women—mother, sisters, lovers—expected a relationship without them. Pain was a different matter.

Pain was an intimate emotion. More personal than passion, more elemental than anger. When it went deep, it found places inside you that should have been left alone.

It had never mattered to him to be considered a rogue, a rake, a playboy—whatever term was being used for a man who appreciated women. Affairs came and went, as affairs were supposed to. They lasted no longer than the passion that conceived them. He was a careful man, a caring man. A lover became a friend as desire waned. There might be spats and hard words during the storm of an affair, but he'd never ended one that way.

It occurred to him that he'd had more spats, more hard words with Juliet than with any other woman. Yet they'd never been lovers. Nor would they be. After pouring a glass of wine, he sat back in a deep chair and closed his eyes. He wanted no woman who compared him with a muscle-bound idiot, who confused passion for lust. He wanted no woman who compared the beauty of lovemaking to—what was it?— a cruise on a water bed. *Dio!*

He wanted no woman who could make him ache so—in the middle of the night, in the middle of the day. He wanted no woman who could bring him pain with a few harsh words.

God, he wanted Juliet.

He heard the knock on the door and frowned. By the time he'd set his glass aside and stood, it came again.

If Juliet hadn't been so nervous, she might have thought of something witty to say about the short black robe Carlo wore with two pink flamingos twining up one side. As it was, she stood in her own robe and bare feet with her fingers linked together.

"I'm sorry," she said when he opened the door.

He stepped back. "Come in, Juliet."

"I had to apologize." She let out a deep breath as she walked into the room. "I was awful to you this afternoon

nd you'd helped me out of a very tricky situation with a
ainimum of fuss. I was angry when you insinuated that I'd
:d that—that idiot on in some way. I had a right to be." She
olded her arms under her chest and paced the room. "It
·as an uncalled for remark, and insulting. Even if by the
:motest possibility it had been true, you had no right to
·lk. After all, you were basking in your own harem."

"Harem?" Carlo poured another glass of wine and of-
:red it.

"With that amazon of a brunette leading the pack." She
·pped, gestured with the glass and sipped again. "Every-
·here we go, you've got half a dozen women nipping at
our ankles, but do I say a word?"

"Well, you—"

"And once, just once, I have a problem with some creep
·ith an overactive libido, and you assume I asked for it. I
·ought that kind of double standard was outdated even in
·aly."

Had he ever known a woman who could change his
·oods so quickly? Thinking it over, and finding it to his
·ste, Carlo studied his wine. "Juliet, did you come here to
·pologize, or demand that I do so?"

She scowled at him. "I don't know why I came, but ob-
·ously it was a mistake."

"Wait." He held up a hand before she could storm out
·ain. "Perhaps it would be wise if I simply accepted the
·ology you came in with."

Juliet sent him a killing look. "You can take the apology
·came in with and—"

"And offer you one of my own," he finished. "Then
·e'll be even."

"I didn't encourage him," she murmured. And pouted.
·e'd never seen that sulky, utterly feminine look on her face
·efore. It did several interesting things to his system.

"And I'm not looking for the same thing he was." He
·me to her then, close enough to touch. "But very much
·ore."

"Maybe I know that," she whispered, but took a step away. "Maybe I'd like to believe it. I don't understand affairs, Carlo." With a little laugh, she dragged her hand through her hair and turned away. "I should; my father had plenty of them. Discreet," she added with a lingering taste of bitterness. "My mother could always turn a blind eye as long as they were discreet."

He understood such things, had seen them among both friends and relatives, so he understood the scars and disillusionments that could be left. "Juliet, you're not your mother."

"No." She turned back, head up. "No, I've worked long and hard to be certain I'm not. She's a lovely, intelligent woman who gave up her career, her self-esteem, her independence to be no more than a glorified housekeeper because my father wanted it. He didn't want a wife of his to work. A wife of his," she repeated. "What a phrase. Her job was to take care of him. That meant having dinner on the table at six o'clock every night, and his shirts folded in his drawer. He—damn, he's a good father, attentive, considerate. He simply doesn't believe a man should shout at a woman or a girl. As a husband, he'd never forget a birthday, an anniversary. He's always seen to it that she was provided for in the best material fashion, but he dictated my mother's life-style. While he was about it, he enjoyed a very discreet string of women."

"Why does your mother stay his wife?"

"I asked her that a few years ago, before I moved away to New York. She loves him." Juliet stared into her wine. "That's reason enough for her."

"Would you rather she'd have left him?"

"I'd rather she'd have been what she could be. What she might've been."

"The choice was hers, Juliet. Just as your life is yours."

"I don't want to ever be bound to anyone, *anyone* who could humiliate me that way." She lifted her head again. '

won't put myself in my mother's position. Not for anyone.''

"Do you see all relationships as being so imbalanced?"

With a shrug, she drank again. "I suppose I haven't seen so many of them."

For a moment he was silent. Carlo understood fidelity, the need for it, and the lack of it. "Perhaps we have something in common. I don't remember my father well, I saw him little. He, too, was unfaithful to my mother."

She looked over at him, but he didn't see any surprise in her face. It was as though she expected such things. "But he committed his adultery with the sea. For months he'd be gone, while she raised us, worked, waited. When he'd come home, she'd welcome him. Then he'd go again, unable to resist. When he died, she mourned. She loved him, and made her choice."

"It's not fair, is it?"

"No. Did you think love was?"

"It's not something I want."

He remembered once another woman, a friend, telling him the same thing when she was in turmoil. "We all want love, Juliet."

"No." She shook her head with the confidence born of desperation. "No, affection, respect, admiration, but not love. It steals something from you."

He looked at her as she stood in the path of the lamplight. "Perhaps it does," he murmured. "But until we love, we can't be sure we needed what was lost."

"Maybe it's easier for you to say that, to think that. You've had many lovers."

It should have amused him. Instead, it seemed to accent a void he hadn't been aware of. "Yes. But I've never been in love. I have a friend—" again he thought of Summer "—once she told me love was a merry-go-round. Maybe she knew best."

Juliet pressed her lips together. "And an affair?"

Something in her voice had him looking over. For the second time he went to her, but slowly. "Perhaps it's just one ride on the carousel."

Because her fingers weren't steady, Juliet set down the glass. "We understand each other."

"In some ways."

"Carlo—" She hesitated, then admitted the decision had already been made before she crossed the hall. "Carlo, I've never taken much time for carousels, but I do want you."

How should he handle her? Odd, he'd never had to think things through so carefully before. With some women, he'd have been flamboyant, sweeping her up, carrying her off. With another he might have been impulsive, tumbling with her to the carpet. But nothing he'd ever done seemed as important as the first time with Juliet.

Words for a woman had always come easily to him. The right phrase, the right tone had always come as naturally as breathing. He could think of nothing. Even a murmur might spoil the simplicity of what she'd said to him and how she'd said it. So he didn't speak.

He kissed her where they stood, not with the raging passion he knew she could draw from him, not with the hesitation she sometimes made him feel. He kissed her with the truth and the knowledge that longtime lovers often experience. They came to each other with separate needs, separate attitudes, but with this, they locked out the past. Tonight was for the new, and for renewing.

She'd expected the words, the flash and style that seemed so much a part of him. Perhaps she'd even expected something of triumph. Again, he gave her the different and the fresh with no more than the touch of mouth to mouth.

The thought came to her, then was discounted, that he was no more certain of his ground than she. Then he held out his hand. Juliet put hers in it. Together they walked to the bedroom.

If he'd set the scene for a night of romance, Carlo would've added flowers with a touch of spice, music with

ie throb of passion. He'd have given her the warmth of
andlelight and the fun of champagne. Tonight, with Ju-
et, there was only silence and moonlight. The maid had
irned down the bed and left the drapes wide. White light
iltered through shadows and onto white sheets.

Standing by the bed, he kissed her palms, one by one.
'hey were cool and carried a hint of her scent. At her wrist
er pulse throbbed. Slowly, watching her, he loosened the
e of her robe. With his eyes still on hers, he brought his
ands to her shoulders and slipped the material aside. It fell
lently to pool at her feet.

He didn't touch her, nor did he yet look at anything but
er face. Through nerves, through needs, something like
omfort began to move through her. Her lips curved, just
ightly, as she reached for the tie of his robe and drew the
not. With her hands light and sure on his shoulders, she
ushed the silk aside.

They were both vulnerable, to their needs, to each other.
'he light was thin and white and washed with shadows. No
ther illumination was needed this first time that they
)oked at each other.

He was lean but not thin. She was slender but soft. Her
kin seemed only more pale when he touched her. Her hand
eemed only more delicate when she touched him.

They came together slowly. There was no need to rush.

The mattress gave, the sheets rustled. Quietly. Side by side
iey lay, giving themselves time—all the time needed to dis-
)ver what pleasures could come from the taste of mouth to
iouth, the touch of flesh to flesh.

Should she have known it would be like this? So easy. In-
vitable. Her skin was warm, so warm wherever he brushed
. His lips demanded, they took, but with such patience. He
ived her gently, slowly, as though it were her first time. As
ie drifted deeper, Juliet thought dimly that perhaps it was.

Innocence. He felt it from her, not physical, but emo-
onal. Somehow, incredibly, he discovered it was the same

for himself. No matter how many had come before, for ei
ther of them, they came to each other now in innocence.

Her hands didn't hesitate as they moved over him bu
stroked as though she were blind and could only gain he
own picture through other senses. He smelled of a shower
water and soap, but he tasted richer, of wine. Then he spok
for the first time, only her name. It was to her more mov
ing, more poetic than any endearment.

Her body moved with his, in rhythm, keeping pace. Sh
seemed to know, somehow, where he would touch her jus
before she felt his fingers trace, his palms press. Then his lip
began a long, luxurious journey she hoped would never enc

She was so small. Why had he never noticed before hov
small she was? It was easy to forget her strength, her cor
trol, her stamina. He could give her tenderness and wait fo
the passion.

The line of her neck was slender and so white in th
moonlight. Her scent was trapped there, at her throat. In
tensified. Arousing. He could linger there while bloo
heated. His and hers.

He slid his tongue over the subtle curve of her breast t
find the peak. When he drew it into his mouth, she moane
his name, giving them both a long, slow nudge to the edge

But there was more to taste, more to touch. Passion, whe
heated, makes a mockery of control. Sounds slipped into th
room—a catch of breath, a sigh, a moan—all pleasure
Their scents began to mix together—a lover's fragrance. I
the moonlight, they were one form. The sheets were ho
twisted. When with tongue and fingertips he drove her ove
the first peak, Juliet gripped the tousled sheets as her bod
arched and shuddered with a torrent of sensations.

While she was still weak, still gasping, he slipped into he

His head was spinning—a deliciously foreign sensation t
him. He wanted to bury himself in her, but he wanted to se
her. Her eyes were shut; her lips just parted as the breat
hurried in and out. She moved with him, slowly, then fa
ter, still faster until her fingers dug into his shoulders.

On a cry of pleasure, her eyes flew open. Looking into
them, he saw the dark, astonished excitement he'd wanted
to give her.

At last, giving in to the rushing need of his own body, he
closed his mouth over hers and let himself go.

# Chapter Eight

Were there others who understood true passion? Wrapped in Carlo, absorbing and absorbed by Carlo, Juliet knew she hadn't until moments ago. Should it make you weak? She felt weak, but not empty.

Should she feel regret? Yes, logically she should. She'd given more of herself than she'd intended, shared more than she'd imagined, risked more than she should have dared. But she had no regrets. Perhaps later she'd make her list of the whys and why nots. For now, she wanted only to enjoy the soft afterglow of loving.

"You're quiet." His breath whispered across her temple, followed by his lips.

She smiled a little, content to let her eyes close. "So are you."

Nuzzling his cheek against her hair, he looked over to the slant of moonlight through the window. He wasn't sure which words to use. He'd never felt quite like this before with any woman. He'd never expected to. How could he tell her that and expect to be believed? He was having a hard time believing it himself. And yet... perhaps truth was the hardest thing to put into words.

"You feel very small when I hold you like this," he murmured. "It makes me want to hold you like this for a long, long time."

"I like having you hold me." The admission was much easier to make than she'd thought. With a little laugh, she turned her head so that she could see his face. "I like it very much."

"Then you won't object if I go on holding you for the next few hours."

She kissed his chin. "The next few minutes," she corrected. "I have to get back to my room."

"You don't like my bed?"

She stretched and cuddled and thought how wonderful it would be never to move from that one spot. "I think I'm crazy about it, but I've got a little work to do before I call it a night, then I have to be up by six-thirty, and—"

"You work too much." He cut her off, then leaned over her to pick up the phone. "You can get up in the morning just as easily from my bed as yours."

Finding she liked the way his body pressed into hers, she prepared to be convinced. "Maybe. What're you doing?"

"Shh. Yes, this is Franconi in 922. I'd like a wake-up call for six." He replaced the phone and rolled, pulling her on top of him. "There now, everything is taken care of. The phone will ring at dawn and wake us up."

"It certainly will." Juliet folded her hands over his chest and rested her chin on them. "But you told them to call at six. We don't have to get up until six-thirty."

"Yes." He slid his hands down low over her back. "So we have a half-hour to—ah—wake up."

With a laugh, she pressed her lips to his shoulder. This once, she told herself, just this once, she'd let someone else do the planning. "Very practical. Do you think we might take a half-hour or so to—ah—go to sleep?"

"My thoughts exactly."

When the phone did ring, Juliet merely groaned and slid down under the sheets. For the second time, she found herself buried under Carlo as he rolled over to answer it. Without complaint, she lay still, hoping the ringing of the phone had been part of a dream.

"Come now, Juliet." Shifting most of his weight from her, Carlo began to nibble on her shoulder. "You're playing mole."

She murmured in drowsy excitement as he slid his har
down to her hip. "Mole? I don't have a mole."

"Playing mole." She was so warm and soft and plian
He'd known she would be. Mornings were made for la:
delights and waking her was a pleasure just begun.

Juliet stretched under the stroke and caress of his hand
Mornings were for a quick shower and a hasty cup of cc
fee. She'd never known they could be luxurious. "Playi:
mole?"

"An American expression." The skin over her rib ca
was soft as butter. He thought there was no better time
taste it. "You pretend to be dead."

Because her mind was clouded with sleep, her system :
ready churning with passion, it took a moment. "Pc
sum."

"*Prègo?*"

"Playing possum," she repeated and, guided by l
hands, shifted. "A mole's different."

"So, they're both little animals."

She opened one eye. His hair was rumpled around l
face, his chin darkened with a night's growth of beard. B
when he smiled he looked as though he'd been awake f
hours. He looked, she admitted, absolutely wonderful.

"You want an animal?" With a sudden burst of energ
she rolled on top of him. Her hands were quick, her mou
avid. In seconds, she'd taken his breath away.

She'd never been aggressive, but found the low, su
prised moan and the fast pump of his heart to her likir
Her body reacted like lightning. She didn't mind that l
hands weren't as gentle, as patient as they'd been the nig
before. This new desperation thrilled her.

He was Franconi, known for his wide range of expert:
in the kitchen and the bedroom. But she was making h
wild and helpless at the same time. With a laugh, she press
her mouth to his, letting her tongue find all the dark, lavi
tastes. When he tried to shift her, to take her because t

eed had grown too quickly to control, she evaded. His
reathless curse whispered into her mouth.

He never lost finesse with a woman. Passion, his pas-
ion, had always been melded with style. Now, as she took
er frenzied journey over him, he had no style, only needs.
Ie'd never been a man to rush. When he cooked, he went
lowly, step by step. Enjoy, experience, experiment. He
1ade love the same way. Such things were meant to be sa-
ored, to be appreciated by each of the five senses.

It wasn't possible to savor when you were driven beyond
he civilized. When your senses were whirling and tangled,
: wasn't possible to separate them. Being driven was some-
hing new for him, something intoxicating. No, he wouldn't
ight it, but pull her with him.

Rough and urgent, he grabbed her hips. Within mo-
1ents, they were both beyond thought, beyond reason....

His breath was still unsteady, but he held her close and
ght. Whatever she'd done, or was doing to him, he didn't
rant to lose it. The thought flickered briefly that he didn't
rant to lose her. Carlo pushed it aside. It was a dangerous
1ought. They had now. It was much wiser to concentrate
n that.

"I have to go." Though she wanted nothing more than to
url up against him, Juliet made herself shift away. "We
ave to be downstairs at check-out in forty minutes."

"To meet Big Bill."

"That's right." Juliet reached onto the floor for her robe,
ipping it onto her arms before she stood up. Carlo's lips
embled at the way she turned her back to him to tie it. It
'as rather endearing to see the unconscious modesty from
woman who'd just exploited every inch of his body. "You
on't know how grateful I am that Bill volunteered to play
hauffeur. The last thing I want to do is fight the freeway
/stem in this town. I've had to do it before, and it's not a
retty sight."

"I could drive," he murmured, enjoying the way the rich
reen silk reached the top of her thighs.

"Staying alive is another reason I'm grateful for Bill. I'll call and have a bellman come up for the bags in—thirty five minutes. Be sure—"

"You check everything because we won't be coming back," he finished. "Juliet, haven't I proven my compe tency yet?"

"Just a friendly reminder." She checked her watch be fore she remembered she wasn't wearing it. "The TV spo should be a breeze. Jacky Torrence hosts. It's a jovial sor of show that goes after the fast, funny story rather than nut and bolts."

"Hmm." He rose, stretching. The publicist was back, h noted with a half-smile, but as he reached down for his ow robe, he noticed that she'd broken off. Lifting his head, h looked up at her.

Good God, he was beautiful. It was all she could think Schedules, planning, points of information all went out o her head. In the early morning sun, his skin was more gol than brown, smooth and tight over his rib cage, nipped i at the waist to a narrow line of hip. Letting out a shak breath, she took a step back.

"I'd better go," she managed. "We can run through to day's schedule on the way to the studio."

It pleased him enormously to understand what had bro ken her concentration. He held the robe loosely in one han as he took a step closer. "Perhaps we'll get bumped."

"Bite your tongue." Aiming for a light tone, she suc ceeded with a whisper. "That's an interesting robe."

The tone of her voice was a springboard to an arousal a ready begun. "You like the flamingos? My mother has sense of humor." But he didn't put it on as he stepped close

"Carlo, stay right where you are. I mean it." She held u a hand as she walked backward to the doorway.

He grinned, and kept on grinning after he heard the clic of the hallway door.

Between Juliet cracking the whip and Bill piloting, the Houston business went like clockwork. TV, radio and prin

1e media was responsive and energetic. The midafternoon
1utograph party turned out to be a party in the true sense of
1e word and was a smashing success. Juliet found herself
 spot in a storeroom and ripped open the oversized enve-
1pe from her office that had been delivered to the hotel.
1ettling back, she began to go through the clippings her as-
.stant had air expressed.

L.A. was excellent, as she'd expected. Upbeat and en-
1usiastic. San Diego might've tried for a little more depth,
1ut they'd given him page one of the Food section in one
1read and a below-the-fold in the Style section in another.
1o complaints. Portland and Seattle listed a recipe apiece
1nd raved shamelessly. Juliet could've rubbed her hands
1gether with glee if she hadn't been drinking coffee. Then
1e hit Denver.

Coffee sloshed out of the cup and onto her hand.

"Damn!" Fumbling in her briefcase, she found three
1umpled tissues and began to mop up. A gossip column.
Vho'd have thought it? She gave herself a moment to think
1en relaxed. Publicity was publicity, after all. And the truth
f the matter was, Franconi was gossip. Looking at it logi-
1lly, the more times his name was in print, the more suc-
·ssful the tour. Resolved, Juliet began to read.

She nodded absently as she skimmed the first paragraph.
hatty, shallow, but certainly not offensive. A lot of peo-
.e who might not glance at the food or cooking sections
1ould give the gossip columns a working over. All in all, it
1s probably an excellent break. Then she read the second
1ragraph.

Juliet was up out of her folding chair. This time the cof-
·e that dripped onto the floor went unnoticed. Her expres-
1on changed from surprised astonishment to fury in a
1atter of seconds. In the same amount of time, she stuffed
e clippings back into their envelope. It wasn't easy, but she
1ve herself five minutes for control before she walked back
1to the main store.

The schedule called for another fifteen minutes, but Carl◀
had more than twenty people in line, and that many again
just milling around. Fifteen minutes would have to b◀
stretched to thirty. Grinding her teeth, Juliet stalked over t◀
Bill.

"There you are." Friendly as always, he threw his arn◀
over her shoulder and squeezed. "Going great guns ou◀
here. Old Carlo knows how to twinkle to the ladies withou◀
setting the men off. Damn clever sonofabitch."

"I couldn't have said it better myself." Her knuckles wen◀
white on the strap of her briefcase. "Bill, is there a phone ◀
can use? I have to call the office."

"No problem at all. Y'all just come on back with me."◀
He led her through Psychology, into Westerns and aroun◀
Romances to a door marked Private. "You just help your◀
self," he invited and showed her into a room with a clu◀
tered metal desk, a gooseneck lamp and stacks upo◀
stacks of books. Juliet headed straight for the phone.

"Thanks, Bill." She didn't even wait until the door close◀
before she started dialing. "Deborah Mortimor, please,◀
she said to the answering switchboard. Tapping her foo◀
Juliet waited.

"Ms. Mortimor."

"Deb, it's Juliet."

"Hi. I've been waiting for you to call in. Looks like we'v◀
got a strong nibble with the *Times* when you come back ◀
New York. I just—"

"Later." Juliet reached into her briefcase for a roll ◀
antacids. "I got the clippings today."

"Great, aren't they?"

"Oh sure. They're just dandy."

"Uh-huh." Deb waited only a beat. "It's the little num◀
ber in Denver, isn't it?"

She gave the rolling chair a quick kick. "Of course it is◀

"Sit down, Juliet." Deb didn't have to see to know h◀
boss was pacing.

"Sit down? I'm tempted to fly back to Denver and ring Chatty Cathy's neck."

"Killing columnists isn't good for PR, Juliet."

"It was garbage."

"No, no, it wasn't that bad. Trash maybe, but not garbage."

She struggled for control and managed to get a very slippery rein on her temper. Popping the first antacid into her mouth, she crunched down. "Don't be cute, Deb. I didn't like the insinuations about Carlo and me. *Carlo Franconi's lovely American traveling companion,*" she quoted between her teeth. "Traveling companion. It makes me sound as though I'm just along for the ride. And then—"

"I read it," Deb interrupted. "So did Hal," she added, referring to the head of publicity.

Juliet closed her eyes a moment. "And?"

"Well, he went through about six different reactions. In the end, he decided a few comments like that were bound to come up and only added to Franconi's—well, mystique might be the best term."

"I see." Her jaw clenched, her fingers tight around the little roll of stomach pills. "That's fine then, isn't it? I'm just thrilled to add to a client's mystique."

"Now, Juliet—"

"Look, just tell dear old Hal that Houston went perfectly." She was definitely going to need two pills. Juliet popped another out of the roll with her thumb. "I don't even want you to mention to him that I called about this—his trip in Denver."

"Whatever you say."

Taking a pen, she sat down and made space on the desk. "Now, give me what you have with the *Times*."

A half-hour later, Juliet was just finishing up her last call when Carlo poked his head in the office. Seeing she was on the phone, he rolled his eyes, closed the door and leaned against it. His brow lifted when he spotted the half-eaten roll of antacids.

"Yes, thank you, Ed, Mr. Franconi will bring all the necessary ingredients and be in the studio at 8:00. Yes." She laughed, though her foot was tapping out a rhythm on the floor. "It's absolutely delicious. Guaranteed. See you in two days."

When she hung up the receiver, Carlo stepped forward. "You didn't come to save me."

She gave him a long, slow look. "You seemed to be handling the situation without me."

He knew the tone, and the expression. Now all he had to do was find the reason for them. Strolling over, he picked up the roll of pills. "You're much too young to need these."

"I've never heard that ulcers had an age barrier."

His brows drew together as he sat on the edge of the desk. "Juliet, if I believed you had an ulcer, I'd pack you off to my home in Rome and keep you in bed on bland foods for the next month. Now…" He slipped the roll into his pocket. "What problem is there?"

"Several," she said briskly as she began to gather up her notes. "But they're fairly well smoothed out now. We'd need to go shopping again in Chicago for that chicken dish you'd planned to cook. So, if you've finished up here, we can just—"

"No." He put a hand on her shoulder and held her in the chair. "We're not finished. Shopping for chicken in Chicago isn't what had you reaching for pills. What?"

The best defense was always ice. Her voice chilled. "Carlo, I've been very busy."

"You think after two weeks I don't know you?" Impatient, he gave her a little shake. "You dig in that briefcase for your aspirin or your little mints only when you feel too much pressure. I don't like to see it."

"It comes with the territory." She tried to shrug off his hand and failed. "Carlo, we've got to get to the airport."

"We have more than enough time. Tell me what's wrong."

"All right then." In two sharp moves, she pulled the clipping out of her case and pushed it into his hands.

"What's this?" He skimmed it first without really reading it. "One of those little columns about who is seen with whom and what they wear while they're seen?"

"More or less."

"Ah." As he began to read from the top, he nodded. "And you were seen with me."

Closing her notebook, she slipped it neatly into her briefcase. Twice she reminded herself that losing her temper would accomplish nothing. "As your publicist, that could hardly be avoided."

Because he'd come to expect logic from her, he only nodded again. "But you feel this intimates something else."

"It *says* something else," she tossed back. "Something that isn't true."

"It calls you my traveling companion." He glanced up, knowing that wouldn't sit well with her. "It's perhaps not the full story, but not untrue. Does it upset you to be known as my companion?"

She didn't want him to be reasonable. She had no intention of emulating him. "When companion takes on this shade of meaning, it isn't professional or innocent. I'm not here to have my name linked with you this way, Carlo."

"In what way, Juliet?"

"It gives my name and goes on to say that I'm never out of arm's length, that I guard you as though you were my own personal property. And that you—"

"That I kiss your hand in public restaurants as though I couldn't wait for privacy," Carlo read at a glance. "So? What difference does it make what it says here?"

She dragged both hands through her hair. "Carlo, I'm here, with you, to do a job. This clipping came through my office, through my supervisor. Don't you know something like this could ruin my credibility?"

"No," he said simply enough, "This is no more than gossip. Your supervisor, he's upset by this?"

She laughed, but it had little to do with humor. "No, actually, it seems he's decided it's just fine. Good for your image."

"Well, then?"

"I don't want to be good for your image," she threw back with such passion, it shocked both of them. "I won't be one of the dozens of names and faces linked with you."

"So," he murmured. "Now, we push away to the truth. You're angry with me, for this." He set the clipping down. "You're angry because there's more truth in it now than there was when it was written."

"I don't want to be on anyone's list, Carlo." Her voice had lowered, calmed. She dug balled fists into the pockets of her skirt. "Not yours, not anyone's. I haven't come this far in my life to let that happen now."

He stood, wondering if she understood how insulting her words were. No, she'd see them as facts, not as darts. "I haven't put you on a list. If you have one in your own mind, it has nothing to do with me."

"A few weeks ago it was the French actress, a month before that a widowed countess."

He didn't shout, but it was only force of will that kept his voice even. "I never pretended you were the first woman in my bed. I never expected I was the first man in yours."

"That's entirely different."

"Ah, now you find the double standard convenient." He picked up the clipping, balled it in his fist then dropped it into the wastebasket. "I've no patience for this, Juliet."

He was to the door again before she spoke. "Carlo, wait." With a polite veneer stretched thinly over fury he turned. "Damn." Hands still in her pockets, she paced from one stack of books to the other. "I never intended to take this out on you. It's totally out of line and I'm sorry, really. You might guess I'm not thinking very clearly right now."

"So it would seem."

Juliet let out a sigh, knowing she deserved the cutting edge of his voice. "I don't know how to explain, except to say that my career's very important to me."

"I understand that."

"But it's no more important to me than my privacy. I don't want my personal life discussed around the office water cooler."

"People talk, Juliet. It's natural and it's meaningless."

"I can't brush it off the way you do." She picked up her briefcase by the strap then set it down again. "I'm used to staying in the background. I set things up, handle the details, do the legwork, and someone else's picture gets in the paper. That's the way I want it."

"You don't always get what you want." With his thumbs hooked in his pockets, he leaned back against the door and watched her. "Your anger goes deeper than a few lines in a paper people will have forgotten tomorrow."

She closed her eyes a moment, then turned back to him. "All right, yes, but it's not a matter of being angry. Carlo, I've put myself in a delicate position with you."

Carefully, he weighed the phrase, tested it, judged it. "Delicate position?"

"Please, don't misunderstand. I'm here, with you, because of my job. It's very important to me that that's handled in the best, the most professional manner I can manage. What's happened between us . . ."

"What has happened between us?" he prompted when she trailed off.

"Don't make it difficult."

"All right, we'll make it easy. We're lovers."

She let out a long, unsteady breath, wondering if he really believed that was easy. For him it might be just another stroll through the moonlight. For her, it was a race through a hurricane. "I want to keep that aspect of our relationship completely separate from the professional area."

It surprised him he could find such a statement endearing. Perhaps the fact that she was half romanticist and half

businesswoman was part of her appeal to him. "Juliet, my
love, you sound as though you're negotiating a contract."

"Maybe I do." Nerves were beginning to run through her
too quickly again. "Maybe I am, in a way."

His own anger had disappeared. Her eyes weren't nearly
as certain as her voice. Her hands, he noted, were twisting
together. Slowly, he walked toward her, pleased that though
she didn't back away, the wariness was back. "Juliet..." He
lifted a hand to brush through her hair. "You can negotiate
terms and times, but not emotion."

"You can—regulate it."

He took both her hands, kissing them. "No."

"Carlo, please—"

"You like me to touch you," he murmured. "Whether we
stand here alone, or we stand in a group of strangers. If I
touch your hand, like this, you know what's in my mind. It's
not always passion. There are times, I see you, I touch you
and I think only of being with you—talking, or sitting si-
lently. Will you negotiate now how I am to touch your hand,
how many times a day it's permitted?"

"Don't make me sound like a fool."

His fingers tightened on hers. "Don't make what I feel for
you sound foolish."

"I—" No, she couldn't touch that. She didn't dare.
"Carlo, I just want to keep things simple."

"Impossible."

"No, it's not."

"Then tell me, is this simple?" With just his fingertips on
her shoulder, he leaned down to kiss her. So softly, so
lightly, it was hardly a kiss at all. She felt her legs dissolve
from the knees down.

"Carlo, we're not staying on the point."

He slipped his arms around her. "I like this point much
better. When we get to Chicago..." His fingers slipped up
and down her spine as he began to brush his lips over her
face. "I want to spend the evening alone with you."

"We—have an appointment for drinks at ten with—"

"Cancel it."

"Carlo, you know I can't."

"Very well." He caught the lobe of her ear between his teeth. "I'll plead fatigue and make certain we have a very quick, very early evening. Then, I'll spend the rest of the night doing little things, like this."

His tongue darted inside her ear, then retreated to the vulnerable spot just below. The shudder that went through her was enough to arouse both of them. "Carlo, you don't understand."

"I understand that I want you." In a swift mood swing, he had her by the shoulders. "If I told you now that I want you more than I've wanted any other woman, you wouldn't believe me."

She backed away from that, but was caught close again. 'No, I wouldn't. It isn't necessary to say so."

"You're afraid to hear it, afraid to believe it. You won't get simple with me, Juliet. But you'll get a lover you'll never forget."

She steadied a bit, meeting his look levelly. "I've already resigned myself to that, Carlo. I don't apologize to myself, and I don't pretend to have any regrets about coming to you last night."

"Then resign yourself to this." The temper was back in his eyes, hot and volatile. "I don't care what's written in the paper, what's whispered about in offices in New York. You, this moment, are all I care about."

Something shattered quietly inside her. A defense built instinctively through years. She knew she shouldn't take him literally. He was Franconi after all. If he cared about her, it was only in his way, and in his time. But something had shattered, and she couldn't rebuild it so quickly. Instead, she chose to be blunt.

"Carlo, I don't know how to handle you. I haven't the experience."

"Then don't handle me." Again, he took her by the shoulders. "Trust me."

She put her hands on his, held them a moment, then drew them away. "It's too soon, and too much."

There were times, in his work, where he had to be very, very patient. As a man, it happened much more rarely. Yet he knew if he pushed now, as for some unexplicable reason he wanted to, he'd only create more distance between them.

"Then, for now, we just enjoy each other."

That's what she wanted. Juliet told herself that was exactly what she wanted—no more, no less. But she felt like weeping.

"We'll enjoy each other," she agreed. Letting out a sigh, she framed his face with her hands as he so often did with her. "Very much."

He wondered, when he lowered his brow to hers, why it didn't quite satisfy.

# Chapter Nine

Burned out from traveling, ready for a drink and elevated feet, Juliet walked up to the front desk of their Chicago hotel. Taking a quick glimpse around the lobby, she was pleased with the marble floors, sculpture and elegant potted palms. Such places usually lent themselves to big, stylish bathrooms. She intended to spend her first hour in Chicago with everything from the neck down submerged.

"May I help you?"

"You have a reservation for Franconi and Trent."

With a few punches on the keyboard, the clerk brought up their reservations on the screen. "You'll both be staying for two nights, Miss Trent?"

"Yes, that's right."

"It's direct bill. Everything's set. If you and Mr. Franconi will just fill out these forms, I'll ring for a bellman."

As he scrawled the information on the form, Carlo glanced over. From the profile, she looked lovely, though perhaps a bit tired. Her hair was pinned up in the back, fluffed out on the sides and barely mussed from traveling. She looked as though she could head a three-hour business meeting without a whimper. But then she arched her back, closing her eyes briefly as she stretched her shoulders. He wanted to take care of her.

"Juliet, there's no need for two rooms."

She shifted her shoulder bag and signed her name. "Carlo, don't start. Arrangements have already been made."

"But it's absurd. You'll be staying in my suite, so the extra room is simply extra."

The desk clerk stood at a discreet distance and listened to every word.

Juliet pulled her credit card out of her wallet and set it down on the counter with a snap. Carlo noted, with some amusement, that she no longer looked the least bit tired. He wanted to make love with her for hours.

"You'll need the imprint on this for my incidentals," she told the clerk calmly enough. "All Mr. Franconi's charges will be picked up."

Carlo pushed his form toward the clerk then leaned on the counter. "Juliet, won't you feel foolish running back and forth across the hall? It's ridiculous, even for a publisher, to pay for a bed that won't be slept in."

With her jaw clenched, she picked up her credit card again. "I'll tell you what's ridiculous," she said under her breath. "It's ridiculous for you to be standing here deliberately embarrassing me."

"You have rooms 1102 and 1108." The clerk pushed the keys toward them. "I'm afraid they're just down the hall from each other rather than across."

"That's fine." Juliet turned to find the bellman had their luggage packed on the cart and his ears open. Without a word, she strode toward the bank of elevators.

Strolling along beside her, Carlo noted that the cashier had a stunning smile. "Juliet, I find it odd that you'd be embarrassed over something so simple."

"I don't think it's simple." She jabbed the up button on the elevator.

"Forgive me." Carlo put his tongue in his cheek. "It's only that I recall you specifically saying you wanted our relationship to be simple."

"Don't tell me what I said. What I said has nothing to do with what I meant."

"Of course not," he murmured and waited for her to step inside the car.

Seeing the look on Juliet's face, the bellman began to
orry about his tip. He put on a hospitality-plus smile. "So,
)u in Chicago long?"

"Two days," Carlo said genially enough.

"You can see a lot in a couple of days. You'll want to get
)wn to the lake—"

"We're here on business," Juliet interrupted. "Only
isiness."

"Yes, ma'am." With a smile, the bellman pushed his cart
to the hall. "1108's the first stop."

"That's mine." Juliet dug out her wallet again and pulled
it bills as the bellman unlocked her door. "Those two
igs," she pointed out then turned to Carlo. "We'll meet
ive Lockwell in the bar for drinks at 10:00. You can do as
)u like until then."

"I have some ideas on that," he began but Juliet moved
st him. After stuffing the bills in the bellman's hand, she
iut the door with a quick click.

Thirty minutes, to Carlo's thinking, was long enough for
yone to cool down. Juliet's stiff-backed attitude toward
eir room situation had caused him more exasperation than
noyance. But then, he expected to be exasperated by
)men. On one hand, he found her reaction rather sweet
d naive. Did she really think the fact that they were lov-
; would make the desk clerk or a bellman blink twice?
The fact that she did, and probably always would, was
st another aspect of her nature that appealed to him. In
atever she did, Juliet Trent would always remain proper.
nmering passion beneath a tidy, clean-lined business suit.
rlo found her irresistible.

He'd known so many kinds of women—the bright young
;enue greedy to her fingertips, the wealthy aristocrat
red both by wealth and tradition, the successful career
man who both looked for and was wary of marriage.
'd known so many—the happy, the secure, the desperate
i seeking, the fulfilled and the grasping. Juliet Trent with

the cool green eyes and quiet voice left him uncertain as t
what pigeonhole she'd fit into. It seemed she had all an
none of the feminine qualities he understood. The only thir
he was certain of was that he wanted her to fit, somehow
into his life.

The best way, the only way, he knew to accomplish th
was to distract her with charm until she was already caugh
After that, they'd negotiate the next step.

Carlo lifted the rose he'd had sent up from the hotel fl
rist out of its bud vase, sniffed its petals once, then walke
down the hall to Juliet's room.

She was just drying off from a hot, steamy bath. If she
heard the knock five minutes before, she'd have growled. *A*
it was, she pulled on her robe and went to answer.

She'd been expecting him. Juliet wasn't foolish enough
believe a man like Carlo would take a door in the face as t
nal. It had given her satisfaction to close it, just as it ga
her satisfaction to open it again. When she was ready.

She hadn't been expecting the rose. Though she knew
wasn't wise to be moved by a single long-stemmed flow
with a bud the color of sunshine, she was moved noneth
less. Her plans to have a calm, serious discussion with hi
faltered.

"You look rested." Rather than giving her the rose,
took her hand. Before she could decide whether or not to
him in, he was there.

A stand, Juliet reminded herself even as she closed t
door behind him. If she didn't take a stand now, she'd ne
find her footing. "Since you're here, we'll talk. We have
hour."

"Of course." As was his habit, he took a survey of h
room. Her suitcase sat on a stand, still packed, but with
top thrown open. It wasn't practical to unpack and repa
when you were bouncing around from city to city. Thou
they were starting their third week on the road, the co
tents of the case were still neat and organized. He'd ha
expected no less from her. Her notebook and two pens w

ready beside the phone. The only thing remotely out of
lace in the tidy, impersonal room were the Italian heels that
t in the middle of the rug where she'd stepped out of them.
he inconsistency suited him perfectly.

"I can discuss things better," she began, "if you weren't
andering around."

"Yes?" All cooperation, Carlo sat and waved the rose
nder his nose. "You want to talk about our schedule here
Chicago?"

"No—yes." She had at least a dozen things to go over
ith him. For once she let business take a back seat.
Later." Deciding to take any advantage, Juliet remained
anding. "First, I want to talk about that business down at
e desk."

"Ah." The sound was distinctly European and as friendly
a smile. She could have murdered him.

"It was totally uncalled for."

"Was it?" He'd learned that strategy was best plotted
ith friendly questions or simple agreement. That way, you
uld swing the final result to your own ends without too
uch blood being shed.

"Of course it was." Forgetting her own strategy, Juliet
opped down on the edge of the bed. "Carlo, you had no
ght discussing our personal business in public."

"You're quite right."

"I—" His calm agreement threw her off. The firm,
oderately angry speech she'd prepared in the tub went out
e window.

"I must apologize," he continued before she could bal-
ce herself. "It was thoughtless of me."

"Well, no." As he'd planned, she came to his defense. "It
sn't thoughtless, just inappropriate."

With the rose, he waved her defense away. "You're too
nd, Juliet. You see, I was thinking only of how practical
u are. It's one of the things I most admire about you." In
tting his way, Carlo had always felt it best to use as much
th as possible. "You see, besides my own family, I've

known very few truly practical women. This trait in yo
appeals to me, as much as the color of your eyes, the te
ture of your skin."

Because she sensed she was losing ground, Juliet sat u
straighter. "You don't have to flatter me, Carlo. It's simp
a matter of establishing ground rules."

"You see." As if she'd made his point, he sat forward
touch her fingertips. "You're too practical to expect fla
tery or to be swayed by it. Is it any wonder I'm enchanted l
you?"

"Carlo—"

"I haven't made my point." He retreated just enough
keep his attack in full gear. "You see, knowing you,
thought you would agree that it was foolish and imprac
cal to book separate rooms when we want to be togeth
You do want to be with me, don't you, Juliet?"

Frustrated, she stared at him. He was turning the ent
situation around. Certain of it, Juliet groped for a han
hold. "Carlo, it has nothing to do with my wanting to
with you."

His brow lifted. "No?"

"No. It has to do with the line that separates our bu
ness and our personal lives."

"A line that's difficult to draw. Perhaps impossible f
me." The truth came out again, though this time u
planned. "I want to be with you, Juliet, every moment
have. I find myself resenting even the hour that you're h
and I'm there. A few hours at night isn't enough for me
want more, much more for us."

Saying it left him stunned. It hadn't been one of his cle
moves, one of his easy catch-phrases. That little jewel h
come from somewhere inside where it had quietly hidd
until it could take him by surprise.

He rose, and to give himself a moment, stood by
window to watch a stream of Chicago traffic. It rushed, th
came to fitful stops, wound and swung then sped on aga
Life was like this, he realized. You could speed right alo

t you never knew when something was going to stop you
ad in your tracks.

Juliet was silent behind him, torn between what he'd said,
1at he'd meant, and what she felt about it. From the very
ginning, she'd kept Carlo's definition of an affair in the
ont of her mind. Just one ride on the carousel. When the
1sic stopped, you got off and knew you'd gotten your
ɔney's worth. Now, with a few words he was changing the
ɔpe. She wondered if either of them were ready.

"Carlo, since you say I am, I'll be practical." Drawing
gether her resources, she rose. "We have a week left on
1r. During that time, we've got Chicago and four other
ies to deal with. To be honest, I'd rather if our only busi-
ss right now was with each other."

He turned, and though she thought the smile was a bit
d, at least he smiled. "That's the nicest thing you've said
me in all these days and all these cities, Juliet."

She took a step toward him. It seemed foolish to think
ɔut risks when they had such little time. "Being with you
't something I'll ever forget, no matter how much I might
nt to in years to come."

'Juliet—"

'No, wait. I want to be with you, and part of me hates the
1e we lose with other people, in separate rooms, in all the
nands that brought us to each other in the first place. But
ther part of me knows that all of those things are com-
tely necessary. Those things will still be around after
re each back in our separate places."

No, don't think about that now, she warned herself. If she
, her voice wouldn't be steady.

'No matter how much time I spend with you in your
te, I need a room of my own if for no other reason than
know it's there. Maybe that's the practical side of me,
rlo."

Dr the vulnerable one, he mused. But hadn't he just dis-
ered he had a vulnerability of his own? Her name was
iet. "So, it will be as you want in this." And for the best

perhaps. He might just need a bit of time to himself to thir
things through.

"No arguing?"

"Do we argue ever, *cara*?"

Her lips curved. "Never." Giving in to herself as much
him, she stepped forward and linked her arms around h
neck. "Did I ever tell you that when I first started setting
this tour I looked at your publicity shot and thought y
were gorgeous?"

"No." He brushed his lips over hers. "Why don't you t
me now?"

"And sexy," she murmured as she drew him closer to t
bed. "Very, very sexy."

"Is that so?" He allowed himself to be persuaded or
the bed. "So you decided in your office in New York th
we'd be lovers?"

"I decided in my office in New York that we'd never
lovers." Slowly, she began to unbutton his shirt. "I decid
that the last thing I wanted was to be romanced and
duced by some gorgeous, sexy Italian chef who had a stri
of women longer than a trail of his own pasta, but—"

"Yes." He nuzzled at her neck. "I think I'll prefer t
'but.'"

"But it seems to me that you can't make definitive de
sions without all the facts being in."

"Have I ever told you that your practicality arouses
to the point of madness?"

She sighed as he slipped undone the knot in her ro
"Have I ever told you that I'm a sucker for a man w
brings me flowers?"

"Flowers." He lifted his head then picked up the ro
bud he'd dropped on the pillow beside them. "Darling,
you want one too?"

With a laugh, she pulled him back to her.

Juliet decided she'd seen more of Chicago in the fli
into O'Hare than during the day and a half she'd been the

ab drives from hotel to television station, from television
ation to department store, from department store to
ookstore and back to the hotel again weren't exactly lei-
urely sight-seeing tours. Then and there she decided that
hen she took her vacation at the end of the month, she'd
somewhere steamy with sun and do nothing more ener-
etic than laze by a pool from dawn to dusk.

The only hour remotely resembling fun was another
opping expedition where she watched Carlo select a plump
ree-pound chicken for his cacciatore.

He was to prepare his *pollastro alla cacciatora* from sim-
er to serve during a live broadcast of one of the country's
p-rated morning shows. Next to the Simpson show in
.A., Juliet considered this her biggest coup for the tour.
Let's Discuss It" was the hottest hour on daytime TV, and
mained both popular and controversial after five consec-
tive seasons.

Despite the fact that she knew Carlo's showmanship
ilities, Juliet was nervous as a cat. The show would air live
New York. She had no doubt that everyone in her de-
artment would be watching. If Carlo was a smash, it would
his triumph. If he bombed, the bomb was all hers. Such
as the rationale in public relations.

It never occurred to Carlo to be nervous. He could make
cciatore in the dark, from memory with the use of only
e hand. After watching Juliet pace the little greenroom
r the fifth time, he shook his head. "Relax, my love, it's
ly chicken."

"Don't forget to bring up the dates we'll be in the rest of
e cities. This show reaches all of them."

"You've already told me."

"And the title of the book."

"I won't forget."

"You should remember to mention you prepared this dish
r the President when he visited Rome last year."

"I'll try to keep it in mind. Juliet, wouldn't you like some
ffee?"

She shook her head and kept pacing. What else?

"I could use some," he decided on the spot.

She glanced toward the pot on a hot plate. "Help you self."

He knew if she had something to do, she'd stop worry ing, even for a few moments. And she'd stop pacing up an down in front of him. "Juliet, no one with a heart woul ask a man to drink that poison that's been simmering sinc dawn."

"Oh." Without hesitation, she assumed the role of pan perer. "I'll see about it."

*"Grazie."*

At the door, she hesitated. "The reporter for the *Su* might drop back before the show."

"Yes, you told me. I'll be charming."

Muttering to herself, she went to find a page.

Carlo leaned back and stretched his legs. He'd have drink the coffee when she brought it back, though he didr want any. He didn't want to board the plane for Detroit th afternoon, but such things were inevitable. In any case, l and Juliet would have the evening free in Detroit—wh American state was that in?

They wouldn't be there long enough to worry about it.

In any case, he would soon be in Philadelphia and ther see Summer. He needed to. Though he'd always had frien and was close to many of them, he'd never needed one as l felt he needed one now. He could talk to Summer and knc what he said would be listened to carefully and not be r peated. Gossip had never bothered him in the past, but wh it came to Juliet... When it came to Juliet, nothing was it had been in the past.

None of his previous relationships with women had ev become a habit. Waking up in the morning beside a wom; had always been pleasant, but never necessary. Every da Juliet was changing that. He couldn't imagine his bedro back in Rome without her, yet she'd never been there. He long since stopped imagining other women in his bed.

Rising, he began to pace as Juliet had.

When the door opened, he turned, expecting her. The tall, willowy blonde who entered wasn't Juliet, but she was familiar.

"Carlo! How wonderful to see you again."

"Lydia." He smiled, cursing himself for not putting the name of the *Sun*'s reporter with the face of the woman he'd spent two interesting days in Chicago with only eighteen months before. "You look lovely."

Of course she did. Lydia Dickerson refused to look anything less. She was sharp, sexy and uninhibited. She was also, in his memory, an excellent cook and critic of gourmet foods.

"Carlo, I was just thrilled when I heard you were coming into town. We'll do the interview after the show, but I just had to drop back and see you." She swirled toward him with the scent of spring lilacs and the swish of a wide-flared skirt. "You don't mind?"

"Of course not." Smiling, he took her outstretched hand. "It's always good to see an old friend."

With a laugh, she put her hands on his shoulders. "I should be angry with you, *caro*. You do have my number, and my phone didn't ring last night."

"Ah." He put his hands to her wrists, wondering just how to untangle himself. "You'll have to forgive us, Lydia. The schedule is brutal. And there's a...complication." He winced, thinking how Juliet would take being labeled a complication.

"Carlo." She edged closer. "You can't tell me you haven't got a few free hours for...an old friend. I've a tremendous recipe for *vitèllo tonnato*." She murmured the words and made the dish sound like something to be eaten in the moonlight. "Who else should I cook it for but the best chef in Italy?"

"I'm honored." He put his hands on her hips hoping to draw her away with the least amount of insult. It wouldn't occur to him until later that he'd felt none, absolutely none,

of the casual desire he should have. "I haven't forgotte
what a superb cook you are, Lydia."

Her laugh was low and full of memories. "I hope yc
haven't forgotten more than that."

"No." He let out a breath and opted to be blunt. "B
you see I'm—"

Before he could finish being honest, the door opene
again. With a cup of coffee in her hand, Juliet walked i
then came to a dead stop. She looked at the blonde wour
around Carlo like an exotic vine. Her brow lifted as she too
her gaze to Carlo's face. If only she had a camera.

Her voice was as cool and dry as her eyes. "I see you'
met."

"Juliet, I—"

"I'll give you a few moments for the... pre-interview,
she said blandly. "Try to wrap it up by eight-fifty, Carl
You'll want to check the kitchen set." Without anoth
word, she shut the door behind her.

Though her arms were still around Carlo's neck, Lyd
looked toward the closed door. "Oops," she said lightly.

Carlo let out a long breath as they separated. "Y
couldn't have put it better."

At nine o'clock, Juliet had a comfortable seat midw;
back in the audience. When Lydia slipped into the seat b
side her, she gave the reporter an easy nod, then looked ba
to the set. As far as she could tell, and she'd gone over eve
inch of it, it was perfect.

When Carlo was introduced to cheerful applause she b
gan to relax, just a little. But when he began preparations
the chicken, moving like a surgeon and talking to his ho:
his studio and television audience like a seasoned p
former, her relaxation was complete. He was going to
fantastic.

"He's really something, isn't he?" Lydia murmured du
ing the first break.

"Something," Juliet agreed.

"Carlo and I met the last time he was in Chicago."

"Yes, I gathered. I'm glad you could make it by this morning. You did get the press kit I sent in?"

She's a cool one, Lydia thought and shifted in her seat. "Yes. The feature should be out by the end of the week. I'll send you a clipping."

"I'd appreciate it."

"Miss Trent—"

"Juliet, please." For the first time, Juliet turned and smiled at her fully. "No need for formality."

"All right, Juliet, I feel like a fool."

"I'm sorry. You shouldn't."

"I'm very fond of Carlo, but I don't poach."

"Lydia, I'm sure there isn't a woman alive who wouldn't be fond of Carlo." She crossed her legs as the countdown for taping began again. "If I thought you'd even consider poaching, you wouldn't be able to pick up your pencil."

Lydia sat still for a moment, then leaned back with a laugh. Carlo had picked himself quite a handful. Served him right. "Is it all right to wish you luck?"

Juliet shot her another smile. "I'd appreciate it."

The two women might've come to amicable terms, but it wasn't easy for Carlo to concentrate on his job while they sat cozily together in the audience. His experience with Lydia had been a quick and energetic two days. He knew little more of her than her preference for peanut oil for cooking and blue bed linen. He understood how easy it was for a man to be executed without trial. He thought he could almost feel the prickle of the noose around his throat.

But he was innocent. Carlo poured the mixture of tomatoes, sauce and spices over the browned chicken and set the over. If he had to bind and gag her, Juliet would listen to him.

He cooked his dish with the finesse of an artist completing a royal portrait. He performed for the audience like a veteran thespian. He thought the dark thoughts of a man already at the dock.

When the show was over, he spent a few obligatory moments with his host, then left the crew to devour one of his best cacciatores.

But when he went back to the greenroom, Juliet was nowhere in sight. Lydia was waiting. He had no choice but to deal with her, and the interview, first.

She didn't make it easy for him. But then, to his knowledge, women seldom did. Lydia chatted away as though nothing had happened. She asked her questions, noted down his answers, all the while with mischief gleaming in her eyes. At length, he'd had enough.

"All right, Lydia, what did you say to her?"

"To whom?" All innocence, Lydia blinked at him. "Oh, your publicist. A lovely woman. But then I'd hardly be one to fault your taste, darling."

He rose, swore and wondered what a desperate man should do with his hands. "Lydia, we had a few enjoyable hours together. No more."

"I know." Something in her tone made him pause and glance back. "I don't imagine either of us could count the number of few enjoyable hours we've had." With a shrug, she rose. Perhaps she understood him, even envied what she thought she'd read in his eyes, but it wasn't any reason to let him off the hook. "Your Juliet and I just chatted, darling." She dropped her pad and pencil in her bag. "Girl talk, you know. Just girl talk. Thanks for the interview, Carlo." At the door, she paused and turned back. "If you're ever back in town without a... complication, give me a ring. *Ciao.*"

When she left he considered breaking something. Before he could decide what would be the most satisfying and destructive, Juliet bustled in. "Let's get moving, Carlo. The cab's waiting. It looks like we'll have enough time to get back to the hotel, check out and catch the earlier plane."

"I want to speak with you."

'Yes, fine. We'll talk in the cab." Because she was al-
.dy heading down the winding corridor he had no choice
t to follow.

'When you told me the name of the reporter, I simply
n't put it together."

'Put what together?'' Juliet pulled open the heavy metal
or and stepped out on the back lot. If it had been much
tter, she noted, Carlo could've browned his chicken on
asphalt. "Oh, that you'd known her. Well, it's so hard
remember everyone we've met, isn't it?'' She slipped into
cab and gave the driver the name of the hotel.

'We've come halfway across the country." Annoyed, he
nbed in beside her. "Things begin to blur."

'They certainly do." Sympathetic, she patted his hand.
etroit and Boston'll be down and dirty. You'll be lucky
emember your own name." She pulled out her compact
give her makeup a quick check. "But then I can help out
Philadelphia. You've already told me you have a…friend
re."

'Summer's different." He took the compact from her.
ve known her for years. We were students together. We
er— Friends, we're only friends," he ended on a mut-
"I don't enjoy explaining myself."

'I can see that." She pulled out bills and calculated the
as the cab drew up to the hotel. As she started to slide
, she gave Carlo a long look. "No one asked you to."

'Ridiculous." He had her by the arm before she'd
ched the revolving doors. "You ask. It isn't necessary to
with words to ask."

'Guilt makes you imagine all sorts of things." She swung
ough the doors and into the lobby.

'Guilt?'' Incensed, he caught up with her at the eleva-
. "I've nothing to be guilty for. A man has to commit
e crime, some sin, for guilt."

he listened calmly as she stepped into the elevator car
pushed the button for their floor. "That's true, Carlo.
u seem to me to be a man bent on making a confession."

He went off on a fiery stream of Italian that had the oth
two occupants of the car edging into the corners. Juli
folded her hands serenely and decided she'd never enjoy
herself more. The other passengers gave Carlo a wide ber
as the elevator stopped on their floor.

"Did you want to grab something quick to eat at the a
port or wait until we land?"

"I'm not interested in food."

"An odd statement from a chef." She breezed into t
hall. "Take ten minutes to pack and I'll call for a be
man." The key was in her hand and into the lock before
fingers circled her wrist. When she looked up at him, s
thought she'd never seen him truly frustrated before. Goc
It was about time.

"I pack nothing until this is settled."

"Until what's settled?" she countered.

"When I commit a crime or a sin, I do so with compl
honesty." It was the closest he'd come to an explosion. J
liet lifted a brow and listened attentively. "It was Lydia w
had her arms around me."

Juliet smiled. "Yes, I saw quite clearly how you w
struggling. A woman should be locked up for taking
vantage of a man that way."

His eyes, already dark, went nearly black. "You're s
castic. But you don't understand the circumstances."

"On the contrary." She leaned against the door. "Car
I believe I understood the circumstances perfectly. I do
believe I've asked you to explain anything. Now, yo
better pack if we're going to catch that early plane." For
second time, she shut the door in his face.

He stood where he was for a moment, torn. A man
pected a certain amount of jealousy from a woman he
involved with. He even, well, enjoyed it to a point. What
didn't expect was a smile, a pat on the head and breezy
derstanding when he'd been caught in another woma
arms. However innocently.

No, he didn't expect it, Carlo decided. He wouldn't tolate it.

When the sharp knock came on the door, Juliet was still anding with a hand on the knob. Wisely, she counted to ten fore she opened it.

"Did you need something?"

Carefully, he studied her face for a trap. "You're not any."

She lifted her brows. "No, why?"

"Lydia's very beautiful."

"She certainly is."

He stepped inside. "You're not jealous?"

"Don't be absurd." She brushed a speck of lint from her eve. "If you found me with another man, under similar cumstances, you'd understand, I'm sure."

"No." He closed the door behind him. "I'd break his e."

"Oh?" Rather pleased, she turned away to gather a few ngs from her dresser. "That's the Italian temperament, I ppose. Most of my ancestors were rather staid. Hand me t brush, will you?"

Carlo picked it up and dropped it into her hand. "Staid— s means?"

"Calm and sturdy, I suppose. Though there was one—my at-great-grandmother, I think. She found her husband kling the scullery maid. In her staid sort of way, she ocked him flat with a cast iron skillet. I don't think he r tickled any of the other servants." Securing the brush a plastic case, she arranged it in the bag. "I'm said to take er her."

Taking her by the shoulders, he turned her to face him. here were no skillets available."

"True enough, but I'm inventive. Carlo..." Still smil-, she slipped her arms around his neck. "If I hadn't un-stood exactly what was going on, the coffee I'd fetched you would've been dumped over your head. *Capice?*"

"*Si.*" He grinned as he rubbed his nose against hers. B
he didn't really understand her. Perhaps that was why
was enchanted by her. Lowering his mouth to hers, he let t'
enchantment grow. "Juliet," he murmured. "There's a lat
plane for Detroit, yes?"

She had wondered if he would ever think of it. "Yes, th
afternoon."

"Did you know it's unhealthy for the system to rush."
he spoke, he slipped the jacket from her arms so that it sl
to the floor.

"I've heard something about that."

"Very true. It's much better, medically speaking, to ta
one's time. To keep a steady pace, but not a fast one. An
of course, to give the system time to relax at regular inte
vals. It could be very unhealthy for us to pack now and ra
to the airport." He unhooked her skirt so that it follow
her jacket.

"You're probably right."

"Of course I'm right," he murmured in her ear. '
would never do for either of us to be ill on the tour."

"Disastrous," she agreed. "In fact, it might be best if
both just lay down for a little while."

"The very best. One must guard one's health."

"I couldn't agree more," she told him as his shirt joir
her skirt and jacket.

She was laughing as they tumbled onto the bed.

He liked her this way. Free, easy, enthusiastic. Just as
liked her cooler, more enigmatic moods. He could enjoy
in a hundred different ways because she wasn't always
same woman. Yet she was always the same.

Soft, as she was now. Warm wherever he touched, lu
rious wherever he tasted. She might be submissive one n
ment, aggressive the next, and he never tired of the swin

They made love in laughter now, something he knew m
than most was precious and rare. Even when the pass
began to dominate, there was an underlying sense of enj
ment that didn't cloud the fire. She gave him more in a n

ent than he'd thought he'd ever find with a woman in a
fetime.

She'd never known she could be this way—laughing,
aurning, happy, desperate. There were so many things she
adn't known. Every time he touched her it was something
ew, though it was somehow as if his touch was all she'd
er known. He made her feel fresh and desirable, wild and
eepy all at once. In the space of minutes, he could bring
er a sense of contentment and a frantic range of excite-
ents.

The more he brought, the more he gave, and the easier it
ccame for her to give. She wasn't aware yet, nor was he,
at every time they made love, the intimacy grew and
read. It was gaining a strength and weight that wouldn't
eak with simply walking away. Perhaps if they'd known,
ey would have fought it.

Instead, they loved each other through the morning with
e verve of youth and the depth of familiarity.

# Chapter Ten

Juliet hung up the phone, dragged a hand through her ha
and swore. Rising, she swore again then moved toward th
wide spread of window in Carlo's suite. For a few momen
she muttered at nothing and no one in particular. Across th
room, Carlo lay sprawled on the sofa. Wisely, he waite
until she'd lapsed into silence.

"Problems?"

"We're fogged in." Swearing again, she stared out th
window. She could see the mist, thick and still hanging ou
side the glass. Detroit was obliterated. "All flights are ca
celled. The only way we're going to get to Boston is to sti
out our thumbs."

"Thumbs?"

"Never mind." She turned and paced around the suite.

Detroit had been a solid round of media and events, ar
the Renaissance Center a beautiful place to stay, but now
was time to move on. Boston was just a hop away by air, 
that the evening could be devoted to drafting out reports ar
a good night's sleep. Except for the fact that fog had driv
in from the lake and put the whole city under wraps.

Stuck, Juliet thought as she glared out the window agai
Stuck when they had an 8:00 A.M. live demonstration on
well-established morning show in Boston.

He shifted a bit, but didn't sit up. If it hadn't been t
much trouble, he could've counted off the number of tim
he'd been grounded for one reason or another. One, he 
called, had been a flamenco dancer in Madrid who'd d
tracted him into missing the last flight out. Better not 
mention it. Still, when such things happened, Carlo

ected, it was best to relax and enjoy the moment. He knew
uliet better.

"You're worried about the TV in the morning."

"Of course I am." As she paced, she went over every
ossibility. Rent a car and drive—no, even in clear weather
was simply too far. They could charter a plane and hope
he fog cleared by dawn. She took another glance outside.
hey were sixty-five floors up, but they might as well have
een sixty-five feet under. No, she decided, no television
oot was worth the risk. They'd have to cancel. That was
at.

She dropped down on a chair and stuck her stockinged
et up by Carlo's. "I'm sorry, Carlo, there's no way around
. We'll have to scrub Boston."

"Scrub Boston?" Lazily he folded his arms behind his
ead. "Juliet, Franconi scrubs nothing. Cook, yes, scrub,
)."

It took her a moment to realize he was serious. "I mean
ncel."

"You didn't say cancel."

She heaved out a long breath. "I'm saying it now." She
iggled her toes, finding them a bit stiff after a ten-hour
ay. "There's no way we can make the television spot, and
at's the biggest thing we have going in Boston. There're a
uple of print interviews and an autographing. We didn't
pect much to move there, and we were depending on the
spot for that. Without it . . ." She shrugged and resigned
rself. "It's a wash."

Letting his eyes half close, Carlo decided the sofa was an
cellent place to spend an hour or so. "I don't wash."

She shot him a level look. "You're not going to have to
anything but lie on your—back," she decided after a
oment, "for the next twenty-four hours."

"Nothing?"

"Nothing."

He grinned. Moving faster than he looked capable of, he
t up, grabbed her by the arms and pulled her down with

him. "Good, you lie with me. Two backs, *madonna,* are better than one."

"Carlo." She couldn't avoid the first kiss. Or perhaps she didn't put her best effort into it, but she knew it was essential to avoid the second. "Wait a minute."

"Only twenty-four hours," he reminded her as he moved to her ear. "No time to waste."

"I've got to— Stop that," she ordered when her thoughts started to cloud. "There're arrangements to be made."

"What arrangements?"

She made a quick mental sketch. True, she'd already checked out of her room. They'd only kept the suite for convenience, and until six. She could book another separate room for the night, but—she might as well admit in this case it was foolish. Moving her shoulders, she gave in to innate practicality. "Like keeping the suite overnight."

"That's important." He lifted his head a moment. Her face was already flushed, her eyes already soft. Almost as if she'd spoken aloud, he followed the train of thought. He couldn't help but admire the way her mind worked from one point to the next in such straight lines.

"I have to call New York and let them know our status. I have to call Boston and cancel, then the airport and change our flight. Then I—"

"I think you have a love affair with the phone. It's difficult for a man to be jealous of an inanimate object."

"Phones are my life." She tried to slip out from under him, but got nowhere. "Carlo."

"I like it when you say my name with just a touch of exasperation."

"It's going to be more than a touch in a minute."

He'd thought he'd enjoy that as well. "But you haven't told me yet how fantastic I was today."

"You were fantastic." It was so easy to relax when he held her like this. The phone calls could wait, just a bit. After all, they weren't going anywhere. "You mesmerized them with your linguini."

"My linguini is hypnotic," he agreed. "I charmed the re-
rter on the *Free Press*."

"You left him stupefied. Detroit'll never be the same."

"That's true." He kissed her nose. "Boston won't know
at it's missing."

"Don't remind me," she began, then broke off. Carlo
uld almost hear the wheels turning.

"An idea." Resigned, he rolled her on top of him and
tched her think.

"It might work," she murmured. "If everyone cooper-
s, it might work very well. In fact, it might just be terri-
"

"What?"

"You claim to be a magician as well as an artist."

"Modesty prevents me from—"

"Save it." She scrambled up until she stradled him. "You
d me once you could cook in a sewer."

Frowning, he toyed with the little gold hoop she wore in
ear. "Yes, perhaps I did. But this is only an expres-
n—"

"How about cooking by remote control?"

His brows drew together, but he ran his hand idly to the
n of her skirt that had ridden high on her thigh. "You
ve extraordinary legs," he said in passing, then gave her
attention. "What do you mean by remote control?"

"Just that." Wound up with the idea, Juliet rose and
bbed her pad and pencil. "You give me all the ingredi-
s—it's linguini again tomorrow, right?"

"Yes, my specialty."

"Good, I have all that in the file anyway. We can set up a
one session between Detroit and the studio in Boston.
u can be on the air there while we're here."

"Juliet, you ask for a lot of magic."

"No, it's just basic electronics. The host of the show—
l O'Hara—can put the dish together on the air while you
k him through it. It's like talking a plane in, you know.
ty degrees to the left—a cup of flour."

"No."

"Carlo."

Taking his time, he pried off his shoes. "You want hi this O'Hara who smiles for the camera, to cook my l guini?"

"Don't get temperamental on me," she warned, while h mind leaped ahead to possibilities. "Look, you write coo books so the average person can cook one of your dishes

"Cook them, yes." He examined his nails. "Not l Franconi."

She opened her mouth, then closed it again. Tread sof on the ego, Juliet reminded herself. At least until you g your way. "Of course not, Carlo. No one expects that. B we could turn this inconvenience into a real event. Usi your cookbook on the air, and some personal coaching fro you via phone, O'Hara can prepare the linguini. He's no chef or a gourmet, but an average person. Therefore, he be giving the audience the average person's reactions. He make the average person's mistakes that you can correct. we pull it off, the sales of your cookbook are going to so You know you can do it." She smiled winningly. "Why y even said you could teach me to cook, and I'm helpless the kitchen. Certainly you can talk O'Hara through c dish."

"Of course I can." Folding his arms again, he stared at the ceiling. Her logic was infallible, her idea creative. be truthful, he liked it—almost as much as he liked the ic of not having to fly to Boston. Still, it hardly seemed fair give without getting. "I'll do it—on one condition."

"Which is?"

"Tomorrow morning, I talk this O'Hara through guini. Tonight..." And he smiled at her. "We have a dr rehearsal. I talk you through it."

Juliet stopped tapping the end of her pencil on the p "You want me to cook linguini?"

"With my guidance, *cara mia*, you could cook a thing."

Juliet thought it over and decided it didn't matter. The
te didn't have a kitchen this time, so he'd be counting on
ng the hotel's. That may or may not work. If it did, once
'd botched it, they could order room service. The bot-
n line was saving what she could of Boston. "I'd love to.
w, I've got to make those calls."

Carlo closed his eyes and opted for a nap. If he was go-
to teach two amateurs the secrets of linguini within
lve hours, he'd need his strength. "Wake me when
've finished," he told her. "We have to inspect the
chen of the hotel."

t took her the best part of two hours, and when she hung
for the last time, Juliet's neck was stiff and her fingers
mb. But she had what she wanted. Hal told her she was a
ius and O'Hara said it sounded like fun. Arrangements
e already in the works.

This time Juliet grinned at the stubborn fog swirling out-
e the window. Neither rain nor storm nor dark of night,
thought, pleased with herself. Nothing was going to stop
iet Trent.

Then she looked over at Carlo. Something tilted inside her
t had both her confidence and self-satisfaction waver-
. Emotion, she reflected. It was something she hadn't
tten into the itinerary.

Well, maybe there was one catastrophe that wasn't in the
oks. Maybe it was one she couldn't work her way through
h a creative idea and hustle. She simply had to take her
lings for Carlo one step at a time.

our more days, she mused, and the ride would be over.
e music would stop and it would be time to get off the
ousel.

t wasn't any use trying to see beyond that yet; it was all
nk pages. She had to hold on to the belief that life was
t one day at a time. Carlo would go, then she would pick
the pieces and begin her life again from that point.

he wasn't fool enough to tell herself she wouldn't cry.
rs would be shed over him, but they'd be shed quietly

and privately. Schedule in a day for mourning, she thoug
then tossed her pad away.

It wasn't healthy to think of it now. There were only fo
days left. For a moment, she looked down at her emp
hands and wondered if she'd have taken the steps she
taken if she'd known where they would lead her. Then s
looked over at him and simply watched him sleep.

Even with his eyes closed and that irrepressible inner li
he had on hold, he could draw her. It wasn't simply a ma
ter of his looks, she realized. She wasn't a woman who
turn her life sideways for simple physical attraction. It w
a matter of style. Smiling, she rose and walked closer to hi
as he slept. No matter how practical she was, how mu
common sense she possessed, she couldn't have resisted l
style.

There'd be no regrets, she reaffirmed. Not now, nor
five days' time when an ocean and priorities separated the
As years passed, and their lives flowed and altered, she
remember a handful of days when she'd had somethi
special.

No time to waste, he'd said. Catching her tongue in h
teeth Juliet decided she couldn't agree more. Reaching u
she began to unbutton her blouse. As a matter of habit, s
draped it carefully over the back of a chair before she u
hooked her skirt. When that fell, she lifted it, smoothed
out and folded it. The pins were drawn out of her hair, o
by one, then set aside.

Dressed in a very impractical lace camisole and string
kini she moved closer.

Carlo awoke with his blood pumping and his head whi
ing. He could smell her scent lightly in her hair, more hea
on her skin as her mouth took command of his. Her bo
was already heated as she lay full length on him. Before
could draw his first thoughts together, his own body f
lowed suit.

She was all lace and flesh and passion. There wasn't ti
to steady his control or polish his style. Urgent and desp

e, he reached for her and found silk and delicacy, strength
d demand wherever he touched.

She unbuttoned his shirt and drew it aside so that their
in could meet and arouse. Beneath hers, she felt his
artbeat race and pound until power made her dizzy. Cap-
ring his lips once again, she thought only of driving him
madness. She could feel it spread through him, growing,
ilding, so that it would dominate both of them.

When he rolled so that she was trapped between the back
the sofa and his body, she was ready to relinquish con-
l. With a moan, dark and liquid, she let herself enjoy
at she'd begun.

No woman had ever done this to him. He understood that
his only thoughts were to devour everything she had. His
gers, so clever, so skilled, so gentle, pulled at the lace
til the thin strap tore with hardly a sound.

He found her—small soft breasts that fit so perfectly in
hands, the strong narrow rib cage and slender waist. His.
e word nearly drove him mad. She was his now, as she'd
en in the dream she'd woken him from. Perhaps he was
l dreaming.

She smelled of secrets, small, feminine secrets no man
r fully understood. She tasted of passion, ripe, shiver-
g passion every man craved. With his tongue he tasted that
eet subtle valley between her breasts and felt her trem-
. She was strong; he'd never doubted it. In her strength,
was surrendering completely to him, for the pleasure of
h.

The lace smelled of her. He could have wallowed in it, but
r skin was irresistible. He drew the camisole down to her
ist and feasted on her.

With her hands tangled in his hair, her body on fire, she
ught only of him. No tomorrows, no yesterdays. How-
r much she might deny it in an hour, they'd become a
gle unit. One depended on the other for pleasure, for
nfort, for excitement. For so much more she didn't dare
nk of it. She yearned for him; nothing would ever stop it.

But now, he was taking her, fast and furious, through doc
they'd opened together. Neither of them had gone there b
fore with another, nor would again.

Juliet gave herself over to the dark, the heat, and to Carl

He drew the thin strings riding on her hips, craving t
essence of her. When he'd driven her over the first peak,
knew and reveled in it. With endless waves of desire,
whipped her up again, and yet again, until they were bo
trembling. She called out his name as he ran his lips dov
her leg. All of her was the thought paramount in his mir
He'd have all of her until she was willing, ready to have
of him.

"Juliet, I want you." His face was above hers again, I
breath straining. "Look at me."

She was staggering on that razor's edge between reas
and madness. When she opened her eyes, his face filled I
vision. It was all she wanted.

"I want you," he repeated while the blood raged in I
head. "Only you."

She was wrapped around him, her head arched back. F
an instant, their eyes met and held. What coursed throu
them wasn't something they could try to explain. It was bc
danger and security.

"Only," she murmured and took him into her.

They were both stunned, both shaken, both content. N
ked, damp and warm, they lay tangled together in silen
Words had been spoken, Juliet thought. Words that w
part of the madness of the moment. She would have to ta
care not to repeat them when passion was spent. They did
need words; they had four days. Yet she ached to hear th
again, to say them again.

She could set the tone between them, she thought. S
had only to begin now and continue. No pressure. She k
her eyes closed a moment longer. No regrets. The extra n
ment she took to draw back her strength went unnoticed

"I could stay just like this for a week," she murmured.
Though she meant it, the words were said lazily. Turning her
head, she looked at him, smiled. "Are you ready for another nap?"

There was so much he wanted to say. So much, he
thought, she didn't want to hear. They'd set the rules; he
had only to follow them. Nothing was as easy as it should've
been.

"No." He kissed her forehead. "Though I've never found
waking from a nap more delightful. Now, I think it's time
for your next lesson."

"Really?" She caught her bottom lip between her teeth.
"I thought I'd graduated."

"Cooking," he told her, giving her a quick pinch where
Italian males were prone to.

Juliet tossed back her hair and pinched him back. "I
thought you'd forget about that."

"Franconi never forgets. A quick shower, a change of
clothes and down to the kitchen."

Agreeable, Juliet shrugged. She didn't think for one
minute the management would allow him to give a cooking
lesson in their kitchen.

Thirty minutes later, she was proven wrong.

Carlo merely bypassed management. He saw no reason to
go through a chain of command. With very little fuss, he
steered her through the hotel's elegant dining room and into
the big, lofty kitchen. It smelled exotic and sounded like a
subway station.

They'd stop him here, Juliet decided, still certain they'd
be dining outside or through room service within the hour.
Though she'd changed into comfortable jeans, she had no
plans to cook. After one look at the big room with its oversized appliances and acres of counter, she was positive she
couldn't.

It shouldn't have surprised her to be proven wrong again.

"Franconi!" The name boomed out and echoed off the
walls. Juliet jumped back three inches.

"Carlo, I think we should—" But as she spoke, sh
looked up at his face. He was grinning from ear to ear.

"Pierre!"

As she looked on, Carlo was enveloped by a wide, whit
aproned man with a drooping moustache and a face as b
and round as a frying pan. His skin glistened with sweat, b
he smelt inoffensively of tomatoes.

"You Italian lecher, what do you do in my kitchen?"

"Honor it," Carlo said as they drew apart. "I thoug
you were in Montreal, poisoning the tourists."

"They beg me to take the kitchen here." The big man wi
the heavy French accent shrugged tanklike shoulders. "I fe
sorry for them. Americans have so little finesse in t
kitchen."

"They offered to pay you by the pound," Carlo sa
dryly. "Your pounds."

Pierre held both hands to his abundant middle a:
laughed. "We understand each other, old friend. Still, I fi
America to my liking. You, why aren't you in Rome pinc
ing ladies?"

"I'm finishing up a tour for my book."

"But yes, you and your cookbooks." A noise behind h
had him glancing around and bellowing in French. Jul
was certain the walls trembled. With a smile, he adjusted l
hat and turned back to them. "That goes well?"

"Well enough." Carlo drew Juliet up. "This is Jul
Trent, my publicist."

"So it goes very well," Pierre murmured as he took J
liet's hand and brushed his lips over it. "Perhaps I will wr
a cookbook. Welcome to my kitchen, *mademoiselle*. I'm
your service."

Charmed, Juliet smiled. "Thank you, Pierre."

"Don't let this one fool you," Carlo warned. "He ha
daughter your age."

"Bah!" Pierre gave him a lowered brow look. "She's l
sixteen. If she were a day older I'd call my wife and tell l
to lock the doors while Franconi is in town."

Carlo grinned. "Such flattery, Pierre." With his hands ooked in his back pockets, he looked around the room. Very nice," he mused. Lifting his head, he scented the air. Duck. Is that duck I smell?"

Pierre preened. "The specialty. *Canard au Pierre.*"

"*Fantastico.*" Carlo swung an arm around Juliet as he led er closer to the scent. "No one, absolutely no one, does to ick what Pierre can do."

The black eyes in the frying-pan face gleamed. "No, you atter me, *mon ami.*"

"There's no flattery in truth." Carlo looked on while an sistant carved Pierre's duck. With the ease of experience, e took a small sliver and popped it into Juliet's mouth. It ssolved there, leaving behind an elusive flavor that begged r more. Carlo merely laid his tongue on his thumb to test. Exquisite, as always. Do you remember, Pierre, when we epared the Shah's engagement feast? Five, six years ago."

"Seven," Pierre corrected and sighed.

"Your duck and my cannelloni."

"Magnificent. Not so much paprika on that fish," he oomed out. "We are not in Budapest. Those were the ys," he continued easily. "But. . ." The shrug was essen- lly Gallic. "When a man has his third child, he has to ttle down, *oui?*"

Carlo gave another look at the kitchen, and with an ex- rt's eye approved. "You've picked an excellent spot. Per- ps you'd let me have a corner of it for a short time."

"A corner?"

"A favor," Carlo said with a smile that would have armed the pearls from oysters. "I've promised my Juliet teach her how to prepare linguini."

"*Linguini con vongole bianco?*" Pierre's eyes glittered.

"Naturally. It is my specialty."

"You can have a corner of my kitchen, *mon ami*, in ex- ange for a plate."

Carlo laughed and patted Pierre's stomach. "For you, *iico*, two plates."

Pierre clasped him by the shoulders and kissed bo
cheeks. "I feel my youth coming back to me. Tell me wh
you need."

In no time at all, Juliet found herself covered in a whi
apron with her hair tucked into a chef's hat. She might ha
felt ridiculous if she'd been given the chance.

"First you mince the clams."

Juliet looked at Carlo, then down at the mess of clams (
the cutting board. "Mince them?"

"Like so." Carlo took the knife and with a few qui
moves had half of the clams in small, perfect pieces. "Try.

Feeling a bit like an executioner, Juliet brought the kni
down. "They're not . . . well, alive, are they?"

"*Madonna*, any clam considers himself honored to
part of Franconi's linguini. A bit smaller there. Yes." Sɛ
isfied, he passed her an onion. "Chopped, not too fine
Again, he demonstrated, but this time Juliet felt more
home. Accepting the knife, she hacked again until the o
ion was in pieces and her eyes were streaming.

"I hate to cook," she muttered but Carlo only pushed
clove of garlic at her.

"This is chopped very fine. It's essence is what we nee
not so much texture." He stood over her shoulder, watc
ing until he approved. "You've good hands, Juliet. No
here, melt the butter."

Following instructions, she cooked the onion and gar
in the simmering butter, stirring until Carlo pronounced
ready.

"Now, it's tender, you see. We add just a bit of flour." F
held her hand to direct it as she stirred it in. "So it thic
ens. We add the clams. Gently," he warned before she cou
dump them in. "We don't want them bruised. Ah . . ." F
nodded with approval. "Spice," he told her. "It's the s
cret and the strength."

Bending over her, he showed her how to take a pinch
this, a touch of that and create. As the scent became mc

easing, her confidence grew. She'd never remember the
nounts or the ingredients, but found it didn't matter.

"How about that?" she asked, pointing to a few sprigs of
rsley.

"No, that comes just at the end. We don't want to drown
Turn the heat down, just a little more. There." Satisfied,
 nodded. "The cover goes on snug, then you let it sim-
er while the spices wake up."

Juliet wiped the back of her hand over her damp brow.
Carlo, you talk about the sauce as though it lived and
eathed."

"My sauces do," he said simply. "While this simmers,
u grate the cheese." He picked up a hunk and with his
es closed, sniffed. *"Squisito."*

He had her grate and stir while the rest of the kitchen staff
orked around them. Juliet thought of her mother's kitchen
th its tidy counters and homey smells. She'd never seen
ything like this. It certainly wasn't quiet. Pans were
opped, people and dishes were cursed, and fast was the
der of the day. Busboys hustled in and out, weighed down
th trays, waiters and waitresses breezed through de-
nding their orders. While she watched wide-eyed, Carlo
ored. It was time to create his pasta.

Unless it was already cooked and in a meal, Juliet thought
 pasta as something you got off the shelf in a cardboard
x. She learned differently, after her hands were white to
 wrists with flour. He had her measure and knead and roll
d spread until her elbows creaked. It was nothing like the
e-minute throw-it-together kind she was used to.

As she worked, she began to realize why he had such sta-
na. He had to. In cooking for a living the way Franconi
oked for a living, he used as much energy as any athlete
 l. By the time the pasta had passed his inspection, her
oulder muscles ached the way they did after a brisk set of
nis.

Blowing the hair out of her eyes and mopping away sweat,
liet turned to him. "What now?"

"Now you cook the pasta."

She tried not to grumble as she poured water into a Dutc[h] oven and set it on to boil.

"One tablespoon salt," Carlo instructed.

"One tablespoon salt," she muttered and poured it i[n]. When she turned around, he handed her a glass of wine.

"Until it boils, you relax."

"Can I turn down the heat?"

He laughed and kissed her, then decided it was only rig[ht] to kiss her again. She smelled like heaven. "I like you [in] white." He dusted flour from her nose. "You're a mess[y] cook, my love, but a stunning one."

It was easy to forget the noisy, bustling kitchen. "Cook?[" ] A bit primly, she adjusted her hat. "Isn't it chef?"

He kissed her again. "Don't get cocky. One lingui[ni] doesn't make a chef."

She barely finished her wine when he put her back [to] work. "Put one end of the linguini in the water. Yes, just s[o]. Now, as it softens coil them in. Careful. Yes, yes, you ha[ve] a nice touch. A bit more patience and I might take you [on] in my restaurant."

"No, thanks," Juliet said definitely as the steam rose [to] her face. She was almost certain she felt each separate po[re] opening.

"Stir easily. Seven minutes only, not a moment more." [He] refilled her glass and kissed her cheek.

She stirred, and drained, measured parsley, poured a[nd] sprinkled cheese. By the time she was finished, Juliet did[n't] think she could eat a thing. Nerves, she discovered wi[th] astonishment. She was as nervous as a new bride on her fi[rst] day in the kitchen.

With her hands clasped together, she watched Carlo ta[ke] a fork and dip in. Eyes closed, he breathed in the arom[a]. She swallowed. His eyes remained closed as he took the fi[rst] sample. Juliet bit her lip. Until then, she hadn't noticed th[at] the kitchen had become as quiet as a cathedral. A qui[ck] glimpse around showed her all activity had stopped and

es were on Carlo. She felt as though she were waiting to
sentenced or acquitted.

"Well?" she demanded when she couldn't stand it any
nger.

"Patience," Carlo reminded her without opening his
es. A busboy rushed in and was immediately shushed.
rlo opened his eyes and carefully set down the fork.
*'antastico!"* He took Juliet by the shoulders and gave her
e ceremonial kiss on each cheek as applause broke out.

Laughing, she pulled off her hat with a flourish. "I feel
e I won a Gold Medal in the decathlon."

"You've created." As Pierre boomed orders for plates,
rlo took both her hands. "We make a good team, Juliet
ent."

She felt something creeping too close to the heart. It just
in't seem possible to stop it. "Yes, we make a good team,
anconi."

# Chapter Eleven

By twelve the next day, there was absolutely nothing left to be done. Carlo's remote control demonstration on the proper way to prepare linguini had gone far beyond Juliet's hopes for success. She'd stayed glued to the television, listening to Carlo's voice beside her and through the speakers. When her supervisor called personally to congratulate her, Juliet knew she had a winner. Relaxed and satisfied, she lay back on the bed.

"Wonderful." She folded her arms, crossed her ankles and grinned. "Absolutely wonderful."

"Did you ever doubt it?"

Still grinning, she shot a look at Carlo as he finished off the last of both shares of the late breakfast they'd ordered. "Let's just say I'm glad it's over."

"You worry too much, *mi amore.*" But he hadn't seen her dig for her little roll of pills in three days. It pleased him enormously to know that he relaxed her so that she didn't need them. "When it comes to Franconi's linguini, you have always a success."

"After this I'll never doubt it. Now we have five hours before flight time. Five full, completely unscheduled hours."

Rising he sat on the end of the bed and ran his finger along the arch of her foot. She looked so lovely when she smiled, so lovely when she let her mind rest. "Such a bonus," he murmured.

"It's like a vacation." With a sigh, she let herself enjoy the little tingles of pleasure.

"What would you like to do with our vacation of five full unscheduled hours?"

She lifted a brow at him. "You really want to know?"

Slowly, he kissed each one of her toes. "Of course. The y is yours." He brushed his lips over her ankle. "I'm at ur service."

Springing up, she threw her arms around his neck and sed him, hard. "Let's go shopping."

Fifteen minutes later, Juliet strolled with Carlo through first tower of the enormous circular shopping center at-hed to the hotel. People huddled around the maps of the nplex, but she breezed around the curve and bypassed e. No maps, no schedules, no routes. Today, it didn't .tter where they went.

'Do you know," she began, "with all the department res, malls and cities we've been through, I haven't had a ince to shop?"

'You don't give yourself time."

'Same thing. Oh, look." She stopped at a window dis-y and studied a long evening dress covered with tiny sil-bangles.

'Very dashing," Carlo decided.

'Dashing," Juliet agreed. "If I were six inches taller it ght not make me look like a scaled down pillar. Shoes." pulled him along to the next shop.

n short order, Carlo discovered Juliet's biggest weak-s. The way to her heart wasn't through food, nor was it ed with furs and diamonds. Jewelry displays barely ned her glance. Evening clothes brought a brief survey ile day wear and sports clothes won mild interest. But es were something different. Within an hour, she'd died, fondled and critiqued at least fifty pairs. She found air of sneakers at 30 percent off and bought them to add an already substantial collection. Then with a careful neuver to pick and choose, she weeded her selection vn to three pair of heels, all Italian.

'You show excellent taste." With the patience of a man ustomed to shopping expeditions, Carlo lounged in a ir and watched her vacillate between one pair then the

other. Idly, he picked up one shoe and glanced at the si
nature inside. "He makes an elegant shoe and prefers n
lasagna."

Wide-eyed, Juliet pivoted on the thin heels. "You kno
him?"

"Of course. Once a week he eats in Franconi's."

"He's my hero." When Carlo gave her his lifted bro
look, she laughed. "I know I can put on a pair of his sho
and go eight hours without needing emergency surgery. I
take all three," she said on impulse, then sat down to e
change the heels for her newly bought sneakers.

"You make me surprised," he commented. "So ma
shoes when you have only two feet. This is not my practi
Juliet."

"I'm entitled to a vice." Juliet pushed the Velcro close
"Besides, I've always known Italians make the best shoes
She leaned closer to kiss his cheek. "Now I know they ma
the best... pasta." Without a blink at the total, she charg
the shoes and pocketed the receipt.

Swinging the bag between them, they wandered fro
tower to tower. A group of women strolled by, earning Ca
lo's appreciation. Shopping during lunch hour, he gaug
as he tossed an extra look over his shoulder. One had to a
mire the American work force.

"You'll strain your neck that way," Juliet comment
easily. She couldn't help but be amused by his blata
pleasure in anything female. He merely grinned.

"It's simply a matter of knowing just how far to go."

Comfortable, Juliet enjoyed the feel of his fingers lac
with hers. "I'd never argue with the expert."

Carlo stopped once, intrigued by a choker in amethy
and diamonds. "This is lovely," he decided. "My sist
Teresa, always preferred purple."

Juliet leaned closer to the glass. The small, delicate je
els glimmered, hot and cold. "Who wouldn't? It's fal
lous."

"She has a baby in a few weeks," he murmured, then
dded to the discreetly anxious clerk. "I'll see this."
"Of course, a lovely piece, isn't it?" After taking it out
the locked case, he placed it reverently in Carlo's hand.
The diamonds are all superior grade, naturally, and con-
t of one point three carat. The amethyst—"
"I'll have it."
Thrown off in the middle of his pitch, the clerk blinked.
Yes, sir, an excellent choice." Trying not to show sur-
ise, he took the credit card Carlo handed him along with
choker and moved farther down the counter.
"Carlo." Juliet edged closer and lowered her voice. "You
ln't even ask the price."
He merely patted her hand as he skimmed the other con-
ts in the case. "My sister's about to make me an uncle
ain," he said simply. "The choker suits her. Now emer-
ls," he began, "would be your stone."
She glanced down at a pair of earrings with stones the
or of dark, wet summer grass. The momentary longing
s purely feminine and easily controlled. Shoes she could
tify; emeralds, no. She shook her head and laughed at
n. "I'll just stick with pampering my feet."
When Carlo had his present nicely boxed and his receipt
hand they wandered back out. "I love to shop," Juliet
fessed. "Sometimes I'll spend an entire Saturday just
ming. It's one of the things I like best about New York."
'Then you'd love Rome." He'd like to see her there, he
covered. By the fountains, laughing, strolling through the
rkets and cathedrals, dancing in the clubs that smelled of
ne and humanity. He wanted to have her there, with him.
ing back alone was going back to nothing. He brought
hand to his lips as he thought of it, holding it there un-
she paused, uncertain.
'Carlo?" People brushed by them, and as his look be-
ne more intense, she swallowed and repeated his name.
is wasn't the mild masculine appreciation she'd seen him
d passing women, but something deep and dangerous.

When a man looked at a woman this way, the woman w.
wise to run. But Juliet didn't know if it were toward him
away.

He shook off the mood, warning himself to tread car
fully with her, and himself. "If you came," he said light!
"I could introduce you to your hero. Enough of my las
gna and you'd have your shoes at cost."

Relieved, she tucked her arm through his again. "Y
tempt me to start saving for the airfare immediately. O
Carlo, look at this!" Delighted, she stopped in front of
window and pointed. In the midst of the ornate display w
a three-foot Indian elephant done in high gloss ceramic. 1
blanket was a kaleidoscope of gilt and glitter and colc
Opulent and regal, its head was lifted, its trunk curled hig
Juliet fell in love. "It's wonderful, so unnecessarily orna
and totally useless."

He could see it easily in his living room along with t
other ornate and useless pieces he'd collected over the year
But he'd never have imagined Juliet's taste running alo!
the same path. "You surprise me again."

A bit embarrassed, she moved her shoulders. "Oh,
know it's awful, really, but I love things that don't belo:
anywhere at all."

"Then you must come to Rome and see my house."
her puzzled look, he laughed. "The last piece I acquired
an owl, this high." He demonstrated by holding out a pal
"It's caught a small, unfortunate rodent in its talons."

"Dreadful." With something close to a giggle, she kiss
him. "I'm sure I'd love it."

"Perhaps you would at that," he murmured. "In a
case, I believe the elephant should have a good home."

"You're going to buy it?" Thrilled, she clasped his ha
as they went inside. The shop smelled of sandalwood a
carried the tinkle of glass from wind chimes set swaying
a fan. She left him to make arrangements for shipping wh
she poked around, toying with long strings of brass be!
alabaster lions and ornamental tea services.

All in all, Juliet mused, it had been the easiest, most re-
xing day she'd had in weeks, maybe longer. She'd remem-
r it, that she promised herself, when she was alone again
d life wound down to schedules and the next demand.

Turning, she looked at Carlo as he said something to
ake the clerk laugh. She hadn't thought there were men
e him—secure, utterly masculine and yet sensitive to fe-
ale moods and needs. Arrogant, he was certainly that, but
nerous as well. Passionate but gentle, vain but intelli-
nt.

If she could have conjured up a man to fall in love
th...oh no, Juliet warned herself with something like
speration. It wouldn't be Carlo Franconi. Couldn't be. He
sn't a man for one woman, and she wasn't a woman for
y man. They both needed their freedom. To forget that
uld be to forget the plans she'd made and had been
rking toward for ten years. It was best to remember that
rlo was a ride on a carousel, and that the music only
ayed so long.

She took a deep breath and waited for her own advice to
k in. It took longer than it should have. Determined, she
iled and walked to him. "Finished?"

"Our friend will be home soon, very soon after we are."

"Then we'll wish him bon voyage. We'd better start
nking airport ourselves."

With his arm around her shoulders, they walked out.
ou'll give me our Philadelphia schedule on the plane."

"You're going to be a smash," she told him. "Though
u might want to try my brewer's yeast before it's done."

"I can't believe it." At eight o'clock, Juliet dropped down
o a chair outside customer service. Behind her, the con-
or belt of baggage was stopped. "The luggage went to
anta."

"Not so hard to believe," Carlo returned. He'd lost his
gage more times than he cared to remember. He gave his

leather case a pat. His spatulas were safe. "So, when do w
expect our underwear?"

"Maybe by ten tomorrow morning." Disgusted, Juli
looked down at the jeans and T-shirt she'd worn on th
flight. She carried her toiletries and a few odds and ends
her shoulder bag, but nothing remotely resembling a busi
ness suit. No matter, she decided. She'd be in the bac
ground. Then she took a look at Carlo.

He wore a short-sleeved sweatshirt with the word *So
bonne* dashed across it, jeans white at the stress points ar
a pair of sneakers that weren't nearly as new as hers. Ho
the hell, she wondered, was he supposed to go on the air
8:00 A.M. dressed like that?

"Carlo, we've got to get you some clothes."

"I have clothes," he reminded her, "in my bags."

"You're on 'Hello, Philadelphia' in the morning at eigh
from there we go directly to breakfast with reporters fro
the *Herald* and the *Inquirer*. At ten, when our bags may
may not be back, you're on 'Midmorning Report.' Afte
that—"

"You've already given me the schedule, my love. Wha
wrong with this?"

When he gestured toward what he wore, Juliet stood u
"Don't be cute, Carlo. We're heading for the closest d
partment store."

"Department store?" Carlo allowed himself to be pull
outside. "Franconi doesn't wear department store."

"This time you do. No time to be choosey. What's
Philadelphia?" she muttered as she hailed a cab. "Wann
maker's." Holding the door open for him, she checked h
watch. "We might just make it."

They arrived a half hour before closing. Though
grumbled, Carlo let her drag him through the old,
spected Philadelphia institution. Knowing time was agai
them, Juliet pushed through a rack of slacks. "What size?

"Thirty-one, thirty-three," he told her with his bro
lifted. "Do I choose my own clothes?"

"Try this." Juliet held out a pair of dun-colored pleated acks.

"I prefer the buff," he began.

"This is better for the camera. Now shirts." Leaving him olding the hanger, she pounced on the next rack. "Size?"

"What do I know from American sizes?" he grumbled.

"This should be right." She chose an elegant shade of lmon in a thin silk that Carlo was forced to admit he'd ive looked at twice himself. "Go put these on while I look the jackets."

"It's like shopping with your mother," he said under his eath as he headed for the dressing rooms.

She found a belt, thin and supple with a fancy little buc- e she knew he wouldn't object to. After rejecting a half zen jackets she came across one in linen with a casual, istructured fit in a shade between cream and brown.

When Carlo stepped out, she thrust them at him, then od back to take in the entire view. "It's good," she de- led as he shrugged the jacket on. "Yes, it's really good. e color of the shirt keeps the rest from being drab and the cket keeps it just casual enough without being careless."

"The day Franconi wears clothes off the rack—"

"Only Franconi could wear clothes off the rack and make em look custom-tailored."

He stopped, meeting the laughter in her eyes. "You flat- : me."

"Whatever it takes." Turning him around, she gave him quick push toward the dressing room. "Strip it off, Fran- ni. I'll get you some shorts."

The look he sent her was cool, with very little patience. here's a limit, Juliet."

"Don't worry about a thing," she said breezily. "The blisher'll pick up the tab. Make it fast; we've got just ough time to buy your shoes."

She signed the last receipt five minutes after the PA sys- n announced closing. "You're set." Before he could do so himself, she bundled up his packages. "Now, if we ca just get a cab to the hotel, we're in business."

"I wear your American shoes in protest."

"I don't blame you," she said sincerely. "Emergen measures, *caro*."

Foolishly, he was moved by the endearment. She'd nev lowered her guard enough to use one before. Because of Carlo decided to be generous and forgive her for crackir the whip. "My mother would admire you."

"Oh?" Distracted, Juliet stood at the curb and held o her hand for a cab. "Why?"

"She's the only one who's ever poked and prodded n through a store and picked out my clothes. She hasn't do: so in twenty years."

"All publicists are mothers," she told him and switch to her other arm. "We have to be."

He leaned closer and caught her earlobe between his teet "I prefer you as a lover."

A cab screeched to a halt at the curb. Juliet wondered it was that which had stolen her breath. Steadying, s bundled Carlo and the packages inside. "For the next f days, I'll be both."

It was nearly ten before they checked into the Cochar House. Carlo managed to say nothing about the separa rooms, but he made up his mind on the spot that she spend no time in her own. They had three days and most that time would be eaten up with business. Not a mome that was left would be wasted.

He said nothing as they got into the elevator ahead of t bellman. As they rode up, he hummed to himself as Jul chatted idly. At the door of his suite, he took her arm.

"Put all the bags in here, please," he instructed the be man. "Ms. Trent and I have some business to see to imn diately. We'll sort them out." Before she could say a wo he took out several bills and tipped the bellman himself. S remained silent only until they were alone again.

"Carlo, just what do you think you're doing? I told you before—"

"That you wanted a room of your own. You still have it," he pointed out. "Two doors down. But you're staying here, with me. Now, we'll order a bottle of wine and relax." He took the packages she still carried out of her hands and tossed them on a long, low sofa. "Would you prefer something light?"

"I'd prefer not to be hustled around."

"So would I." With a grin, he glanced over at his new clothes. "Emergency measures."

Hopeless, she thought. He was hopeless. "Carlo, if you'd just try to understand—"

The knock on the door stopped her. She only muttered a little as he went to answer.

"Summer!" She heard the delight in his voice and turned to see him wrapped close with a stunning brunette.

"Carlo, I thought you'd be here an hour ago."

The voice was exotic, hints of France, a slight touch of British discipline. As she stepped away from Carlo, Juliet saw elegance, flash and style all at once. She saw Carlo take the exquisite face in his hands, as he had so often with hers, and kiss the woman long and hard.

"Ah, my little puff pastry, you're as beautiful as ever."

"And you, Franconi, are as full of..." Summer broke off as she spotted the woman standing in the center of the room. She smiled, and though it was friendly enough, she didn't attempt to hide the survey. "Hello. You must be Carlo's publicist."

"Juliet Trent." Odd, Carlo felt as nervous as a boy introducing his first heartthrob to his mother. "This is Summer Cocharan, the finest pastry chef on either side of the Atlantic."

Summer held out a hand as she crossed into the room. "He's flattering me because he hopes I'll fix him an éclair."

"A dozen of them," Carlo corrected. "Beautiful, isn't it, Summer?"

While Juliet struggled for the proper thing to say, Sum
mer smiled again. She'd heard something in Carlo's voic
she'd never expected to. "Yes, she is. Horrid to work witl
isn't he, Juliet?"

Juliet felt the laugh come easily. "Yes, he is."

"But never dull." Angling her head, she gave Carlo
quick, intimate look. Yes, there was something here oth
than business. About time, too. "By the way, Carlo,
should thank you for sending young Steven to me."

Interested, Carlo set down his leather case. "He's worl
ing out then?"

"Wonderfully."

"The young boy who wanted to be a chef," Juliet mu
mured and found herself incredibly moved. He hadn't fo
gotten.

"Yes, did you meet him? He's very dedicated," Summ
went on when Juliet nodded. "I think your idea of sendir
him to Paris for training will pay off. He's going to be e
cellent."

"Good." Satisfied, Carlo patted her hand. "I'll spea
with his mother and make the arrangements."

Brows knit, Juliet stared at him. "You're going to ser
him to Paris?"

"It's the only place to study cordon bleu properly." Car
gave a shrug as though the matter were everyday. "The
when he's fully trained, I'll simply steal him away fro
Summer for my own restaurant."

"Perhaps you will," Summer smiled. "Then again, pe
haps you won't."

He was going to pay for the education and training of
boy he'd met only once, Juliet thought, baffled. What so
of a man was it who could fuss for twenty minutes over t
knot of his tie and give with such total generosity to
stranger? How foolish she'd been to think, even for a mi
ute, that she really knew him.

"It's very kind of you, Carlo," she murmured after
moment.

He gave her an odd look, then shrugged it off. "Dues are
ant to be paid, Juliet. I was young once and had only a
other to provide for me. Speaking of mothers," he went
smoothly, changing the topic. "How is Monique?"

"Gloriously happy still," Summer told him, and smiled
nking of her mother. "Kyle was obviously the man she'd
en looking for." With a laugh, she turned back to Juliet.
"m sorry, Carlo and I go back a long way."

"Don't be. Carlo tells me you and he were students to-
her."

"A hundred years ago, in Paris."

"Now Summer's married her big American. Where's
ke, *cara*? Does he trust you with me?"

"Not for long." Blake came through the open doorway,
l elegant after a twelve-hour day. He was taller than
rlo, broader, but Juliet thought she recognized a similar-
Power, both sexual and intellectual.

"This is Juliet Trent," Summer began. "She's keeping
rlo in line on his American tour."

"Not an easy job." A waiter rolled in a bucket of cham-
gne and glasses. Blake dismissed him with a nod. "Sum-
r tells me your schedule in Philadelphia's very tight."

"She holds the whip," Carlo told him with a gesture to-
rd Juliet. But when his hand came down, it brushed her
ulder in a gesture of casual and unmistakable intimacy.

"I thought I might run over to the studio in the morning
l watch your demonstration." Summer accepted the glass
champagne from her husband. "It's been a long time
ce I've seen you cook."

"Good." Carlo relaxed with the first sip of frosty wine.
erhaps I'll have time to give your kitchen an inspection.
nmer came here to remodel and expand Blake's kitchen,
n stayed on because she'd grown attached to it."

"Quite right." Summer sent her husband an amused
k. "In fact, I've grown so attached I've decided to ex-
d again."

"Yes?" Interested, Carlo lifted his brow. "Anoth Cocharan House?"

"Another Cocharan," Summer corrected.

It took him a moment, but Juliet saw the moment t words had sunk in. Emotion she'd always expected fr him, and it was there now, in his eyes as he set down glass. "You're having a child."

"In the winter." Summer smiled and stretched out h hand. "I haven't figured out how I'm going to reach t stove for Christmas dinner."

He took her hand and kissed it, then kissed her chee one by one. "We've come a long way, *cara mia*."

"A very long way."

"Do you remember the merry-go-round?"

She remembered well her desperate flight to Rome to f from Blake and her feelings. "You told me I was afraid grab the brass ring, and so you made me try. I won't for it."

He murmured something in Italian that made Summe eyes fill. "And I've always loved you. Now make a toast something before I disgrace myself."

"A toast." Carlo picked up his glass and slipped his f arm around Juliet. "To the carousel that doesn't end."

Juliet lifted her glass and, sipping, let the champag wash away the ache.


Cooking before the camera was something Summer derstood well. She spent several hours a year doing just t while handling the management of the kitchen in the P ladelphia Cocharan House, satisfying her own select clie with a few trips a year if the price and the occasion w important enough, and, most important of all, learning enjoy her marriage.

Though she'd often cooked with Carlo, in the kitcher a palace, in the less expensive area of the flat she still k in Paris and dozens of other places, she never tired watching him in action. While she was said to create with

tensity of a brain surgeon, Carlo had the flair of an art-
. She'd always admired his expansiveness, his ease of
anner, and especially his theatrics.

When he'd put the finishing touches on the pasta dish
'd named, not immodestly, after himself, she applauded
th the rest of the audience. But she'd hitched a ride to the
idio with him and Juliet for more reason than to feed an
l friend's ego. If Summer knew anyone in the world as
:ll as she did herself, it was Carlo. She'd often thought, in
any ways, they'd risen from the same dough.

"*Bravo*, Franconi." As the crew began to serve his dish
the audience, Summer went up to give him a formal kiss
the cheek.

"Yes." He kissed her back. "I was magnificent."

"Where's Juliet?"

"On the phone." Carlo rolled his eyes to the ceiling.
*Dio*, that woman spends more time on the phone than a
w bride spends in bed."

Summer checked her watch. She'd noted Carlo's sched-
: herself. "I don't imagine she'll be long. I know you're
ving a late breakfast at the hotel with reporters."

"You promised to make crêpes," he reminded her,
nking unapologetically of his own pleasure.

"So I did. In return, do you think you could find a small,
iet room for the two of us?"

He grinned and wiggled his brows. "My love, when
anconi can't oblige a lady with a quiet room, the world
ps."

"My thoughts exactly." She hooked her arm through his
l let him lead her down a corridor and into what turned
t to be a storage room with an overhead light. "You've
/er lacked class, *caro*."

"So." He made himself comfortable on a stack of boxes.
ince I know you don't want my body, superb as it is,
at's on your mind?"

"You, of course, *chérie*."

"Of course."

"I love you, Carlo."

Her abrupt seriousness made him smile and take ▌
hands. "And I you, always."

"You remember, not so long ago when you came throu▐
Philadelphia on tour for another book?"

"You were wondering how to take the job redoing ▐
American's kitchen when you were attracted to him and ◣
termined not to be."

"In love with him and determined not to be," she c◣
rected. "You gave me some good advice here, and whe▐
visited you in Rome. I want to return the favor."

"Advice?"

"Grab the brass ring, Carlo, and hold onto it."

"Summer—"

"Who knows you better?" she interrupted.

He moved his shoulders. "No one."

"I saw you were in love with her the moment I stepp▐
into the room, the moment you said her name. We und◣
stand each other too well to pretend."

He sat a moment, saying nothing. He'd been skirt▐
around the word, and its consequences, very carefully ◣
days. "Juliet is special," he said slowly. "I've thought ▐
haps what I feel for her is different."

"Thought?"

He let out a small sound and gave up. "Known. But ▐
kind of love we're speaking of leads to commitment, m▐
riage, children."

Instinctively Summer touched a hand to her stoma▐
Carlo would understand that she still had small fears. ▐
didn't have to speak of them. "Yes. You told me once, w▐
I asked you why you'd never married, that no woman ▌
made your heart tremble. Do you remember what you t▐
me you'd do if you met her?"

"Run for a license and a priest." Rising, he slipped ▐
hands into the pockets of the slacks Juliet had selected ▐
him. "Easy words *before* the heart trembles. I don't wan▐
lose her." Once said, he sighed. "It's never mattered ◣

e, but now it matters too much to make the wrong move.
e's elusive, Summer. There are times I hold her and feel
rt of her pull away. I understand her independence, her
bition, and even admire them.''

'I have Blake, but I still have my independence and my
bition.''

'Yes.'' He smiled at her. "Do you know she's so like you.
bborn.'' When Summer lifted a brow, he grinned. "Hard
the head and so determined to be the best. Qualities I've
ays found strangely appealing in a beautiful woman.''

'Merci, mon cher ami,'' Summer said dryly. "Then
ere's your problem?''

'You'd trust me.''

he looked surprised, then moved her shoulders as though
d said something foolish. "Of course.''

'She can't—won't,'' Carlo corrected. "Juliet would find
asier to give me her body, even part of her heart than her
st. I need it, Summer, as much as I need what she's al-
dy given me.''

Thoughtful, Summer leaned against a crate. "Does she
e you?''

'I don't know.'' A difficult admission for a man who'd
ays thought he understood women so well. He smiled a
e as he realized a man never fully understood the woman
st important to him. With any other woman he'd have
n confident he could guide and mold the emotions to his
1 preference. With Juliet, he was confident of nothing.
'There are times she seems very close and times she seems
y detached. Until yesterday I hadn't fully begun to know
own mind.''

'Which is?''

'I want her with me,'' he said simply. "When I'm an old
1 sitting by the fountains watching the young girls, I'll
want her with me.''

ummer moved over to put her hands on his shoulders.
ightening, isn't it?''

"Terrifying." Yet somehow, he thought, easier now th
he'd admitted it. "I'd always thought it would be ea
There'd be love, romance, marriage and children. H
could I know the woman would be a stubborn American

Summer laughed and dropped her forehead to his. "I
more than I could know the man would be a stubbc
American. But he was right for me. Your Juliet is right
you."

"So." He kissed Summer's temple. "How do I convin
her?"

Summer frowned a moment, thinking. With a qui
smile, she walked over to a corner. Picking up a broom, s
held it out to him. "Sweep her off her feet."


Juliet was close to panic when she spotted Carlo strolli
down the corridor with Summer on his arm. They might
been taking in the afternoon sun on the Left Bank. The fi
wave of relief evaporated into annoyance. "Carlo, I
turned this place upside down looking for you."

He merely smiled and touched a finger to her cheek. "Y
were on the phone."

Telling herself not to swear, she dragged a hand throu
her hair. "Next time you wander off, leave a trail of bre
crumbs. In the meantime, I've got a very cranky cab dri
waiting outside." As she pulled him along, she struggled
remember her manners. "Did you enjoy the show?"
asked Summer.

"I always enjoy watching Carlo cook. I only wish the t
of you had more time in town. As it is, your timing's v
wise."

"Yes?" Carlo pushed open the door and held it for b
women.

"The French swine comes through next week."

The door shut with the punch of a bullet. "LaBare?"

Juliet turned back. She'd heard him snarl that name
fore. "Carlo—"

He held up a hand, silencing any interruption. "What
es the Gallic slug do here?"

"Precisely what you've done," Summer returned. Toss-
g back her hair, she scowled at nothing. "He's written
other book."

"Peasant. He's fit to cook only for hyenas."

"For rabid hyenas," Summer corrected.

Seeing that both of her charges were firing up, Juliet took
arm of each. "I think we can talk in the cab."

"He will not speak to you," Carlo announced, ignoring
liet. "I will dice him into very small pieces."

Though she relished the image, Summer shook her head.
)on't worry. I can handle him. Besides, Blake finds it
using."

Carlo made a sound like a snake. Juliet felt her nerves
ying. "Americans. Perhaps I'll come back to Philadel-
ia and murder him."

Trying her best, Juliet nudged him toward the cab.
ome now, Carlo, you know you don't want to murder
ake."

"LaBare," he corrected with something close to an ex-
)sion.

"Who is LaBare?" Juliet demanded in exasperation.

"Swine," Carlo answered.

"Pig," Summer confirmed. "But I have plans of my own
him. He's going to stay at the Cocharan House." Sum-
r spread her hands and examined her nails. "I'm going
prepare his meals personally."

With a laugh, Carlo lifted her from the ground and kissed
. "Revenge, my love, is sweeter than even your me-
gue." Satisfied, he set her down again. "We were stu-
ts with this slug," Carlo explained to Juliet. "His crimes
too numerous to mention." With a snap, Carlo ad-
ted his jacket. "I refuse to be on the same continent as
"

Running out of patience, Juliet glanced at the scowli
cab driver. "You won't be," she reminded him. "You'll
back in Italy when he's here."

Carlo brightened and nodded. "You're right. Summ
you'll call me and tell me how he fell on his face?"

"Naturally."

"Then it's settled." His mood altered completely,
smiled and picked up the conversation as it ended before t
mention of the Frenchman's name. "Next time we come
Philadelphia," Carlo promised. "You and I will make
meal for Blake and Juliet. My veal, your bombe. You ha
en't sinned, Juliet, until you've tasted Summer's bombe.

There wouldn't be a next time, Juliet knew, but she ma
aged to smile. "I'll look forward to it."

Carlo paused as Juliet opened the door of the cab. "F
tonight, we leave for New York."

Summer smiled as she stepped inside. "Don't forget
pack your broom."

Juliet started to climb into the front seat. "Broom?"

Carlo took Summer's hand in his and smiled. "An c
French expression."

# Chapter Twelve

New York hadn't changed. Perhaps it was hotter than when Juliet had left it, but the traffic still pushed, the people still rushed and the noise still rang. As she stood at her window at the Harley, she absorbed it.

No, New York hadn't changed, but she had.

Three weeks before, she'd looked out her office window at not so different a view. Her primary thought then had been the tour, to make a success of it. For herself, she admitted. She'd wanted the splash.

She realized she'd gotten it. At that moment, Carlo was in his suite, giving an interview to a reporter for the *Times*. She'd made a half-dozen excuses why she didn't have time to sit in on it. He'd accepted her usual list of phone calls and details, but the truth had been, she'd needed to be alone.

Later, there'd be another reporter and a photographer from one of the top magazines on the stands. They had network coverage of his demonstration at Bloomingdale's. *The Italian Way* had just climbed to number five on the bestsellers list. Her boss was ready to canonize her.

Juliet tried to remember when she'd ever been more miserable.

Time was running out. The next evening, Carlo would board a plane and she'd take the short cab ride back to her apartment. While she unpacked, he'd be thousands of miles above the Atlantic. She'd be thinking of him while he flirted with a flight attendant or a pretty seat companion. That was his way; she'd always known it.

It wasn't possible to bask in success, to begin plans on h
next assignment when she couldn't see beyond the ne
twenty-four hours.

Wasn't this exactly what she'd always promised herse
wouldn't happen? Hadn't she always picked her way car
fully through life so that she could keep everything in pe
fect focus? She'd made a career for herself from the grou
up, and everything she had, she'd earned. She'd never co
sidered it ungenerous not to share it, but simply practic
After all, Juliet had what she considered the perfect exa
ple before her of what happened when you let go the rei
long enough to let someone else pick them up.

Her mother had blindly handed over control and h
never guided her own life again. Her promising career
nursing had dwindled down to doctoring the scraped kne
of her children. She'd sacrificed hunks of herself for a m
who'd cared for her but could never be faithful. How cl
had she come to doing precisely the same thing?

If she was still certain of anything, Juliet was certain s
couldn't live that way. Exist, she thought, but not live.

So whether she wanted to or not, whether she thought s
could or not, she had to think beyond the next twenty-fo
hours. Picking up her pad, she went to the phone. The
were always calls to be made.

Before she could push the first button, Carlo strolled
"I took your key," he said before she could ask. "Sc
wouldn't disturb you if you were napping. But I should'
known." He nodded toward the phone then dropped int
chair. He looked so pleased with himself she had to smil

"How'd the interview go?"

"Perfectly." With a sigh, Carlo stretched out his le
"The reporter had prepared my ravioli only last night.
thinks, correctly, that I'm a genius."

She checked her watch. "Very good. You've another
porter on the way. If you can convince him you're a g
ius—"

"He has only to be perceptive."

She grinned, then on impulse rose and went to kneel in
ont of him. "Don't change, Carlo."

Leaning down, he caught her face in his hands. "What I
n now, I'll be tomorrow."

Tomorrow he'd be gone. But she wouldn't think of it.
liet kissed him quickly then made herself draw away. "Is
at what you're wearing?"

Carlo glanced down at his casual linen shirt and trim
ack jeans. "Of course it's what I'm wearing. If I wasn't
aring this, I'd be wearing something else."

"Hmm." She studied him, trying to judge him with a ca-
era's eye. "Actually, I think it might be just right for this
ticle. Something informal and relaxed for a magazine
at's generally starched collars and ties. It should be a
ique angle."

*"Grazie,"* he said dryly as he rose. "Now when do we talk
out something other than reporters?"

"After you've earned it."

"You're a hard woman, Juliet."

"Solid steel." But she couldn't resist putting her arms
ound him and proving otherwise. "After you've finished
ing a hit across the hall, we'll head down to Blooming-
le's."

He nudged her closer, until their bodies fit. "And then?"

"Then you have drinks with your editor."

He ran the tip of his tongue down her neck. "Then?"

"Then you have the evening free."

"A late supper in my suite." Their lips met, clung, then
rted.

"It could be arranged."

"Champagne?"

"You're the star. Whatever you want."

"You?"

She pressed her cheek against his. Tonight, this last night,
ere'd be no restriction. "Me."

It was ten before they walked down the hall to his sui
again. Juliet had long since lost the urge to eat, but her e
thusiasm in the evening hadn't waned.

"Carlo, it never ceases to amaze me how you perform.
you'd chosen show business, you'd have a wall full of O
cars."

"Timing, *innamorata*. It all has to do with timing."

"You have them eating your pasta out of your hand."

"I found it difficult," he confessed and stopped at tl
door to take her into his arms. "When I could think
nothing but coming back here tonight with you."

"Then you do deserve an Oscar. Every woman in the a
dience was certain you were thinking only of her."

"I did receive two interesting offers."

Her brow lifted. "Oh really?"

Hopeful, he nuzzled her chin. "Are you jealous?"

She linked her fingers behind his neck. "I'm here ai
they're not."

"Such arrogance. I believe I still have one of the pho
numbers in my pocket."

"Reach for it, Franconi, and I'll break your wrist."

He grinned at her. He liked the flare of aggression ir
woman with skin the texture of rose petals. "Perhaps I
just get my key then."

"A better idea." Amused, Juliet stood back as he open
the door. She stepped inside and stared.

The room was filled with roses. Hundreds of them
every color she'd ever imagined flowed out of baskets, ta
gled out of vases, spilled out of bowls. The room smell
like an English garden on a summer afternoon.

"Carlo, where did you get all these?"

"I ordered them."

She stopped as she leaned over to sniff at a bud. "C
dered them, for yourself?"

He plucked the bud out of its vase and handed it to h
"For you."

Overwhelmed, she stared around the room. "For me?

"You should always have flowers." He kissed her wrist. Roses suit Juliet best."

A single rose, a hundred roses, there was no in between ith Carlo. Again, he moved her unbearably. "I don't know hat to say."

"You like them."

"Like them? Yes, of course, I love them, but—"

"Then you have to say nothing. You promised to share a te supper and champagne." Taking her hand, he led her ross the room to the table already set by the wide uncur- ined window. A magnum of champagne was chilling in a ver bucket, white tapers were waiting to be lit. Carlo lifted cover to show delicately broiled lobster tails. It was, Ju- t thought, the most beautiful spot in the world.

"How did you manage to have all this here, waiting?"

"I told room service to have it here at ten." He pulled out r chair. "I, too, can keep a schedule, my love." When he'd ated her, Carlo lit the candles, then dimmed the lights so at the silver glinted. At another touch, music flowed out ward her.

Juliet ran her fingertip down the slim white column of a ndle then looked at him when he joined her. He drew the rk on the champagne. As it frothed to the lip, he filled two isses.

He'd make their last night special, she thought. It was so e him. Sweet, generous, romantic. When they parted iys, they'd each have something memorable to take with em. No regrets, Juliet thought again and smiled at him.

"Thank you."

"To happiness, Juliet. Yours and mine."

She touched her glass to his, watching him as she sipped. ou know, some women might suspect a seduction when y're dined with champagne and candlelight."

"Yes. Do you?"

She laughed and sipped again. "I'm counting on it."

God, she excited him, just watching her laugh, hearing r speak. He wondered if such a thing would mellow and settle after years of being together. How would it feel, wondered, to wake comfortably every morning beside t woman you loved?

Sometimes, he thought, you would come together dawn with mutual need and sleepy passion. Other times y would simply lie together, secure in the night's warm He'd always considered marriage sacred, almost myste ous. Now he thought it would be an adventure—one he tended to share with no one but Juliet.

"This is wonderful." Juliet let the buttery lobster d solve on her tongue. "I've been completely spoiled."

Carlo filled her glass again. "Spoiled. How?"

"This champagne's a far cry from the little Reislin splurge on from time to time. And the food." She took other bite of lobster and closed her eyes. "In three weeks entire attitude toward food has changed. I'm going to e up fat and penniless supporting my habit."

"So, you've learned to relax and enjoy. Is it so bad?"

"If I continue to relax and enjoy I'm going to have learn how to cook."

"I said I'd teach you."

"I managed the linguini," she reminded him as she dr out the last bite.

"One lesson only. It takes many years to learn pr erly."

"Then I guess I'll have to make do with the little bo that say complete meal inside."

"Sacrilege, *caro*, now that your palate is educated." touched her fingers across the table. "Juliet, I still wan teach you."

She felt her pulse skid, and though she concentrated, couldn't level it. She tried to smile. "You'll have to w another cookbook. Next time you tour, you can show how to make spaghetti." Ramble, she told herself. Wi you rambled, you couldn't think. "If you write one boo year, I should be able to handle it. When you come arou this time next year, I could manage the next lesson. By th

aybe I'll have my own firm and you can hire me. After
ree best-sellers, you should think about a personal publi-
st.''

"A personal publicist?" His fingers tightened on hers
en released. "Perhaps you're right." He reached in his
ocket and drew out an envelope. "I have something for
ou."

Juliet recognized the airline folder and took it with a
own. "Is there trouble on your return flight? I thought
...." She trailed off when she saw her own name on a
parting flight for Rome.

"Come with me, Juliet." He waited until her gaze lifted
his. "Come home with me."

More time, she thought as she gripped the ticket. He was
fering her more time. And more pain. It was time she ac-
pted there'd be pain. She waited until she was certain she
uld control her voice, and her words. "I can't, Carlo. We
th knew the tour would end."

"The tour, yes. But not us." He'd thought he'd feel con-
lent, assured, even cheerful. He hadn't counted on des-
ration. "I want you with me, Juliet."

Very carefully, she set the ticket aside. It hurt, she dis-
vered, to take her hand from it. "It's impossible."

"Nothing's impossible. We belong with each other."

She had to deflect the words, somehow. She had to pre-
d they didn't run deep inside her and swell until her heart
s ready to burst. "Carlo, we both have obligations, and
y're thousands of miles apart. On Monday, we'll both be
ck at work."

"That isn't something that must be," he corrected. "It's
u and I who must be. If you need a few days to tidy your
siness here in New York, we'll wait. Next week, the week
er, we fly to Rome."

"Tidy my business?" She rose and found her knees were
aking. "Do you hear what you're saying?"

He did, and didn't know what had happened to the words
d planned. Demands were coming from him where he'd

wanted to show her need and emotion. He was stumbli
over himself where he'd always been sure footed. Even nc
cursing himself, he couldn't find solid ground.

"I'm saying I want you with me." He stood and grabb
her arms. The candlelight flickered over two confused fac
"Schedules and plans mean nothing, don't you see? I lc
you."

She went stiff and cold, as though he'd slapped her.
hundred aches, a multitude of needs moved through h
and with them the knowledge that he'd said those words t
many times to count to women he couldn't even rememb

"You won't use that on me, Carlo." Her voice was
strong, but he saw fury in her eyes. "I've stayed with y
until now because you never insulted me with that."

"Insult?" Astonished, then enraged, he shook her. "
sult you by loving you?"

"By using a phrase that comes much too easily to a n
like you and doesn't mean any more than the breath it ta
to say it."

His fingers loosened slowly until he'd dropped her an
"After this, after what we've had together, you'd thr
yesterdays at me? You didn't come to me untouched,
liet."

"We both know there's a difference. I hadn't made
success as a lover a career." She knew it was a filthy thing
say but thought only of defense. "I told you before ho
felt about love, Carlo. I won't have it churning up my
and pulling me away from every goal I've ever set. Yo
you hand me a ticket and say come to Rome, then expect
to run off with you for a fling, leaving my work and my
behind until we've had our fill."

His eyes frosted. "I have knowledge of flings, Juliet,
where they begin and where they end. I was asking you tc
my wife."

Stunned, she took a step back, again as if he'd struck l
His wife? She felt panic bubble hot in her throat. "No.

ame out in a whisper, terrified. Juliet ran to the door and cross the hall without looking back.

It took her three days before she'd gathered enough rength to go back to her office. It hadn't been difficult to onvince her supervisor she was ill and needed a replace-ent for the last day of Carlo's tour. As it was, the first ing he told her when she returned to the office days later as that she belonged in bed.

She knew how she looked—pale, hollow-eyed. But she as determined to do as she'd once promised herself. Pick ) the pieces and go on. She'd never do it huddled in her artment staring at the walls.

"Deb, I want to start cleaning up the schedule for Lia arrister's tour in August."

"You look like hell."

Juliet glanced up from her desk, already cluttered with hedules to be photocopied. "Thanks."

"If you want my advice, you'll move your vacation by a w weeks and get out of town. You need some sun, Ju-t."

"I need a list of approved hotels in Albuquerque for the arrister tour."

With a shrug, Deb gave up. "You'll have them. In the eantime, look over these clippings that just came in on anconi." Looking up, she noted that Juliet had knocked r container of paperclips on the floor. "Coordination's e first thing to go."

"Let's have the clippings."

"Well, there's one I'm not sure how to deal with." Deb pped a clipping out of the folder and frowned at it. "It's t one of ours, actually, but some French chef who's just rting a tour."

"LaBare?"

Impressed, Deb looked up. "Yeah. How'd you know?"

"Just a sick feeling."

"Anyway, Franconi's name was brought up in the inte[r]view because the reporter had done a feature on him. Th[e] LaBare made some—well, unpleasant comments."

Taking the clipping, Juliet read what her assistant ha[d] highlighted. "Cooking for peasants by a peasant," she re[ad] in a mumble. "Oil, starch and no substance..." There w[as] more, but Juliet just lifted a brow. She hoped Summer['s] plan of revenge went perfectly. "We're better off ignori[ng] this," she decided, and dropped the clipping in the tras[h.] "If we passed it on to Carlo, he might challenge LaBare [to] a duel."

"Skewers at ten paces?"

Juliet merely sent her a cool look. "What else have y[ou] got?"

"There might be a problem with the Dallas feature," s[he] said as she gave Juliet a folder. "The reporter got carri[ed] away and listed ten of the recipes straight out of the book[.]"

Juliet's head flew back. "Did you say ten?"

"Count 'em. I imagine Franconi's going to blow when [he] sees them."

Juliet flipped through the clippings until she came to [it.] The feature was enthusiastic and flattering. The timid M[s.] Tribly had used the angle of preparing an entire meal fro[m] antipasto to dessert. Carlo's recipes from *The Italian W*[ay] were quoted verbatim. "What was she thinking of?" Jul[iet] muttered. "She could've used one or two without makin[g a] ripple. But this..."

"Think Franconi's going to kick up a storm?"

"I think our Ms. Tribly's lucky she's a few thousand mi[les] away. You'd better get me legal. If he wants to sue, we'll [be] better off having all the facts."

After nearly two hours on the phone, Juliet felt alm[ost] normal. If there was a hollowness, she told herself it wa[s she] skipped lunch—and breakfast. If she tended to miss wh[ole] phrases that were recited to her, she told herself it was ha[rd] to keep up with legalese.

They could sue, or put Ms. Tribly's neck in a sling, both
which would create a miserable mess when she had two
her authors scheduled for Dallas that summer.

Carlo would have to be told, she reflected as she hung up.
wouldn't be possible, or at least ethical, to crumple up the
pping and pretend it didn't exist as she had with the one
om LaBare. The problem was whether to let legal inform
m, pass it off through his editor or bite the bullet and write
n herself.

It wouldn't hurt to write him, she told herself as she toyed
th her pen. She'd made her decision, said her piece and
pped off the carousel. They were both adults, both pro-
sionals. Dictating his name on a letter couldn't cause her
y pain.

Thinking his name caused her pain.

Swearing, Juliet rose and paced to the window. He hadn't
ant it. As she had consistently for days, Juliet went over
d over their last evening together.

It was all romance to him. Just flowers and candlelight.
could get carried away with the moment and not suffer
y consequences. I love you—such a simple phrase. Care-
s and calculating. He hadn't meant it the way it had to be
ant.

Marriage? It was absurd. He'd slipped and slid his way
t of marriage all of his adult life. He'd known exactly how
'd felt about it. That's why he'd said it, Juliet decided.
'd known it was safe and she'd never agree. She couldn't
n think about marriage for years. There was her firm to
nk of. Her goals, her obligations.

Why couldn't she forget the way he'd made her laugh, the
y he'd made her burn? Memories, sensations didn't fade
n a little with the days that had passed. Somehow they
ned in intensity, haunted her. Taunted her. Sometimes—
often—she'd remember just the way he'd looked as he'd
en her face in his hand.

She touched the little heart of gold and diamonds she
ln't been able to make herself put away. More time, she

told herself. She just needed more time. Perhaps she'd ha
legal contact him after all.

"Juliet?"

Turning from the window, Juliet saw her assistant at t
door. "Yes?"

"I rang you twice."

"I'm sorry."

"There's a delivery for you. Do you want them to bri
it in here?"

An odd question, Juliet thought and returned to her de
"Of course."

Deb opened the door wider. "In here."

A uniformed man wheeled a dolly into the room. Co
fused, Juliet stared at the wooden crate nearly as big as
desk. "Where do you want this, Miss?"

"Ah—there. There's fine."

With an expert move, he drew the dolly free. "Just s
here." He held out a clipboard as Juliet continued to st
at the crate. "Have a nice day."

"Oh—yes, thank you." She was still staring at it wh
Deb came back in with a small crowbar.

"What'd you order?"

"Nothing."

"Come on, open it." Impatient, Deb handed her
crowbar. "I'm dying."

"I can't think what it might be." Slipping the crow
under the lid, Juliet began to pry. "Unless my mother s
on my grandmother's china like she's been threatening
the last couple of years."

"This is big enough to hold a set for an army."

"Probably all packing," Juliet muttered as she put
back into it. When the lid came off, she began to push at
heaps of styrofoam.

"Does your grandmother's china have a trunk?"

"A what?"

"A trunk." Unable to wait, Deb shoved through the
rofoam herself. "Good God, Juliet, it looks like an ele-
nt."

uliet saw the first foolish glitter and stopped thinking.
elp me get it out."

Between the two of them, they managed to lift the big,
ky piece of ceramic out of the crate and onto her desk.
hat's the most ridiculous thing I've ever seen," Deb said
n she caught her breath. "It's ugly, ostentatious and ri-
lous."

"Yes," Juliet murmured, "I know."

"What kind of madman would send you an elephant?"

"Only one kind," Juliet said to herself and ran her hand
ngly down the trunk.

My two-year-old could ride on it," Deb commented and
ted the card that had come out with the packing. "Here
are. Now you'll know who to press charges against."

he wouldn't take the card. Juliet told herself she
ldn't look at it. She'd simply pack the elephant back up
ship it away. No sensible woman became emotional
ut a useless piece of glass three feet high.
he took the card and ripped it open.

*Don't forget.*

he started to laugh. As the first tears fell, Deb stood be-
her without a clue. "Juliet—are you all right?"

No." She pressed her cheek against the elephant and
laughing. "I've just lost my mind."

hen she arrived in Rome, Juliet knew it was too late for
ty. She carried one bag which she'd packed in a frenzy.
'd been lost en route, she wouldn't have been able to
tify the contents. Practicality? She'd left it behind in
York. What happened next would determine whether
eturned for it.

She gave the cab driver Carlo's address and settled b
for her first whirlwind ride through Rome. Perhaps she'd
it all before she went home. Perhaps she was home. D
sions had to be made, but she hoped she wouldn't m
them alone.

She saw the fountains Carlo had spoken of. They rose
fell, never ending and full of dreams. On impulse she m
the driver stop and wait while she dashed over to one
couldn't even name. With a wish, she flung in a coin.
watched it hit and fall to join thousands of other wis
Some came true, she told herself. That gave her hope.

When the driver barreled up to the curb and jerked
halt she began to fumble with bills. He took pity on her
counted out the fare himself. Because she was young an
love, he added only a moderate tip.

Not daring to let herself stop her forward progress,
liet ran up to the door and knocked. The dozens of th
she wanted to say, had planned to say, jumbled in her m
until she knew she'd never be able to guarantee what wo
come out first. But when the door opened, she was read

The woman was lovely, dark, curvy and young. Juliet
the impetus slip away from her as she stared. So soon,
all she could think. He already had another woman in
home. For a moment, she thought only to turn and
away as quickly as she could. Then her shoulders strai
ened and she met the other woman's eyes straight on.

"I've come to see Carlo."

The other woman hesitated only a moment, then sm
beautifully. "You're English."

Juliet inclined her head. She hadn't come so far, riske
much to turn tail and run. "American."

"Come in. I'm Angelina Tuchina."

"Juliet Trent."

The moment she offered her hand, it was gripped. "
yes, Carlo spoke of you."

Juliet nearly laughed. "How like him."

'But he never said you would visit. Come this way. We're
t having some tea. I missed him when he was in Amer-
you see, so I've kept him home from the restaurant to-
to catch up.''

t amazed her that she could find it amusing. It ran
ough her mind that Angelina, and many others, were
ng to be disappointed from now on. The only woman
was going to catch up with Carlo was herself.

When she stepped into the salon, amusement became
rise. Carlo sat in a high-backed satin chair, having an
nse conversation with another female. This one sat on
lap and was no more than five.

Carlo, you have company.''

He glanced up, and the smile he'd used to charm the child
his lap vanished. So did every coherent thought in his
d. ''Juliet.''

Here, let me take this.'' Angelina slipped Juliet's bag
n her hand while she gave Carlo a speculative look.
'd never seen him dazed by a woman before. ''Rosa,
e say good morning to Signorina Trent. Rosa is my
ghter.''

osa slipped off Carlo's lap and, staring all the way, came
uliet. ''Good morning, Signorina Trent.'' Pleased with
English, she turned to her mother with a spate of Ital-

With a laugh, Angelina picked her up. ''She says you have
n eyes like the princess Carlo told her of. Carlo, aren't
going to ask Miss Trent to sit down?'' With a sigh, Anna indicated a chair. ''Please, be comfortable. You must
ive my brother, Miss Trent. Sometimes he loses himself
e stories he tells Rosa.''

rother? Juliet looked at Angelina and saw Carlo's
n, dark eyes. Over the quick elation, she wondered how
y different ways you could feel like a fool.

We must be on our way.'' Angelina walked over to kiss
still silent brother's cheek. As she did, she was already
ning to drop by her mother's shop and relate the story

of the American who'd made Carlo lose his voice. "I h
we meet again while you're in Rome, Miss Trent."

"Thank you." Juliet took her hand and met the sm
and all its implications with an acknowledging nod. "
sure we will."

"We'll let ourselves out, Carlo. *Ciao*."

He was still silent as Juliet began to wander around
room, stopping here to admire this, there to study that.
of every culture was represented at its most opulent
should've been overwhelming, museumlike. Instead it
friendly and lighthearted, just a bit vain and utterly su
to him.

"You told me I'd like your home," she said at length
do."

He managed to rise but not to go to her. He'd left pa
himself back in New York, but he still had his pride. "
said you wouldn't come."

She moved one shoulder and decided it was best no
throw herself at his feet as she'd intended. "You k
women, Franconi. They change their minds. You k
me." She turned then and managed to face him. "I lil
keep business in order."

"Business?"

Grateful she'd had the foresight, Juliet reached in
purse and drew out the Dallas clipping. "This is somet
you'll want to look over."

When she came no farther, he was forced to go over
take it from her. Her scent was there, as always. I
minded him of too much, too quickly. His voice was flat
brisk as he looked at her. "You came to Rome to brin;
a piece of paper?"

"Perhaps you'd better look at it before we discuss
thing else."

He kept his eyes on hers for a long, silent minute b
he lowered them to the paper. "So, more clippings," h
gan, then stopped. "What's this?"

She felt her lips curve at the change of tone. "What I
ought you'd want to see."

She thought she understood the names he called the un-
ortunate Ms. Tribly though they were all in fast, furious
alian. He said something about a knife in the back, balled
e clipping up and heaved it in a scrubbed hearth across the
om. Juliet noted, as a matter of interest, that his aim was
erfect.

"What does she try to do?" he demanded.

"Her job. A bit too enthusiastically."

"Job? Is it her job to quote all my recipes? And wrong!"
censed, he whirled around the room. "She has too much
egano in my veal."

"I'm afraid I didn't notice," Juliet murmured. "In any
se, you're entitled to retribution."

"Retribution." He relished the word and made a circle of
s hands. "I'd fly to Dallas and squeeze my retribution
om her skinny throat."

"There's that, of course." Juliet pressed her lips to-
ther to keep the laughter in. How had she ever thought
e'd convince herself she could do without him? "Or a le-
l suit. I've given it a lot of thought, however, and feel the
st way might be a very firm letter of disapproval."

"Disapproval?" He spun back to her. "Do you simply
sapprove of murder in your country? She overspiced my
al."

After clearing her throat, Juliet managed to soothe. "I
derstand, Carlo, but I believe it was an honest mistake all
ound. If you remember the interview, she was nervous and
secure. It appears to be you just overwhelmed her."

Muttering something nasty, he stuck his hands in his
ckets. "I'll write to her myself."

"That might be just the right touch—if you let legal take
ook at it first."

He scowled, then looked at her carefully from head to
ot. She hadn't changed. He'd known she wouldn't.

Somehow that fact comforted and distressed all at once.
"You came to Rome to discuss lawsuits with me?"

She took her life in her hands. "I came to Rome," she said simply.

He wasn't sure he could go any closer without having to touch, and touching, take. The hurt hadn't faded. He wasn't certain it ever would. "Why?"

"Because I didn't forget." Since he wouldn't come to her, she went to him. "Because I couldn't forget, Carlo. You asked me to come and I was afraid. You said you loved me and I didn't believe you."

He curled his fingers to keep them still. "And now?"

"Now I'm still afraid. The moment I was alone, the moment I knew you'd gone, I had to stop pretending. Even when I had to admit I was in love with you, I thought I could work around it. I thought I had to work around it."

"Juliet." He reached for her, but she stepped back quickly.

"I think you'd better wait until I finish. Please," she added when he only came closer.

"Then finish quickly. I need to hold you."

"Oh, Carlo." She closed her eyes and tried to hang on. "I want to believe I can have a life with you without giving up what I am, what I need to be. But you see, I love you so much I'm afraid I'd give up everything the moment you asked me."

"*Dio*, what a woman!" Because she wasn't certain if it was a compliment or an insult, Juliet remained silent as he took a quick turn around the room. "Don't you understand that I love you too much to ask? If you weren't what you are, I wouldn't be in love with you? If I love Juliet Trent, why would I want to change her into that Juliet Trent?"

"I don't know, Carlo. I just—"

"I was clumsy." When she lifted her hands, he caught them in his to quiet her. "The night I asked you to marry me, I was clumsy. There were things I wanted to say, was

d wanted to say them, but it was too important. What
omes easily with every woman becomes impossible with the
nly woman."

"I didn't think you'd meant—"

"No." Before she could resist, he'd brought her hands to
s lips. "I've thought back on what I said to you. You
ought I was asking you to give up your job, your home,
d come to Rome to live with me. I was asking less, and
uch more. I should have said—Juliet, you've become my
e and without you, I'm only half of what I was. Share
ith me."

"Carlo, I want to." She shook her head and went into his
ms. "I want to. I can start over, learn Italian. There must
 a publisher in Rome who could use an American."

Drawing her back by the shoulders, he stared at her.
What are you talking about, starting over? You're start-
g your own firm. You told me."

"It doesn't matter. I can—"

"No." He took her more firmly. "It matters a great deal,
both of us. So you'll have your own firm one day in New
rk. Who knows better than I how successful you'll be. I
n have a wife to brag about as much as I brag about my-
f."

"But you have your restaurant here."

"Yes. I think perhaps you'd consider having a branch of
ur public relations company in Rome. Learning Italian is
 excellent decision. I'll teach you myself. Who better?"

"I don't understand you. How can we share our lives if
n in New York and you're in Rome?"

He kissed her because it had been much too long. He drew
r closer because she was willing to give something he'd
ver have asked. "I never told you my plans that night. I've
en considering opening another restaurant. Franconi's in
me is, of course, the best. Incomparable."

She found his mouth again, dismissing any plans but that.
Of course."

"So, a Franconi's in New York would be twice the best."

"In New York?" She tilted her head back just enough t see him. "You're thinking of opening a restaurant in Nev York?"

"My lawyers are already looking for the right property You see, Juliet, you wouldn't have escaped me for long."

"You were coming back."

"Once I could be certain I wouldn't murder you. We hav our roots in two countries. We have our business in tw countries. We'll have our lives in two countries."

Things were so simple. She'd forgotten his unending ger erosity. Now she remembered everything they'd alread shared, thought of everything they'd yet to share. Sl blinked at tears. "I should've trusted you."

"And yourself, Juliet." He framed her face until his fir gers slid into her hair. *"Dio*, how I've missed you. I want m ring on your finger, and yours on mine."

"How long does it take to get a license in Rome?"

Grinning, he whirled her in his arms. "I have conne tions. By the end of the week you'll be—what is it?—stuc with me."

"And you with me. Take me to bed, Carlo." She presse against him, knowing she had to get still closer. "I want yc to show me again what the rest of our lives will be like."

"I've thought of you, here, with me." He pressed his li against her temple as he remembered the words she'd hurle at him on that last night. "Juliet." Troubled, he drew awa touching only her hands. "You know what I am, how I' lived. I can't take it back, nor would I if I could. There' been other women in my bed."

"Carlo." Her fingers tightened on his. "Perhaps I sa foolish things once, but I'm not a fool. I don't want to the first woman in your bed. I want to be the last. T only."

"Juliet, *mi amore*, from this moment there is only you
She pressed his hand to her cheek. "Can you hear it?"

"What?"

"The carousel." Smiling, she held out her arms. "It's ever stopped."

*     *     *     *     *

You, too, can write in the
**LANGUAGE OF LOVE** with Silhouette's

# FREE
# ELEGANT STATIONERY

**An elegant box of stationery—perfect for yourself or to give as a gift! Each sheet is beautifully imprinted with specially commissioned artwork from the Nora Roberts Language of Love collection. Every box includes 24 sheets, six each of four different designs, all in full color, plus 24 matching envelopes.**

**This stationery will not be sold in retail stores. See proof-of-purchase on next page for details. (Retail value of stationery: $12.95)**

Silhouette®

LOLSTA1

# NORA ROBERTS
## LANGUAGE OF LOVE

## **FREE Floral Stationery**

Just mail us four proofs-of-purchase from any of the NORA
ROBERTS Language of Love titles 25 to 36, plus $2.75 for
postage and handling (check or money order—please do not
send cash) payable to Silhouette Reader Service, to:

**In the U.S.**

Language of Love Stationery
Silhouette Books
3010 Walden Avenue
P.O. Box 1396
Buffalo, NY 14269-1396

**In Canada**

Language of Love Stationery
Silhouette Books
P.O. Box 609
Fort Erie, Ontario
L2A 5X3

(Offer expires September 30, 1993)

Please allow six weeks for delivery.

---

### ORDER FORM

Name _____

Address _____

City _____ State/Prov _____

Daytime Phone# _____ Zip/Postal Code _____

LANGUAGE OF LOVE
PROOF-OF-
PURCHASE

Silhouette®

097 KAP

097 LOLPOP1